THE PEOPLE
OF PRIDDEN

THE PRIDDEN SAGA: BOOK EIGHT

J. M. TIBBOTT

Disclaimer:
All characters in this book are fictitious, and any resemblance to actual persons, living or dead, is purely coincidental.

Cover Art by Deranged Doctor Designs
Editor: Laura LaRocca

ISBN: 978-1-7390193-8-9

Printed in United States of America
Published by JMT Publishing, Canada
www.jmtpublishing.com

First Edition, 2025

CONTENTS

Dedication

For Robert, always there, never forgotten.

The People of Pridden

Acknowledgements

To so many who have helped me on this extraordinary journey – my critiquing partners and beta readers.

To Ed Greenwood, and Terry Fallis who both helped so much at the beginning with their guidance and kind testimonials.

To my eager readers who request more. You help me focus on my love of telling stories.

To the best editor, an author could have -- Laura. She thumps me when I need it, but is always willing to soothe the lumps and bumps.

To Irene, who, before she retired, helped me sell more books than I thought was possible.

To all readers everywhere for supporting writers. We artists need you, and we thank you.

The People of Pridden

MAP OF PRIDDEN

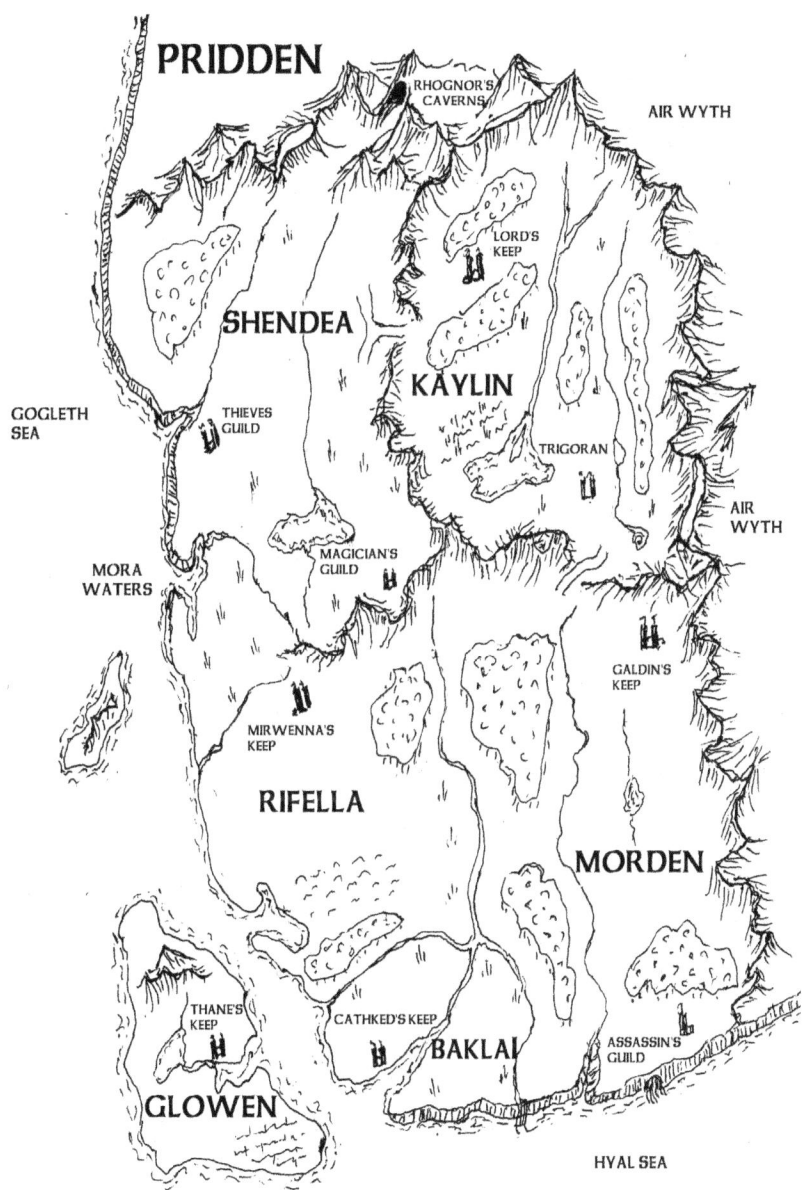

The People of Pridden

LORD OF THE UPPER REGION

Azidon and the Sister Goddesses

The legends declare that Azidon had always been the god of Pridden, but when his daughters were born, he hoped it would be easy for one of them to watch over the people so that he might retire from answering prayers of the foolish inhabitants. He was a tall and well-built male, with dark blond hair reaching to his shoulders, and his eyes were brilliant green. Despite his inspiring presence, He knew he was aging, and wondered if the other inhabitants of Dinession might be considering him past his prime. He had ruled over his own kind for so many passes of Pridden around the star, that he longed to relinquish the throne to someone else.

After much discussion with his mate, he decided to turn over all the daily challenges of the humans who worshipped the gods to his daughters. With two of them, they could spell each other if whenever the needs of the people of Pridden became too demanding. He hoped they would prove to have the stamina to eventually command Dinession, and thus be the ideal guardians for the humans of Pridden.

He called them to his throne room, which was set on the highest pinnacle of all the mountains of Pridden and was

3

concealed from human eyes by the mists and clouds enfold-ing the spires and jagged peaks.

When they answered his call, he invited them to sit while he spelled out their duties as guardians of Pridden.

"Caleesh and Ssayleese, it is time you took on the re-sponsibilities of guardians of the humans on the world below us."

Ssayleese rolled her eyes. "Finally, we have some-thing to do. It is so boring without any purpose, and I often observe things happening to the Priddanese. They are not helping each other, and someone has to do something."

"I am pleased that you are wanting to take care of this world. Our family has always ruled the other gods and goddesses and thus been responsible for all who reside on Pridden and other worlds." He reached out and took their hands in his. "We are fortunate that there are two of you to help control this planet and the humans on it, and although your mother retired to the resting land long since, I am under a remarkable amount of pressure to complete my duty to the worlds that contains the creatures who live here."

He rose from his chair and paced back and forth. "Spend some time becoming used to the people and their general problems, but after a few passes be prepared to seek mates of your own. Naturally you can feel free to call upon any of the other gods to help with specifics. For example, for weather-related situations, Mandeega is experienced and is always willing to be of help. Noomi is perfect for situations of the heart, and Pareen is a fine warrior who can deal with conflicts. However, ultimately, a mate of your own will be the best help you can find."

Caleesh spoke up. "Are there rules we must follow when we deal with these creatures?"

"Yes. What you need to do is implant a thought of you in their minds. The best would be one that shows you as being helpful and all powerful. However, you can never let them see you. They are strange creatures, and if they see you in person, they will cease to respect you as goddesses."

She nodded her head. "I will never let them see me. I will head to the most northern section of this area you call Pridden and will begin my work there."

Ssayleese agreed. "I also will never expose myself to them. I plan to begin working with these strange people living in the south end,"

***

Caleesh began by helping the people in Shendea. While she would not let them catch sight of her, she needed to let them know who was helping them so that they might worship her. She contacted a number of the other gods and goddesses, each with different ideas. She decided the best way to make the people familiar with her name would be to implant the idea while they slept. She chose, for her first subject, a man whose sight began deteriorating. Each night, she entered his dreams as an angelic, ephemeral being who spoke to him and repeated the following mantra to him, "My sight improves every day because of Caleesh, who wishes to heal me." Within three turns, he said the mantra to himself during the day. After twenty-one turns of his dreams of Caleesh, he woke one morning and realized he could see a picture on his wall that he had not been able to distinguish in ages.

The man told his neighbors that the Goddess Caleesh had healed him, and she loved all who lived in Shendea. Within a half a pass, the majority of the people were giving credit to Caleesh for all the benefits Shendeans received.

With the success of her campaign in Shendea, Caleesh began again in Kaylin. The amazing results happened quicker, because Shendeans visited Kaylin often, and the name of Caleesh and her love for the people of Pridden began to take hold. She only needed to imprint a few people in Kaylin before the worship of her name swept over the entire land.

Next, she concentrated on Rifella, and once again, with the Shendeans and Kaylinese giving their praise to Caleesh for the beneficial occurrences, in less than forty turns, Rifella was on board as well.

Glowen took far longer for Caleesh to conquer. Because they were separated from the rest of Pridden by a body of water, they received fewer visitors than the other lands. Thus, she needed to return to a similar method of influencing the Glowens as she did in Shendea.

Caleesh still kept in touch with many of the other gods, but when she met Calanta, the God of Hunters, she fell in love. He was a God of power and stature. He enjoyed a reputation with females. Caleesh knew well he managed to catch the hearts of a number of the other goddesses, but she was unable to lose her feelings for him.

Azidon, who as a leader, followed the lives of all the beings of the Upper Reaches, knew that the result of a mating between a god and a human resulted in unusual progeny. He suspected this might relate to the emergence of a Wielders. Aware of all that occurred in the Upper Reaches, and wanting to ensure the happiness of his daughter, and to be assured that Calanta did not engage with humans, he arranged to meet with him. "It appears that my offspring, Caleesh, has fallen in love with you. What are your plans for her?"

"It is an odd coincidence you should approach me this way. I find Caleesh to be extraordinary. She is beautiful and kind and the majority of the people of Pridden worship her. Quite rightly so. She has helped so many and has saved so many from pain and suffering. I adore her and I wish to request that I may approach her to be my mate."

Azidon clapped Calanta on the shoulder. "I am pleased by your words, and you may approach her to be your mate. Be warned, however, that should you ever hurt her in any way, I would not hesitate to take action." His eyes resembled the cold blue ice on the highest peak of Mont Diffenna.

Calanta's expression changed from a smile to a bare curve of his mouth at his words.

***

Caleesh and Calanta mated while she helped people in Baklai, and thus with the strong emotions released by both of them, the Baklai were the first people to worship the two of them. Within twenty turns the land was completely in thrall with Caleesh and her Hunter God Calanta.

After Caleesh settled into her relationship with Calanta, she became astonished that she had not run into a single worshiper of Ssayleese. She wondered what her sister was doing.

***

Ssayleese headed directly to Morden to establish her right to be part of the Godhead.

She met with all three kinds of snakes and they fascinated her. She attempted to reach the minds of the Mordens by taking over the minds of the snakes. She discovered that syeths were easy to conquer, but found the kokas were sentient. Although she tried to persuade them to consider her a goddess, and they did acknowledge her powers, they refrained from worshiping her. Ssayleese came to the conclusion that she needed to forget about snakes and concentrate on working with the minds of the people of Morden. A number of Mordens adored the poisonous little syeths, so Ssayleese trained them to hiss her name when they were approached by humans. The humans who were fond of the syeths later formed a Guild of Assassins.

When she took time to examine the rest of Pridden,

she noticed that Caleesh had influenced the other lands, but she experienced comfort with Morden and its snakes. She possessed no desire to work as hard as Caleesh would need to, to help such a huge number of people.

The need to remain unseen by humans became the most difficult thing that plagued Ssayleese

Frustrated when she encountered nonbelievers, she sometimes dispatched those who stubbornly refused to think of her as a goddess.

Azidon cautioned her a number of times. "Ssayleese, if too many people see you, they will no longer believe you are a beneficial goddess and may, instead, view you as a threat. Be careful what you do."

However, Ssayleese continued to break the rules. At one point, she spied a human male whom she found intriguing. He was good looking and possessed the body strength of a fine warrior. Ssayleese wanted to not only possess his mind, but his body as well. His appearance stirred intense physical attraction in her. One night, she approached, but he was not asleep, and he saw her. He pulled her to him and did not hold back. They mated wildly and roughly and by the arrival of the morrow, she was caught under his spell rather than the reverse. She came to him the next night and the next, until she became exhausted by his physical assault of her.

She did not return on the seventh night. She needed rest.

When she went to him on the eighth night, he threatened her. "Never do that again. You are not allowed to keep my bed empty." He then took her with a violence she had never experienced before. He ravaged every part of her. Under the relentless pounding Ssayleese did not desire him, instead, she was beset with pain and fear. When she left him on the morrow, she hurt all over. Her body was littered with bruises, her one eye black and swollen and her lip bled, and she felt ripped and torn inside.

Ssayleese made her way to Azidon for his help. She confessed that she had made a terrible error with a human male of extraordinary strength. "I thought I possessed the power, but I was wrong."

Azidon demanded the name of the male who brutalized her.

His name was unknown to her, but she gave directions to his home. When Azidon departed she crawled to her refuge and curled up to sleep and recover.

Azidon, enraged to the point of losing control of his own violent temper, sought out the male who savaged his daughter -- and found him.

Ssayleese's violator, although a strong male, was a mere mortal. Azidon as the leader of all the gods, could create worlds with his strength and power

Azidon seized the man by his legs and whirled him around and around. He then released him to fling him through space like a flaming comet, and when he landed, he plunged deep into the earth. There, he exploded into thousands of shards. No others missed his passing.

Hundreds of passes in the future, the area to which the man had been dispatched, came to be known as The Bowl.

***

Caleesh with an instinct that sisters possess, and convinced that Ssayleese needed her help, visited her sister's home. She was horrified at her appearance. She moved in with Ssayleese to help her recover.

The two sisters decided to change The Bowl from a place of horror to a place of beauty. Ssayleese wanted the memory of this place to give her. She and Caleesh labored for more than two passes to design flowers and trees of extraordinary beauty and fill The Bowl with a massive growth of flowers and lush vegetation and an energy of recovery. They helped new and different creatures inhabit what became a small oasis of new life. Their favorite achievement were the brantors. The huge and gentle creatures were the most spiritual of any they had ever designed. When the sisters completed The Bowl, they showed it to Azidon with a sense of achievement. He approved their effort with pride and with love for his offspring.

After this time, Ssayleese recovered more than enough to be on her own again.

Caleesh returned to helping the people in the five lands she had gathered to her, and spent much time regaining their allegiance. Calanta did his best to help in her stead, but he was more drawn to Baklai than the other lands.

Together they continued to help and aid most of Pridden in times of trouble and of joy.

***

Ssayleese, bonded to Morden in an even stronger sense. She loved the snakes, and even though the Kokas were sentient, they respected Ssayleese and welcomed her interactions with them.

The syeths protected her from even the slightest threat. The shy and rarely seen large constrictors came at her call and wound around her to keep her warm when she needed it. Because it was known that she loved the snakes of their land, the Mordens themselves loved and worshipped her and built a temple to her in the northern part of the land.

This temple remained dedicated to Ssayleese until far into the future when it became the Keep for the current Lord.

Ssayleese spent most of her time in meditation. She never mated again, and remained aloof from most of the gods, with the exception of Caleesh and her parent Azidon.

To this very day, Caleesh and Ssayleese are revered by the people of Pridden.

WYNNETH AND DELETH

The Womb Mates

Barth of Shendea paced up and down outside the birthing room, wincing every time Renneth called out in obvious pain. *I cannot believe we Healers have not prepared a remedy for the pain of birthing.*

The door opened and Breanna, the head of Shendea's healing community, stuck her head out. "You should enter. Your progeny is appearing."

He rushed in and grabbed his mate's hand. "It is time to bear down, Renneth. A new healer is about to be born into this world."

The words were barely out of his mouth when the head and shoulders of the new progeny appeared.

Barth felt such joy. It was a female.

But Renneth did not cease her cries of pain. "When will this be over?" She gasped for breath.

Barth clenched his teeth as his mate clutched his hand so tightly that her nails spiked into his palms and drew blood

Breanna stared in astonishment. "There is another? How extraordinary. You carry womb mates."

Renneth cried out and a second female slid out onto the birthing sheet. She fell back in the bed and breathed a sigh of relief, as Breanna wiped the sweat from her brow with cool cloths, scented with gentle spices.

"I did not plan on such difficult work Barth." Renneth gazed up at him. "Two? This is your fault. I shall choose to sleep alone from now on."

He laughed. "Not my fault alone, my love. You were a willing partner in this. How fortunate I am to now have three beautiful females in my household."

Renneth snorted, but she smiled with indulgence.

***

The two siblings were close, and enjoyed creating mischief in the household. All too often they strained the gentle natures of the staff, and Barth often needed to sooth the frazzled nerves of their minders. Each of the staff, although delighted at the joy exhibited by their charges, waited with eagerness for the day when their healer education was scheduled to begin.

***

High up in the Lord's hold, Breanna and Barth looked on as their young daughters set off for their first lessons in healing. Breanna smiled at her mate. "They look so eager to take these classes."

He nodded. "I cannot believe I am so blessed with beauty in my family."

The Healer Guild had long been established in Shendea, and Wynneth and Deleth, as they had been named, were inseparable. As siblings, they were so alike that their close resemblance gave them the opportunity for pranks.

Most of the time they dutifully attended the lectures that most acquainted them with the valuable Healer techniques. They wished to become important females in Shendea. It was fortunate that both were blessed with exceptional intelligence and they absorbed most of their lessons with ease.

One turn, after their morning meal, Deleth sat staring at her plate and grumbled.. "Potion classes are the most boring lessons ever."

"I love potion classes." Wynneth rubbed at her eyebrow and smirked. "Deleth, I have a plan."

Deleth peered at her with a skeptical frown "What plan? Are you going to get me in trouble? Again?"

Wynneth grinned. "Just the opposite. People cannot tell us apart most times. So, why should I not attend your potion classes? I can always give you any information you need. And…I hate those classes where we have to interpret prophecies. They are so awful that I aways tend to fall asleep in them."

"You do, and Mistress Pliney gets extremely angry with you."

Wynneth giggled. "So, why don't you take my classes in prophecies, because you have already experienced a talent in yourself for pre-cognition."

Deleth laughed out loud. "I forget, Wynneth, that you are almost as brilliant as I am. Excellent idea."

Wynneth just snorted.

***

Many passes later, after the final day of their training, Wynneth and Deleth rushed home to Finrase to tell their parents about their apprenticeship assignments.

Deleth bounced into the seating room, a broad smile on her face. "Our teachers think we are geniuses, because we did so well in all our subjects."

Breanna raised an eyebrow. "I thought you hated potions?"

Deleth turned and winked at Wynneth off to the side. "I do, but I still studied for the exam."

"So where will you be apprenticed?"

Deleth stood tall and proud. "I am being apprenticed to Lord Franklin's official Healer, because she is planning on retiring within the next pass. It will be so wonderful, because his mate is with child, and I will be able to help her with the birthing."

Breanna beamed at Deleth. "Excellent." She peered at Wynneth. "And, where are you assigned?"

"I am to be sent to help Healer Paleth in Kaylin. She has been unwell and wishes to return home to spend the rest of her days in quiet comfort."

Breanna hugged both her progeny. "You are both apprenticed to Healers who look to Lords who are Wielders. Do you know that you are direct descendants of the Healer who discovered that the syeth poison could be rendered to create a potion to cure Red Rash?"

Both Deleth and Wynneth stared at their parents, open mouthed.

They spoke together. "Really?"

Their parents nodded. "You both have large robes to fill, and we are so proud of you."

***

Early one morning, Deleth's mentor summoned her to attend the birth of the future Lord of Shendea. She passed Lord Franklin, pacing the corridors outside the birthing room of his mate. He glanced worriedly at the Healer but refrained from questioning her.

As Deleth entered the birthing room, the senior Healer grabbed her by the hand. "I am glad you are here, Deleth. The poor woman has been in labor for a lengthy time, and she is exhausted. If the young one does not appear soon, we may be forced to remove the progeny from her belly via the cutting process."

Deleth stared at her mentor and gasped. "I am not sure I can help in this. I have never done that before."

"We have no choice if the young one does not appear soon."

At that moment Franklin's mate screamed and panted, and the child slid into Deleth's waiting hands.

"Deleth, you deal with the babe. Clean it and make sure

it is breathing, and bind it well against the cold. I will aid my Lady."

When both patients were cleaned up and ready to be seen by Lord Franklin, Deleth asked him to enter the room. At once, he headed for his mate and grasped her hands. "You were so brave, my love. We have a young male."

Her answering smile was weak. "I would like to name him Rhognor after my warrior ancestor who saved our village from the ravages of a Cathnog."

"Anything you wish, my love."

His weary mate could not keep her eyes open. She slept.

Lord Franklin left the room and asked both Deleth and her mentor to join him in a toast of Orenberry wine to celebrate the birth of his son.

Deleth hid a grin when she realized he had used a Rifellan word for his progeny.

But Franklin caught the grin. "I spent many years in Rifella when I was being groomed to rule Shendea as Lord." He glanced at Deleth's mentor. "I am aware you wish to retire and return to your home in Roothlan, and now that my progeny is born, I give you permission to leave." He turned to Deleth. "I have been told you are more than ready to take on the position of my Healer, so I welcome you to your new life."

***

When Wynneth arrived in Kaylin, Healer Paleth welcomed her to the Keep. The older Healer assigned her to nurse the young Lord Lanerch's ailing parent, who had contracted the Red Rash. "I cannot deal with him by myself any more. I do not possess the strength to handle a man his size."

"Why did he not take the syeth potion to prevent the Red Rash?"

"I am not sure, but I suspect he is like many whose parents had contracted Red Rash and had been cured with the potion. They believed that because their parents took the potion, they were immune. We regret it is not true."

Wynneth frowned. "Can his mate not persuade him?"

"She left us to join with Caleesh over four seasons ago." Paleth shrugged. "Perhaps he is lonely."

Wynneth did her best to attempt to nurse Lord Lanerch's parent back to health, but the Red Rash had not been caught early enough and now it was impossible to rid his body of the disease.

At last, the man succumbed to the Rash, and Lanerch arranged for a funeral pyre to send him to be embraced by Caleesh.

Lanerch sent for Wynneth to come to his office, and when she entered, she found him with Paleth. "Healer Wynneth, Paleth wishes to depart for her home. She has been our Healer in Kaylin for many passes, and now deserves to rest, and heal herself. She has been most complimentary about your abilities, so I wish for you to be my Healer in residence. I know you did your best to help my parent, but he did not admit to having the Rash until it was too late." He sighed. "I am convinced he wished to depart Kaylin and join my female parent with Caleesh. He always said he could not live without her." He stared at Wynneth. "Do you accept the position as my Healer?"

Wynneth nodded her thanks. *Lord Lanerch has a fine reputation as an excellent administrator. I will enjoy being the Healer here in Kaylin.*

During the following days, Lanerch came to rely on Wynneth not only for her healing abilities, but also her willingness to listen to the challenges he often faced. *He is a fine man. I wonder how strong his Wielder abilities are, He is so young, and the people of Kaylin are so tied up in their strict moral views. I suspect they might not respect him as much as they should.*

***

Back in Shendea, Deleth dealt with all the challenges a Healer might encounter in that land, and nursed Franklin's mate when she became ill, which weakened her and she stillbirthed a potential sibling for Rhognor. She could not recover and passed away in the arms of Lord Franklin. Franklin sent for Deleth four turns after his mate had been sent to Caleesh.

"Healer Deleth, my thanks for helping me through these past few turns. And I need to ask for more help."

"What do you wish my Lord?"

"I am concerned about Rhognor. He is an intelligent

young male, and even at his young age of ten passes, he understands the challenges of Lordship. However, he is a gentle male, and is also much caught up in worrying too often about small details. I fear that he may not be strong enough to rule Shendea once I am gone."

"You are correct, Lord Franklin. Rhognor is indeed a gentle young male, but the people of Shendea will appreciate him for this. He will never be feared by his people, but will be much adored by them. As to his attention to small challenges, it is but a minor eccentricity." She patted him on the arm. "Even at his young age, he has a strong friendship with Lady Halfin of the Enchanters' Guild. I foresee a mating between them. Lady Halfin will be the perfect bond mate for him. Have no fear for Rhognor. He has a deep strength. It will make him a fine leader of Shendea."

"You have the sight, Deleth? You foresee him bonding with Halfin?"

"I do, Sire."

Franklin smiled, and clasped Deleth's hand. "Thank you, Healer. You have put my mind at ease."

***

After a lengthy illness, Lord Franklin left Shendea and joined Caleesh, leaving the Lordship to Rhognor, now in his sixteenth pass. Deleth was proved correct. Rhognor had bonded with the Lady Halfin on the previous pass. He ruled Shendea with gloves of velvet and steel determination, and his people adored him. They found his eccentricities of attempting to control minor things around him endearing and often pointed with pride at him when he insisted on arranging his table settings or his clothing, always in precise order. Under Rhognor's rule, Shendea prospered, and their Healers were valued throughout Pridden.

***

Wynneth bolted upright in her bed, as a messenger moth fluttered around her face. She grabbed it and held it to her ear. It was from Deleth. "Wynneth, prepare to ride and meet me at the Lord's Keep in Morden. I have had a vision of trouble for Lord Taliaferro and his family. Leave now, and I will meet you there. There is no time to waste."

Wynneth rose, her heart beating double time, dressed, and prepared a basic travel bag. She ran from her rooms to that of Lord Lanerch, where she asked the guard at the door to request a hasty meeting with the Lord.

When she was admitted, she was frantic to leave to meet with Deleth. "Lord Lanerch, I apologize for disturbing you so early. I must join Deleth in Morden. She has advised me Lord Taliaferro and his family face great danger. Please give me your permission for me to leave now."

Lanerch, his eyes open in astonishment nodded. "Of course, Wynneth. Go now, but let me know what is occurring when you have more information."

"I will, my Lord." She swept from the room and headed

to the stables for a horse. Once in the saddle, she withdrew a moth and brought it to her lips. "I am leaving at once, and I shall see you in just over two turns." She threw the moth in the air, sending the moth to Deleth.

Riding as fast as possible but making sure to spare her mount, she did not stop for sleep. She halted for a brief rest to water her horse and allow it to eat. At Trigoran, she exchanged her tired animal for a fresh one, promising to return it when she could.

***

Wynneth rode up to Taliaferro's Keep just as Deleth appeared, riding fast. Recognized by the guards as Healers, they were admitted at once, and both raced through the halls for Taliaferro's quarters.

The Lord, startled by their appearance, asked them to enter. "Why have you come here?"

Deleth held up her hand. "Where are your mate and your progeny?"

"Why? What is going on?"

Deleth answered, "My Lord you and your family are in great danger. Your Councilor, Gritch, is planning to kill you all so he can assume control of Morden."

"He cannot do that. My guards would never allow such a thing to happen."

Deleth pleaded. "Sire, I beg of you, get ready to leave. He has gathered a huge number of guards who swear allegiance to him, and many of your own guards have been killed or imprisoned."

Taliaferro turned and ran for the bed chamber and shook his mate awake. "Amaris, wake up. Bring Eduardo with you. We must leave this place. We have been betrayed, and all our lives are in danger."

Amaris rose, her face twisted in fear, but before she could leave the room, she doubled over and cried out in pain. "Aah, my child is coming. The shock of such a challenge has brought on my labor. I cannot leave now."

Deleth turned to Wynneth. "You take young Eduardo to Lord Lanerch. I will stay here and deliver Amaris's child and will take the three of them to safety in Shendea."

Wynneth clutched at her sibling. "You must be careful. On my way here when I stopped for food, I heard rumors that Gritch and his army are preparing to breach the walls of the Keep soon and destroy Taliaferro and his family."

"I must deliver the child. I will pretend it was still-born so Gritch cannot seize it. He will be reluctant to prevent me from leaving. Healers are too important in Pridden. I will have one of the female attendants tell him the dead child has been sent to Ssayleese's priests for the fire ceremony. And I will flee with the newborn and his parents to Shendea through the northern tunnel. Wynneth, you must leave now before Gritch seals off the Clog Blue pass."

Wynneth left to search for Eduardo, but turned and called back, "But, if Gritch asks, how will you explain Eduardo's absence?"

Taliaferro spoke up. "I will begin a search in panic for Eduardo. He has been known to hide from everyone before. I will make sure the keep is turned upside down, attempting to find him. When Gritch questions me, I will advise him that Eduardo has been missing for two turns." He caught Deleth by the hand. "Lady Amaris is strong, and Eduardo's birth was quick. I am sure we will not wait long for the appearance of his sibling."

Wynneth, having located Eduardo, returned and faced Taliaferro. "I will deliver Eduardo to Lord Lanerch. I will request that he tells his people that Eduardo is a son of a cousin, and he will be safe until you and Amaris can join us. Lady Amaris cannot logically leave before the birth of Eduardo's sibling. Lord Taliaferro would never leave her so soon after the potential birth. This will also allow us to keep the whereabouts of Eduardo unknown."

After hugging Deleth, Wynneth went back to Eduardo's room to help him pack and flee with him to Kaylin. They left as dusk fell, and with help from a young stable hand, loyal to Lord Taliaferro, rode fast for the Clog Blue pass. As she rode, with Eduardo mounted on the saddle in front of her, Wynneth sent prayers to Caleesh to help her sibling.

***

Wynneth rode through the night, and once in Kaylin, headed straight for Trigoran. Although weary and hun-

gry, rather than seeking an inn, she headed for the Rifellan
Guards' unit in the town.

She burst into the Guards building and cried out in joy
as she recognized one of the guards.

"Agreneth, oh thank Caleesh it is you."

He stared at her. "Healer Wynneth, what brings you to
Trigoran?"

"I need your help. I must get this young male as soon
as is possible to Lord Lanerch. He is under the Lord's protection, but we must gain sanctuary in the Keep."

"Of course, Healer. I will obtain a fresh horse for you
and assign two of our best warriors to accompany you.
They will be ready almost as soon as you have refreshed
yourself, and will have you in the safety of the Keep within
two turns."

True to his word, Wynneth and Eduardo, accompanied
by two strong Rifellan warriors arrived at Lord Lanerch's
Keep in two turns. Lanerch concealed them in one of the
rooms of the inner Keep, and Wynneth and her charge col-
lapsed on beds and slept for almost another turn.

When they woke, Wynneth explained to Lord Lanerch
the challenges that Eduardo faced, and over the next few
turns he introduced Eduardo to his people as the son of his
deceased cousin. He told them all that Eduardo, because of
the death of his parents, had now become his heir. Wynneth
knew that if Eduardo's parents survived, they could handle
the situation. But even without the benefit of a strong sense

of pre-cognition, she suspected that their survival would be a miracle.

***

As soon as Wynneth departed from the Morden Keep, Lady Amaris's water broke. The birth was unusually quick and Deleth concealed the cries of the newborn male, swaddling him against her body for her journey to the northern tunnel leading into Shendea.

"Lord Taliaferro, help me prepare a false still-born so that no one will know your progeny did survive."

"What do you need, Healer Deleth?"

"Bring me two white towels and some extra stuffing to insert between them. Also bring me the cockerel from the yard below this window."

He rushed to obtain the items she requested.

"Thank you, my Lord." Deleth grabbed the cockerel by the neck and snapped it, killing the bird without causing it to suffer. She then slit the throat of the creature, allowing the blood to soak into one of the towels. She wrapped the fowl inside the towel, inserted some extra stuffing, and covered the bundle with the still bleeding afterbirth. Taking the second towel, she dabbed blood onto the outside and made sure the bundle was wrapped and tied.

Opening the door to the birth room, she called out to the guard outside. "You there. The young one did not survive the birth, and I have prepared it for Ssayleese. Take him at once to Lord Taliaferro's Praetor and demand he prepare a pyre now and send this progeny to the goddess. Because this one did not survive his birth, he has never been sanctified by Ssayleese. The pyre must be performed with haste to assure he will be admitted into the goddess's arms." She thrust the bundle into his hands. "Hurry -- Ssayleese never waits long."

The guard stood waiting. "Healer, will not the Lord and Lady Amaris wish to attend?"

"Lady Amaris is too ill, and her mate, the Lord, is too worried for her to attend. He asked that once you have begun the pyre, you then locate Councilor Gritch and request he attend in their stead."

"I will do as you ask, Healer Deleth." He turned away to run down the hallway.

Deleth called out. "Stop. Do you love your Lord and Lady?"

"I do indeed."

"Then under pain of all you hold dear, never refer to me as Healer Deleth. Ever. If Gritch asks of you who I am, only refer to me as one of Lady Amaris's maids."

"I will do as you ask. You are but a stranger to me is all I will admit to."

Deleth thanked him, closed the door, and rushed back to Amaris and her mate. "Come, we cannot wait. Prepare yourselves to come with me to the Tunnel to Shendea. I am sorry we cannot wait for you to heal, Amaris, but we must leave now. I have arranged with my apprentice to have three horses saddled and waiting at the rear entrance to the Keep"

Amaris gazed up at the Healer, tears in her eyes. "Deleth, you and Wynneth have saved my sons but I cannot leave with you. I truly am too weak. The danger we are now facing is too much for me to bear."

Deleth took Amaris's hands in hers. "You and Lord Taliaferro should not be here when Gritch enters the Keep. Please, come with me to the northern tunnel."

Taliaferro shook his head. "We cannot. It is vital that Eduardo and his sibling survive. Amaris and I must remain to ensure that you both escape with our progeny. Only then will Grinch be convinced that our babe never survived and Eduardo is lost somewhere. If we disappear as well, Gritch will be convinced both our progeny survived, and he will never stop searching for them. Please take our babe, whom we have decided to name Markallo, and leave without delay for Shendea."

Deleth, her eyes filled with tears, embraced the two of them, and asked Amaris to express some milk for the babe for the trip. She rushed to the next room, and discarding her blue healer robes, dressed as a peasant woman. Binding the swaddled Markallo to her, she slipped from the inner Keep and, without any sound, made her way to the rear exit.

Waiting there was an apprentice Healer and three horses.

With the help of the young female, Deleth mounted a horse and advised the apprentice to return the other two to the stable. "Thank you for aiding me. If you can, please return to the Lord's quarters and remove my Healer robes. I suggest that as soon as you do, arrange to be as far from the Keep as possible. If you can, pretend to be attending a person who seems to be stricken with Red Rash. The fear of the Rash will keep you safe. There are fearful times about to descend on Morden, and you may have to return to Shendea via the tunnel in the far north of this land."

The young female nodded, blew a kiss to Deleth, and led the two horses back to the stable.

***

Deleth rode as fast as she could, but the babe needed sustenance, and she stopped briefly to give him some of his mother's milk. After riding for another half turn, she came upon a small village and a tiny funeral pyre, for a child still-born. She stopped her horse and slid from the saddle, clutching Markallo to her. The pyre was down to embers only, and Deleth followed a woman who was in obvious grief. "Please forgive me for my presumption, but I believe you have lost your babe."

With red-rimmed eyes, the woman nodded a faint yes.

"Do you have other progeny?"

The woman shook her head. "No, and it is now unlikely we will ever have any."

"Would you be willing to accept a young male as a foster child?"

The woman's face lit up. "My mate and I wish for a

male progeny so often, of course we would."

"I come from a village further to the south, and we were set upon by thieves. This young male's parents were killed, and he is left as an orphan. I must conceal him, and I can only do that if some other female accepts him as her own. Would you be willing to do that?" *If she accepts, and takes Markallo as her own son, he will be just as well hidden as if I managed to escape with him to Shendea.*

The woman stood aside. "You have saved this little one, and I will certainly help keep him alive. Please enter. I will feed the young one, and it would be such an honor to make him part of my family. My mate will be thrilled to be the parent of a male." She called out to her husband. "Fanir, please bring two cups of tea."

Deleth handed the bundled babe to the women, who sat in a comfortable chair.

The woman smiled as she unwrapped the babe's face, and placed him to her breast. "I am called Posy." She gazed down at Markallo, sucking greedily from her. "He is so small. He is like a little mouse."

Deleth thought quickly. "You are correct he is small like a little mouse. I believe that will be a perfect name for him." *Gritch will never even consider a mouse to be the potential Lord of Morden.*

Fanir entered the small parlor bringing two cups of tea, which he placed in front of both women, and stared. "Whose progeny is this, Posy?"

She gazed up at him her face alive with joy. "He is ours, Fanir and his name is Mouse."

Fanir's mouth dropped open, but his eyes shone with pleasure. "He is ours? And he is a male? Caleesh has given us a babe?"

"Yes, Caleesh be blessed, she has sent us this young male via our visitor."

Deleth drank her tea as she watched the two of them, tears trickling down their cheeks as they cuddled and hugged young Mouse. Finally, she rose. "I thank you so much for your hospitality and your amazing help. I must leave now to escape my pursuers."

Posy rose, still holding Mouse and hugged Deleth as best she could.

Fanir kissed her hand, gratitude written on his face. "You never told us your name?'

I can't tell them who I am. "My name is Genron, but if someone comes looking for such a woman, you must never reveal that you have seen me. No matter what happens, you must always insist Mouse is your babe. From now on, Mouse is your progeny. Do you understand how important this is?"

Posy nodded, and Fanir, his brow creased in puzzlement, nodded as well.

The Healer released the breath she was holding. *Thank you Caleesh. This sudden solution must mean that Mouse... er, Markallo has a greater part to play in Pridden in the future.*

Deleth exited the house and climbed on her horse. She wheeled it around and headed north again, bound for Shendea. *I wonder if we'll ever have the chance to tell Eduardo and Mouse about each other?*

The People of Pridden

JAGLOREN

Praetor for Thane Brennan

Jagloren called his mate Dayleeya into his study in Rifella. "I have been summoned to Murwenna's office. I hope she is now willing to send me to a land where I will have more responsibility and perhaps even head a garrison, or at least be the second-in-command to a Praetor."

Dayleeya frowned. "I am aware you and Murwenna were close friends when you were both young, but you should still be careful about being so informal when other people are around."

He snorted at her. "I am always careful. Only you and I are here. No one else can hear us. Plus, we Rifellans are not that formal with each other."

"People who live at the Keep are not, but my parents were both born in Orkanna. I think they over-compensated because Glowen was so close, and they are the most formal people I have ever met. My female parent, in particular, was horrified by the Glowen's attitudes."

Jagloren laughed. "Your female parent is so rigid in her ways she makes my teeth ache. She must have been a Kaylin person in one of her previous lives." He grinned. "She has convinced herself she lived a long string of lives before the one she now lives."

She eyed him. "You might be correct. But no matter what, I am delighted we may be moving to a new land."

"I knew you were becoming bored with always staying near the Keep, when as a warrior, I was always off on some potential exciting adventure. Believe me, Dayleeya, being a warrior in a group in a well-ordered life here in Rifella is not exciting for me either. I am hoping Murwenna will send me somewhere more demanding."

Dayleeya clapped her hands. "I hope it is somewhere we can have a few adventures. I always wanted to be a warrior in my own right, but I was never strong enough to fill such boots."

"Dayleeya, my beloved, you never needed to be a warrior to be the female I wished to mate with."

"I understand that I never needed to impress you with my skills. But I wanted to be an excellent warrior just for me."

"Wherever she chooses to send us, we will create our own type of interesting exploits."

"Do you have any idea where I would like us to be assigned to?"

"No, where?" Before she could answer, he wagged his finger at her. "Now, wait, do not be upset if we are not sent where you want. We can make our own way of having fun in whatever land we are directed to."

"I am aware of what we can or cannot do." She rolled

her eyes. "Stop procrastinating. Go to your meeting with Murwenna and come back immediately to give me the news."

***

Dayleeya began to plan her packing after Jagloran left for his meeting. She examined everything with a critical eye. She understood that postings were always at least six passes, but many decided to remain for lengthier periods when they were sent on their first postings. *I am sure we will need more leathers. I should also order weather-appropriate clothing.* She sat at their desk and finding a pen with ink, began a list of what she suspected they might need.

At the top of her list, she wrote that they should check with Olwyn, the female scheduled to bond with Praetor Arrogol. As Praetor, he is even closer to Lord Murwenna than my own mate, she thought. Rumor had it, he had been chosen to give Murwenna the opportunity to bear a child. If any person knew what was needed in other lands, it would be Olwyn.

She paused in her list making. What they took with them would depend on the position Jagloran received. If he were sent as a mere guard, they would have to take most of their belongings. However, if he obtained the position of second-in-command to a Praetor, he would receive sufficient credits to purchase what they needed in their assigned land. *Before I speak to Olwyn, I should wait to find out what position Jagloran is given, and what land we will be sent to.*

Dayleeya felt so restless and anxious about Jagloran's assignment that she went for a walk to calm herself.

***

Jagloran approached Murwenna's door and spoke to the young guard. "Murwenna has requested I meet with her."

The young male knocked, stuck his head inside and announced him.

Murwenna called out, "Let him in. I need to see him."

"You look as beautiful as ever," Jagloran bowed his head, "My Lord."

She grimaced. "Good grief, Jag. Stop being so serious. Come here, and give me a hug."

He laughed and enveloped her in his best bear hug but apologized when she coughed.

"Do not worry -- you did not break many of my ribs." She grinned at him. "You always gave the best bear hugs when we attended those classes with scholar Tannis. And how is Dayleeya these days? I have not seen her in quite a few turns. Not her fault." She frowned and waved her hands downwards. "Sit. You look uncomfortable standing there."

He sat. "So whose fault is it?"

She sighed. "It is all my fault. I have been so busy dealing with young Cathked. You may not realize that Thane Argonites is unwell, and Cathked is assuming the mantle of many responsibilities in Baklai. His parent has always been so suspicious of Morden, so Cathked, doing his best to please his parent, is asking for more Rifellans to man the border posts."

"Why is that causing you so much trouble?"

"Our Rifellan warriors do not appreciate serving in Baklai. We have all been suspicious of the Mordens since Gritch murdered Lord Taliaferro. Plus, we do not continue to maintain a presence in Morden. Gritch and his minions are as suspicious of us as we are with them. However, the wonderful part is that we can always obtain more horses, thanks to Cathked."

She moved to the table in the center of the room. "Where are my manners? I am complaining too much. I have ordered tea for us." She grinned again. "I also ordered some of those little iced cakes I know you like so much, and that Dayleeya rations."

Jagloran scratched his nose. "So, what do you want to discuss with me?"

She looked down at her hands, folded on the table. "I have been debating back and forth with myself on this. You are one of my oldest and dearest friends." She moved restlessly in her seat. "And this is quite a personal request."

Jagloran pushed away from the table, his mouth open and his eyes wide. "No Murwenna, you cannot in all that is decent want me to take over from Arrogol."

"Are you quite mad? I cannot believe you would think that I would physically mate with Arrogol? Or even you, for that matter. I know we considered each other with interest during our education, but as handsome as you are, I sincerely no longer find you attractive as a mate. I have worked it out with Healer Fenneth."

Jagloran was sure he blushed, because the heat in his face was intense. "Forgive me. I made the error because you said your request was quite personal. I was afraid you had decided to grit your teeth and use me as a lover."

She laughed aloud. "It is personal, but it has nothing to do with procreation. Dear Jag, I would hate to have to grit my teeth with you. And as I said Arrogol will not actually mate with me."

"He will not? Then how?"

"I am only telling you this because you are such a close friend." She blushed slightly. "Fenneth has arranged for the collection of Arrogol's seed, which would be implanted within me. My mate Janella and I have agreed we that prefer this. I believe Olwyn is probably as grateful as we are, that we will use this method."

"Murwenna? You said you had something personal to ask. What is it?"

"Sorry. I do. We are such fine friends that I suspect you will accede to my appeal."

"I do not believe I have ever refused you anything, Murwenna."

"I do recognize you have always agreed to everything I have asked of you." She patted him on the cheek. "I have received an inquiry from Thane Brennan of Glowen. He is new to his Thaneship, and he is attempting to change the ideas of citizens of other lands about the worth of Glowen and their wine and Stinger products. His current Praetor is old and wishes to return to Rifella. In truth, he has never held much sympathy for the Glowens." She took his hand in hers. "I am asking you to be the new Praetor for Thane Brennan. I have seen you grow as a warrior, and I am always impressed by how well you handle yourself with so many varied people. I watch you judge people on their own merit, not gossip."

Jagloren felt a surge of joy within him. A Praetor on his own. He could imagine how excited Dayleeya would be with his news. "Thank you, Murwenna. You have no idea how honored I am." *I can hardly wait to tell Dayleeya, and I can hardly wait to see the delight in her face.*

At that point, their tea and cakes arrived, and Murwenna closed the door behind the young guard.

She poured their tea. "As for your beautiful Dayleeya, I have never seen her be anything but caring to all she meets. I really do believe the two of you will bring pride to Rifella by taking on the position of Praetor to Thane Brennan. I am positive the three of you will be like family with each other."

"Murwenna, my friend, I will gladly become Thane Brennan's Praetor. And Dayleeya will be ecstatic. She is so curious about Glowen and has often expressed a wish to visit there. Although she is a beautiful female, the Glowens are aware that we Rifellans mate for life. I doubt they will make her uncomfortable in their presence, and if they do propose anything to her, she is more likely to pretend that she is flattered, than find fault with them."

"Bless you, my friend. You have taken a load from my shoulders. I would appreciate it if you depart for Glowen as soon as you are able." She smiled with a satisfied gleam in her eye. "Now that is solved. Have your tea, and be sure to eat a couple of cakes. You know Dayleeya would not approve."

He drank his tea, grabbed a cake, and put the whole thing into his mouth. He swallowed with difficulty. "We will depart as soon as we can. It would help if you would agree to advise Dayleeya on what items she will need to take with us. May I have her call on you?"

"By all means." Murwenna paused and a smile lit her face. "Praetor Jagloran, I have called us friends many times, but I now realize you have always been more like a brother to me. My thanks for that."

"I will leave as soon as possible for Glowen, but must take a small amount of time to say farewell to my many friends in Rifella. I must also bid farewell to Arrogol, as I suspect he may have suggested me to you."

Murwenna shook her head. "He did not. Arrogol is a friend, but that is all he is. He would never be a brother to me and I have discovered that in life, family always support one better than friends."

Jagloren grabbed her in a hug again, and laughing he left her rooms. Not all families. He thought about Tiwellan, Janella's sibling. He was family to Murwenna, but Jagloran despised him. He did not trust the male in the least.

***

Dayleeya returned from her walk at the same time as Jagloran arrived from the Keep. She caught the spring in his steps and rushed up to him. "What happened? Are you being posted away from Rifella? What position did you get?"

He grabbed her in a hug and whirled her around. "Stop all the questions, I have such exciting news and I want to tell you everything. Let us head inside, sit down, and take a breath or two. I will make the tea if you promise to wait a while to hear the news."

Dayleeya sat at their small dining table and twitched a bit but managed to tamp down her excitement a little.

Jagloran brought in the biggest teapot, two cups, and a plate of her favorite cookies. He poured the tea and sat beside her. "There is so much news, and you are going to love it. The first thing is, Murwenna has requested I take on the position of Praetor to Thane Brennan of Glowen."

Dayleeya clapped her hands and bounced in her seat. "So, we are going to Glowen? That was the thing I was wishing for most. Why did she decide to ask you to be the Praetor?"

"Thane Brennan asked for a replacement Praetor, because the current one wants to come back to Rifella. She believes you and I are relaxed in our acceptance of people, and are less judgmental than many others."

"I do not think we are judgmental in any way."

He smiled at her. "I agree. I am sure Murwenna wants a better relationship with the Glowens. She has excellent relations with Shendea and Kaylin, and even though the Thane of Baklai is a bit of a challenge, she admires the work he does. The only land she finds more than challenging is Morden. It seems that when Gritch murdered Lord Taliaferro and his family, they also cut off relations with Rifella. They do not want Rifellan warriors in their domain. From what she told me, Gritch has his own warriors now."

"Oh Jag, I was told this by many of my warrior friends. I am nervous about the Mordens myself."

"I suspect that at this time, so is most of Pridden. So, for Murwenna it makes sense to keep good feelings between Rifella and Glowen."

Dayleeya sighed and hugged him. "I am so glad we are mated. When do we have to leave for Glowen?"

"As soon as we are able. By the way, I asked if you could call on Murwenna to get help with what items we will need to take with us and what we will be able to buy in Glowen. She agreed to meet, so you can contact her when you would like her help."

"That would be incredible. I considered asking Olwyn, because of the situation between Arrogol and Murwenna. But speaking with Murwenna would be the best thing." She grabbed Jagloren and kissed him soundly. "You always know exactly how to be the best mate."

He put his arms around her and waggled his eyebrows,

suggesting some impropriety. "It is, my dear, because I have learned to read your mind. I always understand what you want."

She smacked him on the nose. "Let me go, you big fool. I need to begin making some new lists." When he resisted, she pushed him away. "You will have to wait for your reward until after our evening meal. I have too much to do now."

"Dayleeya, we are moving to Glowen." He frowned at her but could not resist grinning a bit. "Be careful about denying me my rights as your Praetor."

"Don't be silly. No self-respecting Glowen female will attempt to have her way with you. I happen to know Thane Brennan has warned his people that Rifellans are off the menu from now on."

Jagloren shook his head. "You should allow me some self-delusion. It is the only kind thing you can do."

She snorted and left the room to find parchment and a pen for her list.

***

The trip from Rifella via the Mora Waters was calm, and Dayleeya explored every inch of the ship. Jagloran spent most of his time lounging on deck, reading all the information Murwenna had given him regarding Glowen and Thane Brennan. Everything during the voyage had been handled with as much ease as possible.

Their entrance at the Netht Dowron bought them to the

docks on the north side of the river.

Thane Brennan's representative, Molatana, met them and gathered them and their four packing cases of goods. He loaded up a couple of horse-drawn carts and whisked them off to their new house in the village area surrounding the Keep.

He chatted during the trip to the Keep. "This busy area contains the homes of many of those who hold responsible positions at the Keep—the Rifellan guard unit members, the Horse Master, and a number of the managers of specific sections of Glowen. Only a few kitchen workers and immediate councilors to Brennan lived within the Keep."

Jagloren asked if he and Dayleeya would be living in the area surrounding the Keep.

Molatana nodded. "You will indeed. The outside village gives the inhabitants there the opportunities to enjoy stables attached to their homes and plenty of space to house their progeny and aging parents. You will appreciate the sense of freedom that will give you."

Molatana handed them the keys. "Thane Brennan wishes you to take your time unpacking so that by the time you meet with him, the stress of moving will have abated. Your two horses will be brought within the next day, and a young male will accompany them. He will be your permanent help with the stables, and he lives not far from you." With those words, he left to return to the Keep.

***

Four turns after Jagloran and his mate disembarked, they were still unpacking in their new home.

Jagloren paused in opening the final carton. "Our luck has been excellent with our arrival here, but we still have not had an audience with Thane Brennan."

Dayleeya dropped herself onto a chair. "I think he is being extremely kind and giving us time to settle in." She stretched her back. "We only have this last carton to empty, and I do not really care for unpacking. Could we head over to the Keep dining hall and have our noon-turn meal?"

Jagloren was just about to reply when someone knocked at the door. "I wonder who that is?"

He opened the door and a young woman in blue robes stood on their porch, smiling. "You must be Jagloren and" -- she looked inside the house --"and you must be Dayleeya. I am Marreth, Healer for Thane Brennan."

Dayleeya called out. "Come in Marreth, we are just pausing from our unpacking. We're considering heading to the Keep for our noon-turn meal."

"You do not need to do that. Thane Brennan has sent me to request you join him and his mate, Lilliwon for a meal in his quarters."

"Perfect. We have been wanting to meet with him. Will you also be at the meal?"

"No. I have dined with him many times, but now the Thane only wishes to hand me some instructions. If you would follow me."

47

"Can you give us a minute or two? I need to wash my face and Jagloren needs to locate a clean shirt."

"Please do what you need to."

***

Dayleeya returned to the room with a different blouse and a pair of long black slacks.

Jagloren raised an eyebrow. "I would say you did more than wash your face, mate of mine."

"Well, I could not look like a vagabond, could I?"

Marreth laughed at them and headed toward the door. "Thane Brennan is not a formal person, but I prefer not to keep him waiting too long."

The three left the Rifellans' home and walked across the cobbled roadway to the front gate of the Keep, which stood open.

Jagloran eyed the entrance. "I have visited most of the Keeps on Pridden, and I rarely see the entrances open. Do Glowens not feel the need for protection?"

Marreth looked at hm, curiosity wrinkling her forehead. "Protection from what?"

"People who may wish to rob you or those who might be criminals."

"Praetor, you are most often hired to protect a land, so that is a logical thought on your part. However, Glowen is quite different. First, they have few visitors from other areas. Glowen is also fortunate to have an excellent bounty of food, so no citizen wants for a comfortable life. And if you are aware of the reputation of Glowens for physical pleasures, you will also discover they have no desire for aggression. I do suspect there are some who want more and may be tempted to rob or steal. That is so rare, that if someone did, they would be caught and handled with incredible speed."

Jagloren pondered her words. "I suspect being a Praetor in Glowen may not be an onerous or demanding position."

Marreth laughed. "You are probably correct. However, I will tell you that once the star disappears below the horizon, we do close the gates."

***

By the time they arrived at Brennan's door, Marreth had expanded on the history of pleasure in Glowen and why that accounted for a crime rate of almost zero.

She knocked and Brennan himself came to the door, and grinned at them, giving the appearance of genuine pleasure at their presence. He was an attractive man with short black hair and the extraordinary eyes common to the Glowens. He had the build of a strong warrior, used to fighting, but his eyes twinkled. "Come in, come in. I have been most anxious to meet with you Praetor Jagloren." He extended his hand. "And you must be the beautiful Dayleeya I have heard so much about."

Jagloren placed his hand on Dayleeya's waist. *I hope the Thane is not attempting to flirt with my mate?*

A glorious woman, her hair streaked with silver stands, standing further back stepped forward. "Praetor, do relax. My mate cannot help himself. He adores all attractive things in life and is compelled to express his admiration. However, it does not mean he wishes to possess whatever he admires. I apologize, I should have introduced myself. I am Lilliwon." Her voice was smooth and rich, unlike the gruff voice of her spouse.

Dayleeya took Brennan's hand. "I thank you Thane Brennan for your admiration. No woman can have too many admirers."

The Thane turned to his mate. "I told you Lilliwon, these Rifellans are cultured people and fully understand why I would admire them. And please, Dayleeya, we do not stand on ceremony here in Glowen. Please call me Brennan."

She smiled. "I will, Brennan."

The Thane ushered them all to seats at the enormous table in the center of the room. The flatware gleamed a rich silver, and the crisp white napkins beside the delicate thin glassware spoke of wealth and admiration of fine things.

Brennan turned to Dayleeya. "Do you like the glasses for the wine?"

"They are magnificent. I have never seen such fine work."

"Glowen is most fortunate. We have one of the finest glass blowers on all of Pridden. His name is Garren pen Darren. If there is anything you wish to have in your home just because it is beautiful, please meet with him."

"From what you have told me, there are many beautiful items which might tempt me."

Brennan patted her hand like an indulgent parent. "My Lilliwon is an expert on artwork. Please make sure you ask her anything you want."

Once the meal was complete, they excused themselves. Dayleeya mentioned she still needed to unpack a few more things, and Jagloren told his Thane that he wished to take a tour of Glowen with one of his men to understand how people lived and worked in this land."

"Excellent, Praetor. Here is a supply of chits so that you can purchase anything you need. You will not be challenged by the physical desires of our people. They are well aware to refrain from acting in their normal manner with you."

Jagloren and Dayleeya took their leave and headed back to their home.

***

Two passes later, Jagloren was touring Glowen for the fifth time and had left Dayleeya at home this journey. By accident, she had consumed Orenberry skins, and although it was only a small dose of the poison on the fruits it still was sufficient to make her unwell enough to avoid travel.

Jagloren did his best to take an evaluation trip through Glowen at least twice per pass. He had never encountered any problems and on the contrary, always found some new products to take home for Dayleeya.

On this particular occasion, he met up with a woman rumored to be from another world. She encountered an enormous challenge because she was unprepared for the Glowen's physical predilections. As a result, she managed to insult some, attracted one too many, and annoyed others. Her travel companion, Mouse, admitted to Jagloren that Kat, as she was named, was unbelievably irresponsible and stubborn as well. Jagloren suggested they travel with as much speed as possible and seek help from Thane Brennan.

He was relieved to leave them behind and make his way back to his home with all possible speed. He missed Dayleeya and wished she had travelled with him.

***

His mate, languishing at home and recovered, at last, from her bout with Orenberry poisoning, had travelled with her mate on two different occasions, and always found the excursions delightful. *I so enjoyed it when we stopped at the furred stingers' village. Between those gorgeous fragrant candles and the scented ritual oils, I always find ways to titillate Jagloren.* She often wondered about the actual physical relationships between Glowens. *Can they really be satisfying? I cannot imagine desiring a second physical relationship. Jagloren is more than enough mate for me. He keeps me happy.*

She brightened when she caught the sound of the door

opening. "Is that you?"

"I hope you think so. Were you expecting another?"

She hugged him. "Not yet. Although I missed you, and I wondered if Glowens avoid that by having extra lovers. It was fortunate you were not gone long. So, what goodies did you bring me?"

"Am I only good for bringing you presents? As if I would forget you." He opened the large leather backpack he had travelled with. "I found some of your favorite things." He grinned at her. "Plus, I bought a few unusual pieces of art." He handed her a picture painted by an artist he had met in Kamerdow.

"Jagloren, it is fantastic. How odd for you to notice something like this."

"Well, I met an odd woman."

Dayleeya's eyebrows climbed almost up to her hairline.

He grimaced at her. "She was unusual because she apparently came from another world. And she ran afoul of the Glowens and their customs, so I suggested she leave with haste and seek Brennan's help as soon as possible. I did not want to become involved in her challenges, so I parted company from her and her guide at my first opportunity."

"Did she suggest this for me?"

"Yes. I told her of some of the things you liked, and she also purchased the scented ritual oils, so I assumed she might be right when she suggested I buy this for you."

"You did well. Thank you for my gifts." Dayleeya giggled. "However, you know very well you will get to enjoy my oils as well."

He grabbed her around the waist and pulled her to him, his voice gruff. "I missed you."

She kissed him, and ran her tongue over his lips. "Go and lock the door."

He shuffled backward to the door without taking his eyes off her.

She picked up the scented ritual oil, opened it, and dabbed it on her neck.

Licking her lips, she glided toward the bedroom, smiling to herself.

PENROW

The Master Builder of Kaylin

Aflinda strode through his front door and flinched at the sound of shrieks from his offspring. He looked around for Engrin, his mate. He found her in the kitchen preparing their morning meal. "Ah, there you are. The Brynosh will be ready to harvest in three more turns. I know you will want to be caring for Penrow, so I have managed to find two new workers to help with the gathering of the stalks."

He flinched again at the shrieks emanating from the bedroom area. "Why is he making so much noise? He sat at the table and poured tea for them both.

Engrin set a plate of food in front of him, and sat down with another, sighing. "I have misplaced his favorite toy. As usual, he wants it. Now."

Aflinda drank from his tea. "Master Godrith will be delighted at the quality of the Brynosh this season. This is one of the best yields we have enjoyed in many passes."

Engrin patted him on the arm. "I am so grateful you have found help. This progeny of ours is a young devil. Although he can only stand up for a few moments, his ability to crawl has intensified. He moves with such speed I have to run to keep up with him. He removed all the pots and pans from the cupboards, but now he is settled in the enclosure you constructed for him, yelling for something."

"Should we take him anything?"

"I am going to give him those pretty blocks of wood you created. The most interesting thing is that those are the playthings he enjoys the most. He keeps putting them on top of one another into building shapes, until he knocks the entire construction over. I took them away from him because he kept knocking them over, which was causing me an aching head. Obviously, I will have to return them to him."

"After the noon meal on the previous turn, I found him beside the back door, putting small rocks into piles." Aflinda laughed. "Perhaps he will become a builder of homes."

Engrin rolled her eyes. "Oh, no. It will cost an enormous amount to apprentice him to a builder. Perhaps you would best be putting credits aside for his education." She suddenly shrieked. "Penrow, stay in your barrier." She rushed over to the door to the reading room, and plucked him from the edges of the construction intended to keep him safe. "Aflinda, I need someone to help me with him. He is so strong for such a young one. Before we know it, he will be dragging me across the floor. Plus, he appears able to escape any attempt I make at containing him."

Her mate sighed heavily. "And he is not yet walking?" He rubbed at his jaw. "I will speak to Praetor Bardu and ask if he can suggest a youngish male we can hire."

"Not too young. He will need to be stronger than this imp of ours."

***

"Excuse me, Sir Aflinda, may I enter?"

Aflinda turned around in his seat and saw Krenna, the young Rifellan who had been helping Engrin with Penrow's care. "Of course, come in. Please do not tell me Penrow has become too much of a burden. He is only five passes old now."

"Not at all. He and I have become fast friends. He may be much younger than me, but he is as smart, -- perhaps, I suspect, smarter than I. He never ceases to astonish me with his knowledge."

"I am not surprised to hear you say this. He never stops asking questions. Engrin has sent him to many learned men and women to get his questions answered. However, it never appears quite enough. I have no idea how we will handle him when he reaches ten passes."

"I wish to speak with you about him and the speed with which he is learning. Penrow is enamored with building, and I am convinced that what he really wishes is to become a builder in his own right. I would like to suggest you apprentice him to Master Builder Janset in Shendea."

"We would like nothing more than to give him the opportunity, but we are not a wealthy family. Master Janset's instruction is costly, and we cannot afford to send him there."

"I may be able to help you solve that. My male parent is a close friend of the Master, and Praetor Bardu is his cousin. My parent owes Praetor Bardu an extraordinary amount for help he received in the past. I have spoken to the Praetor, and he is willing to ask my parent to approach the Master to request he accept Penrow as an apprentice for a reduced fee. If I asked my parent myself, he would probably say no. He does not yet trust my judgment."

"Truly? Praetor Bardu and your parent would do that for us?"

"Yes. The Praetor has been the recipient of Penrow's questioning a number of times, and he is convinced your progeny has a significant future as a builder."

"Krenna if you can accomplish that for Penrow, we will be forever in your debt. Please do whatever you can. Engrin and I thank you with all our hearts."

Krenna bobbed his head. "I will speak to the Praetor now." He turned and left the room.

Aflinda sat for a moment thinking about opportunity, and then jumped up in excitement. "Engrin. Engrin. Where are you? I have the most extraordinary news."

She appeared at the doorway to his work office, eyes wide. "What is it?"

He caught her up in his arms and danced around the room, startling her so she laughed and said, "What? Again."

He sat her down and told her what Krenna had promised.

She burst into tears.

Aflinda opened his mouth, astonished at her reaction. "Why are you crying? This is exceptional."

"It is remarkable. I am overwhelmed with the idea that we can give our talented Penrow the education he needs to live his best life. My tears are those of joy, not sorrow."

During the next ten turns, Penrow's parents prepared him for the journey to Shendea to be apprenticed to Master Janset. While both of them were sad that they would miss their young one, Penrow appeared too excited, to consider being homesick.

When his parents waved farewell to him, they prepared to have some emptiness in their lives.

As Penrow disappeared around a bend in the road, Aflinda turned to his mate. "Do you realize this will be the first time we will be alone in our home since Penrow birthed?"

"I do. And I have missed our evenings together. We have always had to be so quiet because Penrow woke up so easily."

He put his arms around her and kissed her. "I do believe a celebration is in order."

She responded to him, grabbing his hand and leading him to the bedroom. "However, Aflinda, you must take care not to spread the seed of another Penrow in my body."

He laughed and began removing clothes on their way to the big comfortable bed.

***

For six passes, Penrow worked with Master Builder Janset. Every day, he learned something new. He discovered the way to build walls of stone without any cement in between, the careful cutting of stone so the resulting walls kept the interior warm and dry, the carving of wood to create staircases and window frames, how to match wood planks to each other so that floors blended well; and how strong foundations kept a house upright and helped it to last for hundreds of passes.

Penrow continued to ask questions. "Master, in the Clog Neran, we have extraordinary stone, set with crystals of many, and I would like to be able to build with it to create beautiful dwellings. Can you advise me the best way to cut this type of stone?"

"Hmm. I have never had the opportunity to work with that stone. We should work on it together, and both of us will learn the best use of it."

With Janset often suggesting they work on a project together, Penrow soon began to feel confident enough to consider starting his own business back in Kaylin. Janset then taught him the way to draft the outlines and interiors of buildings of new and unusual designs. As his reputation grew, many of Janset's customers allowed Penrow to design their houses when the Master was busy and unable to begin their projects without delay.

At the end of his seventh pass, the Master called Penrow to his office. "Penrow. How many houses have you designed for my customers this pass?"

"Four or five, Master. I have lost track."

"I believe it is time for you to return to Kaylin and begin your own business of building houses there. We will spend the next fifteen turns or so practicing tracking your business so that you can always tell whether you are moving forward, or have. When you decide to bond with a woman, I would suggest she maintain your records, leaving you free to seek out new building materials and create new designs."

Penrow hung his head. "While I would enjoy learning the way to keep records of my business, I am afraid I might never meet a female I would like to mate with."

Janset laughed. "You have only just attained your journeyman status, and will now begin to enjoy attention from many of the young females who are available. Once your own business is flourishing, I am convinced it will not be long before you become a Master."

"Many thanks for all your patience, Master Janset. I will send a moth to my parents to advise them when I will be returning home."

***

While Janset began to instruct Penrow in the intricacies of business practice, he spent more time eating in the kitchens of Garrin. Since visitors needed to pass through the village to meet with Lord Rhognor, Penrow met citizens of many other lands. One remarkable night, a group of Glowens were enjoying the benefits of the kitchen, when a woman of extraordinary beauty, caught Penrow's attention

Her skin glowed golden, and her hair, smooth and silky, shone like a black waterfall under the lights of the kitchen.

He turned to one of his Rifellan friends at the table. "Who is that glorious woman with the Glowen group?"

"I believe she is the daughter of a wealthy Glowen couple who are of supreme importance in the wine industry. You are good looking enough to appeal to her. Go and talk to her."

Penrow stood, nervous, feeling strange emotions he did not understand, approached the table. "Excuse me."

The young female turned to look at him and Penrow was struck by the bolts of light from the sky. Her eyes, with dark blue rims, presented the palest blue irises he had ever seen. Transfixed by those eyes, Penrow stared at her.

He stammered. "I am Penrow, a journeyman Builder of houses."

She gazed at him, her mouth slightly open and breathed a reply. "I am Altona."

They stared at each other without moving.

At last, Altona spoke. "I am overheated in this room. May we stroll in the cool air outside?"

All Penrow could manage was a nod. She took, and they headed outdoors.

They rambled along the paths, bewitched with each other. When Penrow pulled her behind a tree and leaned in for a kiss, she responded immediately and pressed her body to his.

Breathless and almost unable to contain himself, he reached for her. He wanted to mate with this woman now, and he ran his hands over her body, taking possession of her breasts and pressing his arousal to her without being able to cease.

She pulled back a bare minimum. "Who are you? Why do I want you with such desperation?"

"I do not know. I suspect Caleesh is suggesting we should bond. Will you come with me to my house?"

Her breathing was erratic. "Yes. I am a Glowen. We act quickly when we know what we wish. So yes, now, take me to your house."

Once inside his home, they undressed, clothing flying everywhere, and naked, they fell on the bed and joined their bodies in the way that men and women do when obsessed with each other.

***

The following morn when they woke, Penrow gazed at Altona and reached for her again.

She opened her eyes and responded to his ministrations. "I cannot resist you Penrow. I adore you and never wish to leave you."

"Will you agree to bond with me and be my mate, forever?"

"I wish no other to share my bed. I am yours always."

***

After forty more turns, they departed for Kaylin after obtaining approval of Altona's parents. Penrow was thrilled to learn she was expecting progeny.

They went to the home of his parents, and there, bursting with pride, he announced Altona's state.

In the subsequent turns, the two startled his parents because they spent so much time loving each other.

Engrin glanced at Aflinda as they sat at the morning meal, and grinned at him. "When we first met, did we mate as often as our Penrow and his Altona do?"

He shook his head. "No, I do believe they have been more active than we ever were."

Engrin smiled and ducked her head. "No wonder she is already expecting progeny."

"You should be delighted. We will soon have a young babe in our house, since I followed your wishes and refrained from planting another Penrow in your body."

She rolled her eyes at him, but grinned. "I am delighted to see our Penrow so happy with his mate. I often worried it might be difficult for him to find someone who would accept him. Based on the amount of time they spend in their bed he should build a home for them soon. He will need many rooms to house all his progeny."

Aflinda stared at her. "You possess magic. He has already shown me the drawings for the house he plans to build for them. And, yes, he has included many rooms for the numerous offspring he intends to have."

"Has he said where he will build it?"

"He has decided upon land adjacent to Clog Neran. He has always been fascinated by the crystals in the stone from there."

"How ever did he manage to obtain the rights to the land?"

"You are aware he has always been a friend of Praetor Bardu, because he helped him become apprentice to Master Builder Janset. The Praetor's mate is Irina, and her sibling is the Metal Master, Liandock, who lives at Lanfair. The Metal Master interceded on Penrow's behalf with Lord Eduardo."

Engrin shook her head in apparent wonderment. "Our Penrow is well connected in Pridden. I am so proud of the male he has become."

Aflinda breathed a sigh of contentment. "I find it difficult to wait to discover what else he accomplishes."

***

Over the next two seasons, Penrow spent as many turns as possible working on his new home which he referred to as Mammac. He left Altona in the care of his parents, which she appreciated, as she grew bigger and bigger with her progeny.

When their home was ready enough for Altona to join him, he hired a cook, a cleaner, and a healer to help with the household and the pending birth. He brought Altona to their house in a carriage, making sure the wheels were well sprung, so the journey remained as comfortable as possible. He had built the rooms for the two of them and their forth coming progeny all on one floor, assuming Altona would not wish to be up and down stairs with a newborn. The second wing of the house contained two stories, with rooms for younger ones on the lower floor, and the second-floor bedrooms reserved for older siblings as they grew.

Engrin accompanied Altona in the carriage to the new home, prepared to help the young female on her journey to Mammac.

When they arrived, Altona exclaimed at the beauty of colored crystals winking in the sunlight. "Oh Penrow, the house is like a huge jewel."

Laughing, Penrow lifted her from the carriage and carried her in his arms to the most comfortable couch in the house. Engrin had not seen him for more than two seasons and marveled at how tall and how strong he had become, so much so that he reminded her of drawings of the massive growlers that had been rumored to live in the high reaches of Clog Arth. They were reputed to be frightening and vicious. But through every turn, Penrow's face wreathed in smiles once Altona was ensconced in their new home. It was clear that her family's appreciation of all things pleasant in food, wine, and life in general had captured Penrow's fancy. He often took Altona for sedate walks on the property and he always found small flowers to present to her. When they returned from their stroll through the grounds, he consumed flagons of wine and plenty of food, while Altona ate only small amounts.

Soon, however Altona had difficulty handling walking anywhere. Her belly became huge, and she ached all over. She spent little time laughing with Penrow and preferred to sleep for seemingly endless periods.

The Healer approached Engrin and asked to speak with her outside. "I am worried about the lady Altona. She is far bigger than I anticipated, and her energy is flagging. I would like you to remain here to help me with the birth, and I have already sent a moth to Healer Wynneth requesting an additional healer to help us."

"Oh no. Is she in danger?"

"I hope not, but we may have to cut her open to allow the babe to live."

"Will that endanger Altona?"

"No more than allowing her to go through the natural birthing process."

"Do you know why she is so huge?"

"I do not. At first, I wondered if she was having womb mates, but I can detect no other heart-beat, so that is not the challenge."

Engrin sighed. "I too am worried. I will stay and help you as much as I am able."

***

Turns passed, and Altona's health declined. Even Penrow began to look worried. "Is she going to be fine?"

The Healer, patted him on the shoulder. "I hope so. If she has not birthed by the morrow, we will have no choice but to cut the babe from her."

Penrow frowned. "Will she live through that?"

"Many females have needed the cut, and it has saved their lives. This is why we will need to do this to Altona."

***

On the morrow, both Healers and Engrin wheeled Altona into an empty room, which they had set up to perform the cut. Wynneth, who arrived herself to help with the birthing, administered a sedative, supplied by the Glowens. Altona's eyes became heavy-lidded and she dropped off to sleep. Wynneth proceeded with the cutting. The babe drawn from Altona was female and Engrin smiled at the thought of how Penrow would deal with a female progeny.

Wynneth handed the babe to the other healer, and began to close the wound. Before she could go further, she gasped. "There is another babe, but it does not live. It has been inside Altona too long and has caused an illness inside her. I will do my best to cleanse her, but I do not know if I can remove all the sickness."

Engrin stared at Wynneth. "Will she survive?"

"I do not know. I am afraid she has had this sickness inside her for far too long."

Wynneth did her best and with her brow now soaked with sweat, closed up the cut.

While the other Healer prepared the new babe, Engrin and Wynneth eyed Altona with close scrutiny, waiting for her to wake.

They watched anxiously when her eyelids fluttered, and she groaned. Her words were slurred. "Penrow, I love you. Call her Illian." Her breath rattled in her throat, her eyes closed, and she was gone.

When Engrin told Penrow the news, he roared and pounded his fist into the closest wall, creating a hole in the plaster. He retreated to one of the rooms on the second floor and refused to see his progeny.

Wynneth brought in a lactating female to feed the new babe and cautioned Engrin that she and the other Healer should persuade Penrow to meet with his progeny. "He needs to bond with this little female.

Engrin picked up the swaddled babe. "I have an idea." She walked up to the second floor and entered the room where Penrow lay on his bed, sobbing.

He snapped at her. "Take that creature away. It killed my Altona."

"She did not kill your Altona. There was a second babe who had ceased to live inside her. That babe created a sickness in Altona, and that was what sent her to Caleesh."

Engrin stood beside the bed. "Sit up, Penrow. This is your progeny. Altona gave her life for her and requested she

69

be called Illian. Do not treat Altona's sacrifice with such disdain. Hold Illian. She needs you."

The minute the babe was placed in his arms, she gave a little burp, gurgled and smiled at him. The change in the big man was instantaneous. A single tear ran down his left cheek. He growled, gruffness in his voice. "She is beautiful, like her parent." He looked up at Engrin. "Altona wanted her to be called Illian?"

"She did. And she wanted you to love her."

***

So Penrow accepted Illian as his, and she thrived.

Illian grew up loved by the Herculean bear of a man and in her turn, learned to love all the things he adored. Over time she became fascinated by buildings and materials of wood, stone, glass, and crystals.

Penrow did not feel the need to send her to apprentice with Janset. He was now a Master in his own right and Janset had aged and would not accept novice builders any more.

Illian began her training with Penrow while she was still less than fifteen passes, and Penrow gave her the journeyman badge when she reached nineteen.

Engrin and Aflinda came for the ceremony and were delighted to view the wonderful relationship that had developed between Penrow and Illian. They growled at, each other, and fought as though they were deadly enemies. The truth was they were as close as any parent and offspring could be.

Liandock, the Metal Master, often joined them for meals, but Illian was never drawn to him. She often took her pleasure with visiting males, but she never permitted them to enjoy more than one night with her.

Both gained fame as Master Builders.

Illian continued to design and build family houses and farm structures.

However, Penrow turned his hand to bridges and vast meeting areas. He had even been hired by Lord Eduardo to create an addition to the Lord's Keep.

Penrow gained the love of many people throughout Pridden and was kept young by constantly warring with his much-loved progeny. Everyone who came into contact with him remarked about his warmth and his love of life.

But Penrow never forgot Altona. He remained unmated for the rest of his life.

CATHKED

Thane of Baklai

Thane Argonites was enthralled by a pair of the most extraordinary dark brown eyes. He had never met Evanor before, but he viewed her as one of the most beautiful women in the land. Her ebony skin glowed with health, and he knew it would feel like silk beneath his fingers. When she smiled and flashed brilliant white teeth at him it became a miracle. When many of his people glimpsed his blue eyes and the patches of blond in his hair, a genetic gift from his Rifellan female parent, they tended to be suspicious. Their apparent distrust of him, convinced him that he would be without a mate. His entire life was colored by the what he interpreted as the people of Baklai's reluctant acceptance of him as their Thane. Their evident distrust increased when he inherited the post upon his male parent's departure from life. He had been well-trained to handle his duties as a Thane, but he wondered how long he would last, living with the distrust of the Baklai.

His skin the color of cinnamon, and the streaks of blonde among his black curls, caused his people to be wary of him, even though they accepted his right to rule their land. But Evanor not only accepted him, she gave him the love that he craved with such desperation, and when, after only half a season, she agreed to bond with him, he sensed that, at last, he had attained the status of a true male of Baklai.

His own female parent had been united with Caleesh not long after his birth. His remaining parent considered him responsible for the departure of the woman who bore him. Now, mated with a strong and beautiful woman who was full Baklai born, the odd result was that his people appeared to relax around him. Many would assert, that he became easier to be around. He now appeared less insecure about himself.

Within the fifth pass of their union, Evanor presented him with a male offspring. The second miracle in Argonites's life was that young Cathked possessed rich brown skin, dark brown curly hair, and piercing brown eyes. No one viewed him as anything but a true Baklai.

Argonites kissed his exhausted mate as soon as he saw Cathked. "He is perfect, my love. No one will ever question his right to rule Baklai. He is the perfect Baklai warrior."

Evanor gazed at him through tired eyes. "No one really ever judged you as an imperfect Thane. Only your own attitude did that." She sighed and blinked at him. "Please allow the healer to finish her ministrations to help after my strenuous birthing. Go and brag to your friends about your perfect offspring."

He left her with reluctance. Friends? He hmphed to himself. *Evanor does not realize she is my only friend.*

***

A few turns later, Argonites sat writing out some additional duties for his immediate guards and councilors when he stopped, and put his pen down on the table. *Friends? Evanor referred to friends.* True, there were no males with whom he drank at various inns. But there were a number of men he trusted. As he thought about it, there were a number of males in whom he placed complete trust. *Surely, friends are those you trust, are they not?* What would happen if he reached out to them and revealed a little more of himself. Would he then be permitted to refer to them as friends?

My mate has just birthed my heir. It is a time to celebrate. He stood up and tugged at the tassel in the corner.

A young male knocked on the door, and Argonites said, "Please advise Gayzella, my Head of House; Galakis, the Hunter Master; Penabon, the Horse Master; and Makinti, Praetor for Baklai, plus my two councilors, to all join me in my rooms for a meeting after the mid-turn meal. Also, will you request that the kitchens supply us with tea and small snacks for the meeting?"

"Yes, Sire, I will make these arrangements for you."

***

Seated at the immense wooden table in his meeting room, Argonites greeted his advisors as they entered one after the other, and settled into their seats. Praetor Makinti, a handsome young Rifellan with bronze skin, blond hair, and blue eyes, sat on his right side. Makinti, an impressive male, also wore a scar, like a physical award, running over his eye and down his right cheek. He had earned this in a battle when he was only eighteen passes and, at that time had yet to become a seasoned warrior. Next to him sat Hunter Master Galakis, a serious, almost humorless male. He was about the same age as the Thane and his skin, eyes, and hair were all the same dark brown. Unlike younger males who tended to have wild hair, he wore his cut short and neat. It fitted with his air of dedicated responsibility.

On Argonites's left sat Horse Master Penabon, a powerfully built Baklai warrior with dark-brown skin, brown eyes, and shaggy black hair. Nearly as tall as the Thane, his demeanor seemed always somber in his dealing with people. He related far more to horses than his Baklai companions. The males who worked with him were convinced he might understand and speak the same language as the horses he trained.

Gayzella, the Thane's Head of House, sat beside Penabon. As the only woman in the room, the men treated her with the deference she deserved. It was due to her abilities that all ran without challenges. As a female who had served for many years at the Keep, the Thane held her in high esteem.

Argonites's two councilors were ensconced in the last two seats at the table.

Argonites waited until two kitchen helpers entered the room and placed mugs of Orenberry wine and tea for Gayzella on the table. He asked one of the helpers to close the door as they left.

The people around the table looked at him with expectation.

He drank from his wine glass. "I have called you all here because I need advice and a little help."

There were murmurs of interest.

"As you may be aware, my mate, Evanor, has given birth to my heir, Cathked. We have waited many passes for this blessing in our lives, and now there is an heir to the Thaneship in Baklai. I would like to ask all of you to supply me with ideas on how this should be celebrated with our people."

Each of them offered congratulations, except for Gayzella, who not only was aware of the birth but had already gifted Evanor with a tiny coverall for the babe.

Makinti stood. "Thane Argonites, are both Evanor and Cathked well enough to travel?"

He nodded. "They are. It has been more than twelve turns since Cathked birthed. Why?"

"You could perhaps consider having a brief parade around the courtyard of the inner Keep and a further short tour of the outer village. We can arrange a comfortable carriage for her, and pad it with many blankets. This would give many of the people a chance to view the babe now. Of course, I would suggest we keep it a reasonable length."

"Praetor, do you think this would be a safe endeavor?"

"I do, my Thane. We have been blessed with an exceptional harvest, and thus, the Baklai people are happy and well fed. With Lord Taliaferro as Lord in Morden, there have been no border skirmishes. He is an excellent leader in Morden and wishes to have fine relations with our land. While there are a number of Mordens who dislike our people, they all need our horses, and are willing to maintain peaceful relations with us."

"Excellent. Makinti, even though I would, under normal circumstances, use my Praetor to lead this parade, I would prefer Penabon to be responsible this time. Our people have often appeared to be uncomfortable with me as Thane because of my strange coloring and half-breed genes. I therefore think that a Baklai-born warrior is the best person to pick."

"I agree, Argonites." Makinti turned to the Hunter Master. "Penabon, are you amenable to lead this parade displaying our heir to Thane Argonites through the Keep and the immediate area?"

Penabon bowed his head to Argonites. "I am honored to do so, my Thane."

Argonites rose from his chair. "Thank you all for your kind words and your help. When Cathked takes over as Thane of Baklai, I hope that all of you are still serving in your current positions. He will be a fortunate leader."

They all nodded goodbye, and began to file out of the room, but Makinti stopped and asked Argonites if he might have a word.

When the room cleared Makinti faced the Thane. "Sire, I am so pleased you called upon your councilors to ask for our help in this. I know you experienced much difficulty when you took over the leadership of Baklai. Your male parent neglected you after your female parent perished at the teeth and claws of a hissar."

Argonites shook his head. "I cannot claim that neglect by my parents created difficulty for me. I blame the odd coloring in my skin and hair from the recessive Rifellan genes that showed up after my birth. My people did not trust me. Although I believe that, thanks to my mate, Evanor, they are slowly changing their minds."

"Nevertheless, my Thane. You created two valuable achievements today. The first is that your councilors considered it to be an honor to be told of something personal about you. The second is that they believe you have shown trust in them. It is so important that you continue to establish stronger relationships with your councilors. Allow them to see more things about you that are personal. And you can trust your advisors. They are committed to you as their Thane."

Argonites put out his hand. "Thank you, Makinti. You have given me valuable advice today. I do trust my councilors, and it is you, Praetor, whom I trust the most."

***

Argonites continued to give his councillors insights

into his life. They learned very quickly that he adored Evanor and, unlike many Baklai males, experienced no unsettled thoughts about his mate. Baklai developed like many other lands, and although it appeared to be a patriarchal society, in reality, the women controlled many aspects of Baklai life. Their society was, in truth, an egalitarian one. But Baklai had once been a patriarchy, and the males were not yet completely ready to accept the benefits of real equality with their females. They tended to view the females with a sense of discomfort. However, Argonites, who had been viewed for much of his life as flawed, appeared comfortable with the values of both males and females. His progeny, Cathked, as he grew, possessed no doubts, and appeared precisely in tune with the egalitarian point of view, maintaining that view as he grew to manhood. Evanor had beautiful dark brown, almost black skin, and so Cathked showed none of the Rifellan recessive gene coloring.

When Cathked reached nineteen passes, Argonites, who aged poorly, joined with Caleesh.

Cathked took over as Thane of Baklai, and he attained the growth of a fine young male. Because of his additional worship of the Hunter god Calanta, and his admiration of the magnificent and spiritual Hunter birds, his people gave him the nickname of Hunter Cathked. Every person in the land acknowledged him as extremely handsome. His dark, piercing-brown eyes and the rich brown of his skin found great favor with the unmated females. In addition, he was quite tall for a Baklai and rode one of the biggest horses available, which he handled with skill. As he continued to rule as Thane, the Mordens, who lived adjacent to Baklai, changed and became even more unpredictable. With the murder of Lord Taliaferro and his family by Gritch, according to others in Morden, the lines between Cathked's eyes deepened, and his ability to distrust became stronger with each passing season. He kept his beard shadow short, which served to add to his sober appearance. He did not laugh at much, and the constant strain of leadership of a land next door to Morden, showed in his demeanor.

His councillors, the very same ones who had aided his parent, encouraged him to arrange celebrations of harvest, of plantings, and of the mating and birth of horses. Horses were Baklai's finest product, and they obtained many items from other lands, including Rifellan guards for protection, from the sale their horses. Although Cathked attended these celebrations, he only did so because it was expected of a Thane. He did his best to seem involved, but for a sober young male like Cathked, these joyous occasions were an anathema to him. He was well aware that the posting of Rifellan warriors in his land kept the Mordens from raiding Baklai to steal horses, but to him, the presence of that tenuous border continued to prey on his mind. He perceived Morden to be like an enormous weight upon his shoulders.

However, at one such celebration, something odd happened. Cathked met Kerdinon, a young Baklai-born female, whose male parent hailed from Morden. Cathked disliked the male from the start, but fell in love with his progeny at his first sight of her. Cathked's councilors surveyed the pair with hope. Was it possible that this young female might bring a lightness to their Thane? She appeared to be as smitten with him as he was with her.

However, the course of love does not always run easily or without challenges. While Kerdinon's Baklai parent expressed delight that her progeny had attracted the Thane and eagerly suggested a mating between the two, her Morden parent was after benefits for himself. Cathked refused to be part of a bargaining session with a Morden, so this chore was left to his councilors to handle.

However, both Cathked and his councilors underestimated Kerdinon's own powers in dealing with her parent. She advised him that if he persisted in attempting to gain a position in Cathked's advisory group, she would have him banished to Morden, and he would never again be permitted to visit Baklai. Her parent backed down from his demands.

Thus, Kerdinon made it clear to the Thane she was willing to mate with him, and that her parent would not interfere. The two became a bonded pair, and Kerdinon gained what she wanted, to be acknowledged as Lady Kerdinon, bonded mate of Thane Cathked. For her, life became perfect.

***

During the first five passes of their bonding, Baklai

prospered under the Thane's rule. The sale of horses increased, and the latest Mating of Horses resulted in two stallions and five fillies. The farms located in Baklai produced enough foodstuffs that all its people enjoyed a comfortable living within the borders of their land. Baklai, revealed now as a land of peace, allowed all the inhabitants to believe they were safe and at ease. Morden had not even attempted to venture over Baklai's border, as the Rifellans continued to guard the borders for the Thane. This sense of security also helped the people maintain their well-being.

Cathked's councilors monitored the land next to theirs with trepidation, waiting for an indication of hostility from Galdin, who it was rumored had dispatched Gritch and, thus gained the Thaneship for himself. But all remained calm.

What Cathked did not know, was that Kerdinon had become bored with her life. Her parents, when she lived at home, acceded to her every whim, but the Thane, so involved in the running of Baklai did not spend the time with her that she felt she deserved. Had he been aware, he might have seen it as a challenge and done what he could to spend more time with his spoiled young mate.

***

Three passes later a strange female arrived in Baklai, under a huge cloud. Her valuable horse had been killed aboard a boat from Glowen. When she applied for a new mount, Cathked, convinced she had neglected the animal, was reluctant to approve.

However, it appeared that the female, Kat, enjoyed the protection of Lord Eduardo of Kaylin. This put a different light on the Thane's dealings with her.

In the end, Cathked did approve a horse for her, since Eduardo guaranteed payment, but he found the woman disconcerting.

Then the unthinkable happened. Kat, found illegally viewing a Mating of Horses, was arrested immediately. This was no minor flouting of a rule -- it was a matter of gross misconduct, punishable by death. No female had ever been allowed this privilege and the males of Baklai were enraged that she had ignored Baklai law. Cathked became apoplectic. He threw her into a Baklai prison and prepared to pass the ultimate sentence for her irresponsible behavior.

Two unusual things happened. While Kat admitted she had broken Baklai law, she gave a reasonable explanation for this, based upon the rules under which she lived in her own home. Her apology and well-spoken explanation, almost persuaded Cathked to be lenient. What, in reality, turned the sentence of death aside, was the fact that Eduardo considered her valuable to him. Plus, of course, her guide, Mouse's, extraordinary defense of her conduct, altered his decision. Cathked had encountered Mouse before, and both trusted and respected him. The sentence of death was dropped, but the Thane insisted that the woman be escorted out of Baklai by an accompanying guard.

Mouse and the assigned guard, Kesiad, escorted Kat from the Thane's Keep to the Rifellan border Keep, a journey intended to last only two turns.

On the way to the Rifellan Keep, the three spent the night at a border hut. During the night, they were attacked by a group of unknown guards. Kat, caught in one of the sleeping rooms, was captured, bound, and gagged to prevent her from escaping. It was here that the Assassin Ssestin found her, cut her bonds, and left her a knife as a weapon.

By extraordinary luck, Cathked and a division of his personal guards were on their regular inspection of the border against Morden insurgents. A young stable hand had slipped from the hut and, when he encountered the Thane's group, advised him of the attack.

The Thane's unit speeded up and, when they arrived at the hut, immediately set about defeating the unknown attackers. His guard unit seized them all, killing most by hurling them over the cliffs into the gorge of the Left Farralawn River.

Then Cathked discovered, to his horror, that Kerdinon had betrayed him, He gaped at her in disbelief. She had killed Kesiad with specific intent, captured Kat, and intended to turn her over to Galdin. Guaranteed a sizable fee and a promise of a position of power in Morden in order to perform her treasonous deeds, Kerdinon had joined forces with Galdin. To Cathked, it appeared that what she most desired was a position of power.

Cathked shook his head in astonishment. "You made a pact with Galdin?"

"He promised I would help him rule Morden. I thought it might be the way to bring peace between our two lands."

The Thane had difficulty believing Kerdinon had acted in such a treasonous manner, but everything was confirmed by Kat and the young assistant who managed the hut. In an instant, his love for Kerdinon turned into a violent, red rage.

Kerdinon reached out to him. "Cathked, it is not what you think--"

"Stop. By Calanta, you cannot expect me to believe you. I know you covet power, but how might you ever believe anything that vile male told you? You betrayed me and our people. Worse, you have committed an act of treason so odious, I cannot bear to look at you."

In Cathked's eyes, Kerdinon did not warrant a trial. Deaf to her entreaties and screams of fear, the Thane himself threw her over the cliffs of the Left Farralawn River, and within seconds, her screams stopped abruptly.

He did this without giving thought to his action. Cathked, a Thane who had evaluated Kat's actions with limited empathy, gave no quarter when it came to high treason.

***

Cathked continued to rule Baklai, now without a mate, but never considered bonding with any other female. His people respected him in his strict adherence to the rules of their land but walked softly in his presence. He reverted to his more sober and suspicious self. All trusted his word without question. However, he was also feared.

Baklai flourished as the only provider of horses in Pridden, and the Rifellans continued to protect Cathked and his people from the Mordens.

Baklai, not a land filled with mirth, but with common sense, prospered. Its people continued to live lives of hard work and dedication to their horses.

LADY HALFIN

The Last of the Enchanters

Near the Carrog Kennin, Shale sat with her mate, Griffin, discussing the challenges faced by their offspring, Halfin. "She has all the gentle nature of a full Enchanter already, but she has no other friends."

"She does not appear to be lonely."

"She is not lonely. She has every bird and animal this side of Dizerth always keeping her company. But she needs to be with other young Enchanters."

"Shale, you are her female parent. Can you not encourage her to mix with other Enchanters?"

"How can I? I cannot locate any others."

"What?" He narrowed his eyes. "Have you consulted with Frennor or with Ivanor?"

She sighed. "Frennor joined Caleesh this most recent pass without leaving progeny in his wake. And Ivanor's mate never produced any progeny before *she* left us to join Caleesh." She gave an even deeper sigh. "I have questioned every Enchanter family, and none have born offspring since they mated."

"Our Halfin is only four passes, I am sure there will be new young ones of our race before she is of age to mate,"

Shale shook her head. "I know of none who are still young enough themselves to produce viable progeny. I also doubt that if Halfin mates with a non-Enchanter, she will be able to produce a babe blessed with her abilities."

"How has everything managed to change so much? Are the Enchanters about to become eradicated from Shendea?"

"Not only Shendea, Griffin, but all of Pridden. I have a suspicion. The Healers have expanded their abilities, not only in Shendea, but are now welcome everywhere in Pridden. Perhaps Caleesh has decided to allow the Healers to replace us."

"Replace us? How can such a thing be?"

"Consider what is happening. At a time that our Enchanters are not producing babes with our talents, the Healers are expanding all over Pridden." She sighed. "All things change, and from what I observed, Caleesh is replacing those with our abilities with Healers. Their talents are similar to ours when it comes to the nature of our world, but they also possess an ability to help with physical problems that our people are sometimes challenged with."

"Your words make sense, Shale, but they are also the cause of sadness in me. Come, let us walk in the forest and go to the grove. We will ask Caleesh to give us wisdom enough to understand what is happening to our people. The goddess may even give us a way to help continue our line."

He took her by the hand and they left their home to walk the paths made by the passage of animals. They walked in silence, listening to the conversations of the birds, and the low murmurs of small animals who lived beneath the forest floor.

Finally, they entered a small clearing, bare of all bushes, but the ground was covered in long pine needles and shorter spruce ones. A green fragrance filled the air and curled around their nostrils, calling up peace and well-being.

A gnarled and lengthy log rested in the middle of the glade, facing a huge stump, on which someone had carved the word "allor". Others often referred to it as an altar. This became the sacred space where devotees deposited offerings for Caleesh in the form of flowers, fruit, or other growing plants. Strands of ivy hung from the tree behind the altar, like a curtain, hiding the bower of a gentle and cherished female. Caleesh meant much to all who lived in Shendea.

The two Enchanters walked to the log and sat, facing the chancel.

Griffin bowed his head. "Caleesh, we come before you to request help and knowledge in our time of confusion. We have searched for a potential mate for our beautiful Enchanter offspring, but cannot find any other of our people on Pridden. Are our kind ordained to be replaced by others? Does this mean our beautiful and gentle Halfin will never find a mate?"

Shale joined him in his prayers to the goddess. "Pease aid us in our confusion Caleesh. We are helpless without your guidance."

The two sat with bowed heads, breathing in the air in the forest, filled with the aromas of living creatures and the wonders of the creations of nature.

Silence reigned.

A tiny breeze stirred the ivy hanging from the trees and it became a wilder wind that parted the strands, exposing a carving of a glorious female on the massive oak.

The two raised their heads and gazed at the carving, hearts pounding in their chests. The wind played with their hair and filled their ears like the breath of angels. "Your family will not produce more offspring. Your end is near, and the earth will not continue your line. Halfin is an extraordinary female and is the last of her kind. But she will mate, and will enjoy her abilities until her end. She will long be remembered for what she achieved. There is one faint hope. If her mating is with a male of great abilities, she may be able to produce an offspring with Enchanter abilities. This is a possibility whose outcome is unknown to me. But for now, return home and do your best with the time you have left. No matter what the outcome, Enchanters will always be remembered on this world."

The wind died down, and the vines fell back in place. The birds began to sing again.

Shale turned to Griffin and held onto him. Tears run down her face, but she was not sad. "We are the last, Griffin, yet I have no regrets. Our Halfin will find a mate who will love her. Even if she does not bear a babe with Enchanter abilities, she will leave a mark on this world as the last of the Enchanters."

He stood, held out his hand, and brought her to her feet. "We should return home."

They left the clearing, and headed down the green paths to the unique little house they called home. The small wooden structure nestled in the far western edge of the Hanford Forest had become a haven for them. Constructed from young oak logs and with the seams filled with emerald green moss, it welcomed them with warmth and comfort.

***

For the next fourteen passes, Halfin grew into an exquisite female. Her talent with the animals of the forests, and her abilities with all growing things were unsurpassed by any other being. She laughed and sang and loved her family.

In her eighteenth pass, Healer Deleth visited her. The Healer asked Halfin if she could meet with her parents.

Shale appeared and welcomed Deleth into their home, just as Griffin exited his office.

Halfin ran to make tea while the other three sat in the lounging room.

Deleth asked Shale and Griffin if they would be willing to help her.

They agreed at once.

"My Lord Rhognor is touring Shendea, which he does on a regular basis, but I am worried about him." She sighed.

"He is not himself, and appears concerned about unknown things. I cannot determine the cause of his unrest. Would you consider meeting with him to determine the basis of his mental turmoil?"

"Of course. We would be more than willing."

"I am relieved. We will meet you at the town of Magwin in four turns. We will have rooms arranged for all three of you."

***

Halfin, excited to be traveling to Magwin, skipped along the path rather than ride in the cart with her parents. She chatted with the birds that accompanied them. She called back to her parents, "The birds say Magwin is celebrating the arrival of Lord Rhognor, and they are happy that we will visit as well."

Griffin glanced at Shale. "We are so fortunate. Enchanters are almost always welcome. Believe it or not, I learned of a rumor that many turns ago, the Magwins did not welcome visitors and tended to be a bit suspicious of them."

Shale laughed. "How odd. We have never encountered suspicion when we have visited before." She leaned forward. "Halfin, please join us again in the cart. Magwin is only a short distance away, and we should present ourselves as well-mannered and relaxed."

"I will. I must admit I would like to rest a bit."

Griffin stopped the horse, and put his hand out to guide

Halfin into the back seat.

On her way, she patted the animal and thanked it. The horse whinnied and tossed its head up and down. Halfin burst out laughing. "He said he is glad I cannot walk for more distance than he can. He would not appreciate giving up his job as our horse and letting me perform it instead."

Griffin hid a smile. "Please assure him, we would never allow you to replace him."

The horse whinnied again.

Griffin, his brow furrowed, turned to Shale. "Unlike Halfin, I have never been able to understand the speech of animals, and I always assumed they could not understand me. It appears I may have been incorrect."

Shale grinned. "You have other talents my love. Talents I find most appealing."

They turned a corner on the road and Magwin appeared before them. The town possessed a well-built and sturdy wall, but the gates stood open. Flags and bunting were draped from every house top and the crenelations atop the walls. These walls were much like the Keeps of larger villages, where the walls had walks for archers to stand if the Keep were ever attacked. At the entrance, Griffin reigned in the horse, and the three descended from the cart.

A portly man hustled out of the gates from the inner courtyard to greet them. "Welcome. Welcome. You are the Enchanters from the forest?" He gave them no time to respond. "I am Burgermaster Flank, and Magwin welcomes you. Come, let me show you to the house we have reserved for you." He turned and walked through the gates, then snapped his fingers at a young male. "Take this horse to the stables, groom it, feed it, and place it in our best stall."

Flank hurried through the gates. "Follow me."

Shale and Griffin glanced at each other, hiding grins, and followed.

Flank led them past a series of brightly colored wooden houses to a small pink-and-gray one and handed them a key. "Please, make yourself at home. We have stocked your house with foodstuffs and plenty of tea. Lord Rhognor is in our largest house and awaits your arrival. My own progeny, Cranik, will be with you soon to take you all to meet with the Lord." He bowed his head and bustled away.

***

The three shook the travel dust from their clothes and then ate a light snack. Shale brushed Halfin's hair and tied it back in loose plaits. "Now you look more presentable."

At that moment there was a knock on the door. When Griffin opened it, a young male stood on the doorstep, smiling. "My name is Cranik, and Burgermaster Flank ordered me to bring you to Lord Rhognor. Would you please follow me?"

They locked the door and followed him to a huge building constructed from stone rather than wood. The exquisite stonework consisted of a series of perfectly square. blocks held together with pitch-black mortar. While the walls were stark, it was an almost regal display. Cranik escorted them with pride to the door and requested that the Rifellan guard admit them to Lord Rhognor.

They thanked Cranik and followed the Rifellan into the interior. At a beautiful door carved with leaves and flowers, the guard knocked, pushed open the door, and announced them to the male inside. Deleth, the female responsible for their invitation, was already seated.

They entered and were invited to sit in seats opposite the Lord, and the Rifellan guard moved to the corner of the room.

Rhognor was a tall, slender male, with bushy eyebrows. He had pale skin, but his eyes were the brilliant blue of a noon-time sky.

Halfin leaned toward Shale and whispered, "He has beautiful eyes. I believe he is an excellent Lord for Shendea."

Shale barely registered her words. She was fixed on the expression on Rhognor's face. He looked as if he had been struck by sky fire during a rain storm. He stared at Halfin. *The Lord is transfixed by my progeny. He cannot take his eyes off her.*

She glanced over at Deleth, who was also watching the Lord closely, a ghost of a smile on her mouth. Shale cleared her throat and broke the spell in the room. "We wish to thank you, my Lord, for inviting us to visit with you."

Rhognor tore his gaze from Halfin, and called to the

Rifellan. "Would you please arrange for the kitchen to supply us with refreshments?"

"Yes, my Lord." He left to hand over the order.

Deleth spoke up. "Lord Rhognor, I have not properly introduced our visitors. This is Lady Shale and Sire Griffin of the Enchanters. The younger Halfin, their progeny, is also an Enchanter." She turned to the others. "Lady Shale, Sire Griffin and Lady Halfin, this is Lord Rhognor of Shendea."

Rhognor nodded at them. "We are well met." But he kept staring at Halfin, his eyes fixed on her and his mouth slightly open

Halfin sat, eyes lowered and gazed at him every now and then and blushed.

A kitchen assistant brought in tea and cakes and placed the tray on the table. She bobbed at them and left with haste.

Deleth poured tea for them all and began a conversation in an attempt to reakax Rhognor time to relax. "My Lord, I mentioned to Lady Shale that you have not been as erudite as you are wont to be, and I wondered if these Enchanters could determine what might be troubling you. You may not know this, but Enchanters often have healing remedies unknown to we Healers."

He gazed at them his brow wrinkled in curiosity. "I did not know that. You are the first Enchanters I have ever met. Are there many others of you?" He drank from his cup.

Shale shook her head sadly. "Lord Rhognor, I regret to tell you we are the last of our kind."

He paled a little. "That is so unfortunate. Can nothing be changed to allow more Enchanters to be born in Shendea?

"We had hoped to find a male Enchanter for Halfin to bond with. However, it appears that what you have sitting with you are all the Enchanters remaining on your land."

Rhognor stood and walked over to Shale and took her hand in his. "I am so sorry for your challenges, Lady Shale. I only wish I could help in some way."

"My Lord, you have a reputation in Shendea for being a most caring ruler, and we are convinced that if our situation had a solution, you would find it. We do thank you for your commiserations."

He returned to his seat and regarded Lady Shale with compassion in his eyes.

They sat in silence and drank their tea. Conversation, it seemed, had ceased.

Deleth coughed and stood. "My Lord, I promised Lady Shale that I would show her and Sire Griffin the gardens in Magwin. May I be excused to fulfill my promise?"

He answered offhandedly. "Of course." He turned to Halfin. Would you prefer to visit the gardens, or perhaps you would be more comfortable simply to sit and enjoy more tea?"

Halfin blushed. "I do believe I would prefer more tea, my Lord."

Deleth and the other two left to view the gardens.

***

As they left the house where Rhognor was billeted, Deleth turned to Shale and Griffin. "I did not mean to trick you, but I felt sure when I heard of Halfin that she might be the perfect female for our Lord. He has been most melancholy of late, and I was convinced he thought he might never find a mate. He is a gentle and loving leader, but he does have a few oddities. His people find them endearing, but they have never attracted women to him."

Shales tilted her head. "How strange, Deleth. He is such a handsome young male."

"He is, and he does attract women, but never seems to be aware if they wish him to begin a relationship."

Griffin frowned at her. "Did you plan this?"

Deleth shook her head. "Not really. But I hoped. I hoped so much. Rhognor has been so lonely. He is an unusual male. The people of Shendea adore him, but they do not offer friendship. He needs a loving companion, a mate. I am convinced he has seen that in Halfin, which is why I suggested we walk and leave them alone. I do not believe it will be long before he asks if you will allow her to be his mate."

Griffin peered at her. "She is young Deleth. Will she be ready for a mating?"

Deleth smiled and nodded. "She will be ready. Rhognor is a compelling young male. He is easy to love."

Shale grinned. "Well, we might as well head back and have our own tea."

When they arrived at the hall where they had met Rhognor, the room lay empty and the tea cold.

Griffin stood in the center of the room. "Where are they?"

Deleth walked toward the back of the house where the bedrooms were located. Empty. All was quiet. She walked to the tassel in the corner. "I shall order a light meal, so we may celebrate."

Shale laughed. "I believe, Deleth, that he and Halfin are attracted to each other, and they both recognize it. You saw their faces when they met."

Griffin raised his eyebrows. "I suggest you two should leave them alone to find out about each other."

***

Just after the other three left, Rhognor poured more tea for Halfin and handed the cup to her. "You are a full Enchanter, Halfin?'

"I am. I speak with birds and animals, and I love plants and flowers and the beauty of nature."

"Halfin. Your name conjures up delicate creatures, beauty, and serenity."

Halfin put a hand to her face to ease the heat. Only the cool beauty of his blue eyes kept her from bursting into flame.

Rhognor stood. "Halfin, put your cup down."

She did so, but she twisted her brows. *What does he want? He is so handsome I could never refuse him anything.*

He held out his hand, and pulled her to her feet so she stood in front of him.

He gazed at her. "I rarely act in haste, but…I have never met anyone like you before, and cannot help myself. Are you sure you are not a witch who has put a spell on me?" He leaned in and kissed her.

His lips were warm, soft, and gentle.

She gazed into his eyes and swallowed. She stroked his face. "I am also bewitched."

He breathed her name and kissed her again. The kiss exploded like the fireworks prepared by the Magicians Guild.

"Halfin, I do not want you to ever leave."

"I would die if I did."

"I know you love the outdoors and the woods and nature. Could you live with me at my Stronghold?"

"What is it like?"

"It is like a Keep but is carved out of the solid rock of a mountain called Bar Braich"

"Is there any starlight in it?"

"Not yet, but I can have it created just for you."

"Then the answer is yes, Rhognor. I can live with you in your rock"

He took her by the hand. "We should have a lengthy walk in the forest and you can show me all you love, so we can reproduce it at the Stronghold."

They headed out the door of the house along a grass-strewn path through the forest.

For most of the turn, they strolled, admiring the abundant greenery and small bushes ablaze with flowers of every shade. Halfin stopped, turned, and put her hand on his heart. "I have something to show you. We have been walking toward my home, and this is my favorite place in this forest." She left the path they had been following, and began to walk between a pair of lush green trees. She looked back and beckoned him to follow her.

Rhognor was stunned at the scene before him. A small glade, surrounded by trees and flowering bushes, with soft green moss covering the ground welcomed them both. She moved to one of the larger sections of moss and sat down, patting the space beside her.

He joined her. "This is extraordinary. I have never seen anything so beautiful."

She smiled at him. "Wait a little. The star is leaving for the evening, and the light is growing faint. Watch."

He gazed around, wondering what she hinted at. Suddenly the glade exploded with small flittering lights, and a mist rose to enclose them in a private magical world.

"What do you call this secret place? It is the most wonderful glade I have ever seen."

She smiled again. "I call it, the Bower."

They sat in silence, drinking in the sight of nature's lights. The moon cast beams of light that sliced through the mist.

Halfin stood and gazed down at him. "We should leave.

My parents will be wondering where we are, and I need food."

He stood up, took her hand and they walked back to the house together.

***

Her parents and Healer Deleth were waiting at the house when they returned.

Shale hugged her progeny. "We wondered where you were. We were a little concerned when the light began to fade."

"I showed Lord Rhognor some of the things I like most about our forest."

"Were you impressed with what you saw, my Lord?"

"I was, but I would prefer it if you both were less formal with me. Would you call me Rhognor when we are alone. I have asked Halfin if she will agree to our bonding, and I am thrilled that she has said yes."

Shale's eyebrows formed a slight frown. "She plans to join you at the Stronghold, Rhognor?"

"Yes. Before you worry about her leaving the forest, I will create one for her within my Keep. And, of course, I shall visit all of Shendea every pass, and she will accompany me. Halfin will always be able to feel the warmth of starlight on her face."

Shale and Griffin both beamed at his words, and Shale took his hand. "Congratulations Rhognor." She hugged Halfin again. "And congratulations my wonderful offspring."

Rhognor moved to the corner of the room and tugged on the tassel. "I will order meals for the five of us. You will join us, Healer Deleth?"

"I would like nothing better. I am so happy for you and Halfin. You are perfect for each other."

When the guard knocked and poked his head around the door, Rhognor ordered an evening meal for them all.

The guard left.

They all began to talk about bonding ceremonies, details of living in a stone Keep, and forests, and before they knew it, their meals had arrived.

***

For two more turns, they discussed what they needed to accomplish to make the people of Shendea aware of the good news.

Exhausted from all the planning and talking, Halfin asked Rhognor if they could visit the Bower.

He sighed. "Oh yes. This is all exhausting, is it not?"

They left after an early evening meal and headed straight for the Bower. When they arrived and were seated inside, the star began to sink below the horizon, so the flitting lights and the mist surrounding the glade had created a haven for them. The Bower had turned into a cozy space in a secret part of nature's forest.

Halfin took his hand. "Rhognor, we have one more turn

here before we head to your Keep."

"Yes, why?"

"I love you, and I want you so desperately. I am so ready to be bonded with you, and I cannot stand the delay. We are here in one of the most spiritual of places. I wish you to love me now. We do not have to admit this to anyone, except ourselves."

He sighed. "Halfin, you have no idea how much I wish this to happen. The Bower will become our most beloved place. I have avoided kissing you too much because I feared I would not be able to control myself."

"Do not avoid it any longer, my love."

"Halfin, I love you." He kissed her with his warm, gentle lips, and guided her onto the biggest mound of moss, covered now in the mist. They sank into it and found each other.

Their mating was slow, gentle, and filling, and she cried out in joy.

Spent, they fell apart but continued to gaze at each other.

I love this wonderful male. I am one with him.

Rhognor reached over and kissed her again. "My beautiful mate. I cannot believe I have found you at last. I have waited so very long for you." He touched her breast and she responded again.

They mated once more, and now exhausted, they lay with each other, and drifted into the most satisfying sleep either had ever experienced.

***

Four turns after Rhognor and Halfin arrived at the Stronghold, Halfin asked him for a favor. "I would like to have some birds living with us. I so miss the beautiful sounds they make, and I have no animals to talk to."

Rhognor appeared horrified. "I have been so neglectful. I shall remedy this immediately."

He had prepared the most beautiful indoor forest for Halfin. He had dedicated a substantial hall, filled it with rich earth, a variety of flowers, and much lush greenery. He had lights arranged to follow the same rhythm as the star outside the Stronghold. Now, he accompanied Halfin to the forest where she asked a number of birds to join her and invited a few of the smaller animals. They returned to the Stronghold and released them into the indoor forest garden. Halfin then spoke with the birds and the animals, and they all told her the garden was a pleasure to be in. All were agreed, as it was Halfin they really wanted to be with.

The Stronghold was a happy place for Halfin and her animals, and Rhognor was a happy mate. The Shendeans were proud of their Lord and often pointed out to visitors what an extraordinary person he had become. They even loved his eccentricities.

Halfin disliked the bitterness of cold during the snowy season in the north of Shendea and never ventured out of the Stronghold during that time. However, when the warm growing season arrived, she often left to visit her parents, and took her birds and animals with her. Some remained in the forests, and others might take their places, but many returned with her to her home with Rhognor. However, every pass, on the same turn as their mating, they returned to the Bower and made love there to celebrate their bonding.

***

A number of passes later, a strange woman, named Kat, purported to be from another world came to visit. It was most unfortunate that trouble seemed to follow this woman to Shendea. Halfin discovered that Kat attempted to remove a boradai from her land and had to consider arresting her. But Assassins entered Shendea, and in the melee, a syeth bit the Lady Halfin. She did not survive the poison coursing through her veins.

Rhognor, struck half mad by the death of Halfin, led a vengeful charge on the Assassins, and discovered that his own councilor, Hesginn was responsible for the invasion. He took it upon himself to dispatch the Gray Magician and returned to the Hanford Forest to make the preparations that would enable Halfin to join Caleesh.

All of Shendea joined him in mourning her loss.

Rhognor would never even consider mating again.

He continued to visit the Bower every pass on the same turn as he and Halfin had done. He sat alone on the moss and remembered. He had become so familiar with the birds and animals Halfin loved that they sat beside him in the Bower. They, too, missed Lday Halfin, because with her passing, the time of the Enchanters was over.

The People of Pridden

GARREN PEN DARRYN

The Glass Blower

Two young males stood, mouths open, watching as their parent, Banquin pen Darryn, handling a long tube. A blob of molten and brilliant red glass hung from the end. Banquin blew through the tube with steady and careful breaths, turning it as he blew, to keep the glass centered at the end of the pipe. With specific precision, his lungs formed a bubble that expanded the globe of crimson glass into a long and graceful cylinder. Banquin's assistant, with slow precise movements, guided the tube to the highly polished surface of the rolling table. With huge gloves to protect him from the heat, he rolled the glass creation to keep the shape even. Banquin continued to blow, expanding the cylinder, while his assistant applied pressure to create a narrowing near the end, and the crimson glass took on the shape of a glorious and delicate vase.

Garren, the eldest of the young males, gazed mesmerized and longed to blow glass into beautiful shapes all on his own.

After Banquin completed the glass vase, he returned it to the cooling oven. When Garren asked for permission to make a vase of his own, he refused. "You are not yet tall enough or strong enough to handle the pipe, Garren. Have patience for one more pass, and I will begin your training then as a glass blower."

"Why must I be taller and stronger? I can already carry large sacks of glass shards, and I can stand tall enough to peer into the kilns."

"If a stack of shards grows too heavy, you can set it down and adjust the way you hold it. You cannot do that with a substantial amount of molten glass on the end of the tube. I have seen too many young males falter and burn themselves beyond their ability to heal. Trust me, I will be able to tell when you are ready to handle the dangers of forming glass."

Garren shuffled. "I do trust you, but I long so much to be able to create the same beauty you can."

Banquin smiled at him. "I know you feel a strong desire to do so, but a glass blower can never afford to act in an impatient manner. You would put not only yourself in danger, but others as well."

Garren's younger sibling, Brinner, shook his head. "I do not wish to heat glass. I think it is too dangerous. I prefer using paints to make copies of the land around us."

Banquin grinned at his youngest. "I am pleased you do not wish to blow glass. I would not be comfortable having to supervise two of you working with such heat and danger." He patted Brinner on his head. "You are very talented as a painter. I suspect you will have an excellent reputation in Pridden after you have practiced your craft for more passes."

***

True to his word, one pass later, Banquin invited Garren to come to his studio for his first lesson in the art of glass. "You are ready to learn how to manipulate glass. We will not begin with blowing, but by constructing small glass sculptures. If you learn to handle the small and the delicate, switching later to creating through blowing will be the best way to make use of your talents. To attempt to reverse that process will be much more difficult. Making small glass animals or birds or other items that attract people to your artistry, will be the most efficient way to be assured that all your creations are valued. Working with melted glass to develop something dainty and graceful will enable you, when you begin blowing glass, to produce a gauzy appeal in the vases, plates, and bowls you create."

Thus, Garren began his instruction with his parent for the next seven passes. When he began producing his small sculptures on his own, he sometimes became impatient that the glass did not always bend to his will as quickly as he wished. Those times cost him burns. His parent would make him stop what he was doing each time, put the work-in-progress in the annealing oven to gradually cool down, and cease work for the day. Once the complete work cooled, Banquin placed it on a shelf. He would then suggest Garren begin the same job again, but practice extreme patience this time.

Once the final work cooled, Banquin would invite Garren to bring both the failed and completed pieces to his office, and they would have tea and discuss the results. Garren saw at once that impatience not only caused him pain with burns, but also interfered with the beauty of the piece. He kept the ruined pieces on a high shelf to remind him how important it was to be clear, concise, and patient when dealing with molten glass. He also understood why his parent possessed a reputation of such renown in Pridden.

By that time, he was already making a name for himself because of his abilities.

A young female from Rifella, Maleena, arrived one day to request a figurine of what she referred to as a sylph. Garren sat down with her and asked her to sketch an example to give him an idea of what she wanted him to produce.

She produced a picture of what she called a faerie. It was a young female reaching upward, surrounded by wind, with translucent draperies flowing around her. Darren was intrigued. The figurine would be a challenge to produce, so he asked Maleena to give him four or five turns to study it and plan how he would proceed.

Four turns later, Garren was ready to begin the creation that she desired.

Maleena arrived at his workshop with her chaperone, Duenna. As Garren's two assistants began heating clear glass rods in the kiln, he watched the way the light of the fires caught and bounced off Maleena's blond hair, burnishing them with faint red highlights. The company of her chaperone told him she was not mated.

He removed his shirt and donned the shop shirt, which

consisted of padded cotton, loose enough to allow air to flow around his chest to keep him cool.

He pulled on a pair of protective gloves, reached into the kiln for the heated glass rod, and began working with tweezers to pull the glass into the shape of a torso. Bit by bit, he pulled and shaped arms extending from the torso, and then he placed the section in the annealing oven.

He removed another heated rod and teased a shape of the lower body, with the beginning of a skirt flowing from the figure. This too was placed in an annealing oven.

He removed the gloves and stepped over to his bench, inviting Maleena to sit while he described how he planned to create the figurine she wanted. "I cannot do any more today. This is a creation that is so complex, it requires careful and concentrated work. "Tomorrow I will continue with the lower torso, but I would like to ask you a few more questions. Would you accompany me to my office, and I will order tea for us? I can then make further notes so I am clear about the design."

They headed to his office with Duenna to discuss the figure in greater detail.

For the next four turns, Maleena scrutinized Garren as he molded the slender legs of the figure standing on tip toe, straining against an invisible wind with its skirt flowing away from the body.

Duenna kept the two of them in her sight with the sharp eyes of an eagle.

Each night as Maleena said goodnight, she blushed when Garren bowed to her.

When Garren left his workshop, his parent inspected his work for the day. After the third turn, he invited Garren to join him for a late meal.

As his progeny entered his office, Banquin suggested he sit. "We need to have a conversation."

Garren raised his eyebrows. "Have I done something that is not correct?"

Banquin shook his head. "Not at all. The work you have done is exemplary. It is the work of a master. You are destined to surpass me as a glass blower. I am so proud of you and of how you have learned techniques even I have never used." He beamed. "No, there is no challenge with your work. I am worried you are beginning to fall for the Lady Maleena. The two of you have spent much time together, and I recognize a relationship beginning to form. Her family enjoy a high ranking in Rifellan society, and they will never allow a union of their most precious daughter with a Glowen."

"Why would they find fault with me?"

Banquin shrugged. "They would not find fault with you but your citizenship as a Glowen. Throughout Pridden, our citizens have earned a reputation for being less than committed in our relationships with each other. You must be aware of this, because I know you have been sought after by a number of already mated women. Our ways are different from many others in Pridden. Most of our relationships are casual, and enjoying more than one mate is normal for us -- more so when we are younger. But Maleena's parents are Rifellan, and they will never approve of a union between you and her." He sighed. "You need to back away from going further with her. Now!"

Garren hung his head. *My parent is correct. I have seen enough among my Glowen friends that our ways are not looked upon well by others in Pridden.* He raised his head and looked Banquin straight in the eyes. "You always speak with wisdom. I will fit the cloak on the figurine on the morrow. Once it is removed from the annealing oven, I will never set eyes on Maleena again. Her parents will call for her to return to Rifella in two turns."

"Rest easy Garren. You will enjoy significant success as a glass blower, and you will travel to other lands in my stead as your reputation increases. Many potential mates will be available to you."

***

On the following turn, after Garren completed his morning meal, he headed to his studio and began bringing the kiln to the desired temperature. Once it was heated, he placed a larger than normal clear glass rod inside and gathered his tools around him. He carefully joined all the pieces of the figure and set the result inside the annealing oven to await the final addition of the cloak.

Within minutes, Maleena and Duenna appeared at the

117

doorway to his studio, and he motioned them to chairs off to the side.

As he walked over to the kiln to withdraw the now pliable glass rod, Garren smiled at Maleena. "Your figurine is almost complete now. I am going to create the cloak and fix it in place. Once that is done, your faerie will be complete and will only need to spend a few hours in the annealing oven. You will be able to take it home when your parents come for you on the morrow." Although he appeared calm, Garren's heart ached with loss.

He did not don gloves. Instead, using jacks and tweezers began pulling and forming the malleable glass rod into a thinner and thinner swirling sheet of the cloak. He worked steadily, manipulating the glass while turning it with extreme care, in the flame emitted by the kiln. Sweat beaded his forehead, and an assistant dabbed at it with a towel wrapped around a length of wood. He did not speak, but worked with razor-sharp concentration on the glass coming from the heated rod. At last, a diaphanous spiral of glass, fine enough to appear almost invisible, emerged from the tweezers. Garren used sheers to cut the cape from the master tube and gently deposited it onto a heated metal block. Without hesitating, he placed the delicate final piece into a second annealing oven. This would reduce the stresses built up in the manipulated glass and add strength and durability.

He turned to Maleena. "I would suggest you and your companion retire to the dining lounge and have a meal. I need to wait until both items have cooled to the same temperature, and then combine them. Once that is done the final figurine will be cooled, little by little, until it can be removed from the oven and be allowed to finish the cooling process until it is at room temperature. You will not be able to view it again until the morrow."

He appreciated that his parent had been correct. It was obvious, by the way Maleena viewed the ovens that her desire was directed at the glass figure, not at him.

He sighed, shook his head at his own mistake in interpreting her emotions, and began to tidy his workshop. He sent his helpers off to their homes, but requested that his most valued assistant, Dungred, arrange for a light meal and tea to be delivered to the workshop for them both.

As they ate and drank, they discussed the day's accomplishments. "We achieved much today," Garren said. "My thanks for your seamless assistance."

"Master Garren, it has been my most exciting day in this studio."

Garren laughed. "I am not a Master yet."

Dungred shook his head. "What lies in those two ovens, says that you are."

Distracted by Dungred's words, Garren gazed at the two ovens without speaking for a few moments. "They are both the same temperature. I can combine both pieces now."

He picked up a glass blower's paddle and removed the figurine from the first oven and placed it on the rolling table.

He then extricated the cloak from the other and deposited it on the same table.

Using the flame from the primary kiln, Garren brought the two pieces together, employing a delicate jack to merge both into a final creation. Once he was happy with the look of the combination, he returned it to be annealed once more to ensure that all stresses would be removed, and that the finished piece would retain its strength for as long as was needed.

He and his assistant cleaned up the studio. Garren peered once more at the temperature gauge of the oven and nodded in satisfaction. "Perfect. You may head home. We will be able to remove the figure first thing on the morrow."

His assistant bowed to him. "Good eve, Master."

Garren smiled and shook his head. "Dungred, I am not a Master."

His assistant just smiled at him and wordlessly left the studio.

***

After their morning meal together, Banquin and Garren walked to the studio to remove the finished piece from the now cool oven.

On the forming table, Garren placed a small stand that would hold the figure in place and, donning soft cotton gloves, reached into the oven's now cool interior and removed the figure with cautious hands. He placed a small dab of warmed glue on the stand and inserted the left foot. He held it in place while the glue hardened and set, and the miniature faerie remained upright on the stand.

It was magnificent. The tiny creature reached up, face toward the heavens, holding an edge of the cloak in her left hand. An unseen wind blew the hair back from her face, and the gossamer cloak swirled and whirled about her, thin as fine silk, and although made of glass, it manifested movement as if blown by a gentle breath of air. The expression on the tiny face expressed joy.

While he had been affixing the figurine to the stand, his parent witnessed the process in silence.

Banquin breathed a soft breath, and gazed at Garren, whose face was lit with excitement. "You have seen your own creation. What do you feel for Maleena now?"

"I am grateful she gave me the opportunity to create something extraordinary."

"Excellent. When I said before that you will gain an exceptional reputation, I was correct. You will travel all over Pridden, and you will indeed have the opportunity to meet many potential mates."

Garren sighed. "Thank you for your encouragement, but I will never surpass your skill or fame in glass creation."

Banquin swallowed, his eyes bright with emotion, He placed his arm on Garren's shoulder. "Look at what you have done. You have already surpassed me."

Garren, startled by his father's words gazed at him.

"Do you mean that?"

"I do. I must use a Rifellan word. I am so very proud of you, my son."

At that moment, a gentle knock distracted them both.

Garren called. "Come."

Maleena and a Rifellan couple entered.

The elder female stepped forward. "We have come to view the figure Maleena requested that you created for her. May we?"

"Of course." Garren stepped back to allow them to study the completed figure.

Maleena and her parents, all wide-eyed, opened their mouths and exhaled in awe.

"It is the most beautiful thing I have ever seen." Maleena's eyes glowed with reverence.

She glanced briefly at him, but her face, filled with an expression of love for the beauty of the piece, turned again to the statue framed in the lights of the studio.

Watching her, Garren at last understood her apparent infatuation of him had, in truth been a deep admiration of his abilities as a creator of works in glass. This time his heart did not hurt. The expression not only on her face, but also those of her parents, spread warmth through his body. Plus, the pride on his parent's face cemented the realization within him that he was indeed a worthy artist. *I really am a Master.*

***

Over the next number of passes, Garren travelled throughout Pridden fulfilling commissions, and his fame continued to spread. He was delighted that his younger sibling Brinner also achieved a sterling reputation for his paintings.

The now aging Banquin no longer travelled but helped to keep track of and manage his progenies' assignments. Content to remain in the background and enjoy the accomplishments of his sons, he sensed his life as complete. More and more when he thought of them the Rifellan word of "sons" came to his mind. The tenor of it was more personal, and it appealed to his emotions. He often wondered why his family always possessed brown eyes, rather than the blue-rimmed pale eyes of other Glowens. He also wondered what other land his ancestors had come from and why he perceived such an affinity for the Rifellans.

***

Many passes later, after Banquin joined with Caleesh, Garren remained unmated, and wondered if he would ever find a mate as perfect for him as his female parent had been for Banquin. He was working glass at his permanent studio in the market attached to Thane Brennan's Keep, when out of nowhere, a woman caught his eye. She resembled Rifellan royalty, with red hair in a mass of curls that looked like a crown of fire, and her eyes were different colors — one a soft brown and the other as green as newly grown grass. For

123

an instant, he was attracted to her, but suspected she was not bond-mate material.

He realized he presented a picture of a strong male because he wore only a vest of Rifellan-type armor, and because of the heat, sweat poured from him. Lifting huge bags of glass had strengthened his body so that his chest and arms were those of a warrior. Many females had remarked that these attributes were enticing in the extreme. He lifted a long blowpipe filled with cerulean glass from the furnace and began rolling the tube on the metal table. From the corner of his eye, he sensed she was watching with interest and could not resist attempting to attract her attention further. When he completed the vase, his assistant cut it from the end of the blowpipe and placed it in an oven to anneal.

Garren used a towel to dry his sweating body and walked over to the counter. "Are you looking for something unusual, my Lady?"

"It is such a shame, but I am traveling and cannot carry much with me, even though I find your work beautiful."

He was so taken with this woman, whose name he learned was Kat, that he gifted her a glass ring with intertwined bands of pale pink and deep emerald. He noticed the pink matched a bracelet on her wrist and was surprised when he caught sight of a pendant half hidden by her shirt. It glowed an astonishing emerald, the exact shade in the second band of the ring.

Her next question took him by surprise. "Are you by

any chance a Wielder?"

He shook his head. "I have no idea what a Wielder is."

She seemed disappointed and she bid him goodbye.

He frowned as she walked away and disappeared among the stalls of the market. *I wonder if I will see her again. Somehow, I suspect she still has a part to play in my life.*

***

More than three passes later, Garren received an unexpected messenger moth from Kat, asking him to aid her in returning to her own world. He set out to travel to Kaylin, since he had promised her, when they said farewell as she left Glowen, that he would help when she needed his presence to return home.

When he arrived at Lord Eduardo's Keep in Kaylin, he was introduced to a number of people from the lands who had made similar promises to Kat. At his first morning meal in the Keep dining hall, he met a young apprentice healer who was preparing to be sent to her first position. A compelling young female, he was delighted to discover her intended destination was Glowen. He was even more delighted when he learned her name was Linneth.

They spent the entire first part of the turn wandering the halls of the Keep and talking about their hopes and desires.

Linneth gazed up at him, smiling. "Garren you are not what I expected a man from Glowen would be."

"No doubt you imagined we are all overbearing lechers who have many, many women in our lives, but are often reluctant to take a bond mate."

She laughed. "Not quite that bad. But you are quiet, and I suspect you are a gentle man who is not at all like the reputation of Glowen males. You have never had a permanent mate?"

"I have never been fortunate enough to meet a woman who could distinguish me as being beyond the reputation of my homeland."

"Perhaps you just have not been ready before this time."

He gazed down at her and felt warmth emanating from his heart. "Perhaps." *I believe she is the one, and now the time is right.*

HAYDAR

The Horse Master of Kaylin

Haydar had two problems. While all Baklai are quite petite, Haydar was the smallest one in the family was much shorter than either of his siblings. His biggest challenge was that he was also much cleverer than their friends, which made him the brunt of many unkind jokes. His family in Baklai had a tiny patch of land that they farmed to supply them the bare necessities for living but, it appeared unlikely that he would be able to add to the family income.

Haydar's biggest desire was to be a trainer of horses. He adored horses and as soon as he reached his sixteenth year, made the rounds of all the horse owners and begged them for a job. They either laughed or sneered at him.

"You are far too little to work with our horses. We breed some of the biggest in Baklai. You would not be able to control them and could be injured. We cannot take the risk of hiring you."

Haydar was disconsolate. He ached to work with horses, and suspected that they, liked him in return and, rather than trampling him, were careful around him. He often felt that he and the horses, managed to communicate with each other. He had no proof of this, it was simply a strong suspicion o his part. He begged his parents to give him ideas of how to be hired to work with horses. He was willing to do anything around a stable, but he was still refused again and again.

Haydar's male parent, who had little time for his smallest progeny, was impatient. "You have to learn to stand up for yourself and be more aggressive."

While it was probably good advice for either of Haydar's siblings, it was of minimal use to him. However, Haydar decided that perhaps his parent had a point. The first thing he did was visit farms with horses, offering to help with anything around the farm. He listened to every conversation the farmers had about their horses and often picked up minor things they wished the horses could do.

He recognized that the farm closest to that of his parents had fifty horses, but only three riders to take them for exercise. Haydar was convinced the horses wanted more exercise. The farmer had hired him to clean the stalls when the horses were in the paddocks. One day, Haydar sidled up to the farmer. "May I ask you something, Sire?"

"It is Haydar, is it not? What do you wish to know?"

Haydar frowned and raised his eyebrows. "Do horses have friends?"

"What a peculiar question. Why do you ask?"

"Well, it is just because I see that the dark brown gelding you often ride, appears to be in the company of the big bay a great deal. I was just wondering if they are friends."

"Interesting. But I am sure it is just a coincidence."

"I asked, Sire, is because if they are friends, when you ride the gelding, would the bay run with him without a rider and also receive exercise?"

"What a ridiculous idea."

"I am sure you are correct, Sire. You know so much about horses. It was just a silly thought."

***

Within a couple of turns, Haydar observed that most of the riders had other riderless horses with them when they exercised. By the end of the season, the farmer needed only five riders to keep all his horses exercised. Haydar was convinced the horses thanked him for his intervention.

Soon, after the evening meals, he began walking to local farms, carrying a step stool. He would quietly approach the horses, who never whinnied or were disturbed by him. He placed his step stool beside each one and climbed up to their heads. He whispered in their ears that he loved them and was proud of them. He would give them suggestions if the farmer had a challenge with them. The horses would nod their heads up and down and sometimes face him and blow sweet hay-scented breath in his face. He was convinced they understood him. He decided they must be listening to him since the running of riderless horses had worked so well.

He was careful not to stay too long because he was afraid of being caught. One night, he stood on his usual stool, whispering to his favorite horse.

"Who are you?"

The voice was so unexpected, he overbalanced and fell from the step stool and scraped himself on the rough ground. He scrambled to his feet, attempting to rub the dirt from his skin.

When he gained his senses, he saw a young female standing and watching him. She had caught him speaking to the horses.

He stammered, "Who are you?"

"I asked first, you stupid thing."

He thought with haste about what to say, and realized he should not give his real name. "Er…I am Grisanno."

"That's not a Baklai name. Who are you in reality?"

This female was not scared of him.

"I am not answering any more questions until you tell me who you are."

"I am Mayrin, and this is my parent's farm. You better be honest with me, or I will call them and they will have the Guards come and put you in jail."

Haydar's heart sank. He had tried to be so careful, and now he was going to be in such trouble, and it might cause trouble for his parents. "I cannot tell you. I was not hurting the horses. They like me."

"You were trying to steal a horse. Tell the truth. I should call my parents right now."

"Please do not. The horses do like me. I will prove it."

Mayrin stared at him squinting her disbelief. "So, prove it."

He stared at her and edged back toward the horse he had been whispering to. Using a soft voice, he looked up at the animal. "Please tell this Mayrin female that I am not a horse thief."

The horse lowered its head and rubbed its nose on Haydar's head. It looked at Mayrin and gave a soft whinny, butted Haydar, and rested its chin on his shoulder.

"Did it just talk to you?" she asked.

Haydar reached up, stroked the horse's nose, and placed his hands on either side of its jaw. "Please tell her you trust me and that I am a friend."

The animal gave little nickers and rubbed his head over Haydar. Haydar reached up and brought the head down to him so he could kiss it on its nose. It nickered again and rested its chin on Haydar's head.

Mayrin laughed. "He does appear to like you. Do you bring him food all the time? Is that why?"

"No, I just talk to him and tell him stories he likes. We are friends, and I think he believes I am interesting."

"I believe you. I have never seen a horse act like this before. So, tell me your name and why you are sneaking around our farm."

Haydar sighed. "I am Haydar, and I am not sneaking around your farm. I love horses and have a great desire to become a trainer. I have asked and asked all of the owners of horses in this area, but none will hire me."

The horse nickered and nodded its head up and down.

Mayrin laughed again. "It seems the horse says you are telling the truth. So, why will they not hire you?"

"They say I am too short to work with the horses, and that I might be injured and it would make the horses dangerous to others."

The horse snorted.

Haydar glanced up at the animal. "You see. He also agrees it is not true. No horse will ever hurt me. They are my friends."

She smiled at him. "I do understand why you feel you have to sneak around. I also love horses, but my parents will only let me work with the smallest mares. They never let me ride them. I would adore to work with some of the bigger males, and I am positive they would not injure me in any way. My parents just want me to find a mate and be out of their way so I am no longer a challenge to them."

"I have a suggestion. Let us meet each other after the evening meal, and we can spend time with all the horses, and I will introduce you to some of the bigger males. I will also help you to ride some of the mares. I can work with the horses, and I know which are having problems. If you observe what your parent and his workers are doing with them, I can help, and they will never know."

"You have helped my parent with his horses?"

"Yes." He told her of the riderless horse situation.

"I do not believe that. My parent has a reputation of being one of the best trainers in the area. Other trainers copy the way he works."

"I know. Your parent began using riderless horse to give more animals the exercise they needed. He told another farmer, who began using the same method. It was successful for him as well. So, he told another, and so on. Your parent has the reputation for being an innovator."

She glanced at him sideways. "It does sound logical."

"It is true." He gazed at her keeping his eyes firmly on her face. "So will you meet with me in the evenings to be with horses?"

She opened her mouth and took a huge breath. "Oh, yes. That would be wonderful. I am so glad I met you, Haydar. We will have so much fun with the horses. I must go in, and you should leave, because one of my parent's helpers will be doing his scheduled rounds of the stables in a moment."

Haydar picked up his stool. "I will meet you on the morrow's eve."

They both went their separate ways, Haydar grinning from ear to ear.

***

Haydar and Mayrin continued to meet in secret, her to ride the horses and Haydar to train them to be valuable creatures who enjoyed the services they performed on the farms on which they lived.

After a while, Haydar suggested they move to other farms and ride and teach other horses.

At first, Mayrin was frightened to switch from her parents' farm but soon realized they needed to be familiar with as many horses as possible. Haydar watched her riding some of the mares, and his heart nearly burst with pride at her accomplishments.

One day when Haydar was working to clean up around Mayrin's parents' farm, Mayrin came out of the house, and pretended to meet him for the first time. She invited him for the noon-turn meal and, when asked by her parent why she had done so, she replied calmly that she spotted him working hard, and he seemed to be a nice young male.

Her parents were delighted to meet Haydar in their house. Because Mayrin was often so aggressive with other young males, they viewed Haydar with approval. It appeared he was the first young male she seemed to approve of.

Haydar and Mayrin continue to meet each day at the farm, as well as their secret meetings. One evening while walking home from another horse farm, they stopped to sit in the light of the moon, and talk about what they had accomplished that evening. Haydar was overcome by the light of the moon on her silky hair, and the sense of romance in the air. He gazed at her shyly and admitted, "I must admit I like being with you, Mayrin. I wish we could spend more time together."

Mayrin lowered her eyes and stared at her feet. "I like

you too."

They sat in silence until she stood up. "We better return home before our parents discover we are not in our beds."

He stood, took her hand, and they walked home, hand in hand. That night, he dreamed about her and smiled in his dreams.

***

For the next twelve turns, they walked everywhere holding hands, except when other people were around. Haydar was so happy when he was with Mayrin that he could not imagine being separated from her.

One night he could not help it, and he leaned down and kissed her. He felt her trembling lips beneath his, and he knew he was in love. "Mayrin, I want to be with you always. I wish we could become bond mates and live together and have a family."

She smiled at him. "I would like that more than anything. But you must ask my parents if they will agree to us becoming bonded."

He was so happy she agreed with him, he kissed her again. "I will do that on the morrow. I hope they will agree, because I am old enough. I am already twenty-two passes."

***

On the morrow, Haydar took extra care with his appearance, which puzzled both his parents. He combed his hair so that not a single hair was out of place. He wore his cleanest long pants and a new shirt that his female parent had recently bought for him. He set out for the farm where Mayrin lived, and rather than heading for one of the stables to get brooms and other equipment he used every day, he headed straight to the main house. He knocked and waited.

Mayrin's male parent opened the door and stared down at him. "Haydar. What are you doing here so early this morrow?"

"I have come to ask your permission, Sire."

"Permission? For what?"

Haydar was quaking inside, but his heart needed an answer more than he needed to run from the challenge. "I would like to request your permission to become the bond mate of your offspring, Mayrin."

"Are you serious?"

"Yes, Sire."

"Come in. Come in." He escorted Haydar to the living room area, told him to sit, and plunked a glass of water beside him. "Wait here." He left the room and, within a few moments, returned with Mayrin's female parent.

The two of them sat opposite Haydar.

"Say again what you requested before."

Haydar cleared his throat. His mouth was so dry he thought he was in the desert. He sipped water from the glass next to him. "I would like your permission to become the bond mate of your progeny, Mayrin."

Mayrin's parents beamed at each other. Her female parent, mouthed, "At last".

Her male parent smiled at him. "You are quite sure it is Mayrin that you wish to bond with?"

"Yes Sire. I am in love with her, and I believe she shares my feelings."

"Excellent, and I am more than willing to give my permission. However, we should meet with your parents and discuss the dowry and make arrangements for the bonding ceremony. Do you have plans where the two of you will live? Do you plan to continue to work for me? What other ideas do you have after you are bonded?"

"Much of this I shall discuss with my own parents, Sire." *Plans? I have no clue as to how I will be able to earn enough for this. I will think about this later.*

"Excellent. I will write your parents a note to suggest a time when we can all meet. I will have it delivered to your parents on the morrow."

***

Mayrin's parents waited until Haydar was out of their sight and then they laughed and hugged each other.

Her female parent was ecstatic. "I thought this would never happen. Mayrin is twenty-four passes and still not mated."

Her mate nodded. "Haydar may not be the best possible mate for her. He is too short to work with horses, and the amount I pay him for what he does here is without a doubt not sufficient for them to live well, but at least she will be mated."

"Perhaps we can help them with occasional gifts. I would not want our offspring to starve."

"I promise, we will help where we can."

She kissed him. "We should tell Mayrin of her good fortune."

***

After the next twenty turns, Mayrin and Haydar had a small celebration at his parent's home to mark their official bonding. They had agreed upon a most generous dowry of two horses. Of course, because Haydar was so short for a Baklai, the horses were both small-sized mares. Her parents also agreed to gift Haydar with enough wood to build a little house for the two of them.

Haydar was a young man with enormous ambition. He worked long and hard, and within about ten turns, had a tiny, but comfortable house ready for the two of them.

However, his desire to become a horse trainer was all consuming, so he and Mayrin continued their evening adventures, riding and speaking with the horses belonging to most of the surrounding farms.

Late one evening, back in their cozy house, he broached the subject of his deepest desire again. "Mayrin, I will never be able to bring you any luxuries in life until I can begin to train horses. I regret that in our mating we have to be so careful, because with what I am earning now, we cannot support a young one."

Along with her love of horses, Mayrin also was desperate for offspring. "We must do something different from what we have been attempting thus far. Why do you not take one of the mares my parents have given us and ride to Kaylin to ask Lord Eduardo to hire you. I know he has no Horse Master."

"How do you know that?"

"You question me? Baklai supplies horses to every land in Pridden. And I always listen to the male workers when they gossip with each other. All conversations are about horses." She blushed. "Well, most are."

"While your idea has much merit, I would not be admitted to see Lord Eduardo without an introduction. I have to discover another way to be heard by him." He frowned and bit his lip. "I believe I have a solution. I once met Praetor Makinti when he came through this area on his security rounds. I also got the opportunity to speak to his horse. It is a massive animal, and most feisty. I do believe the Praetor was upset when I came so close to his horse. However, I also suspect he was surprised when his animal did not attempt to bite or chase me."

He stopped. "Wait, what do you mean when you mentioned most conversations were about horses?"

Mayrin blushed again. "Well, they sometimes spoke about females."

"And you listened to those conversations?"

"No I left with alacrity when that happened."

Haydar peered at her under a lowered brow. "I hope so. I am sure those conversations were most unseemly."

"Haydar. Forget those conversations. We were discussing you speaking with Praetor Makinti. Why would that be better than speaking face-to-face with Lord Eduardo?"

Haydar grinned. "Because Praetor Makinti is a long-time friend of Bardu, who is Praetor to Lord Eduardo."

"That is the most wonderful idea of all. When will you speak with him?"

"We are not far from Eeglos, and the horse I spoke to last eve told me the Praetor was on his way there."

Mayrin gasped. "You mean the horses also tell you news about people and other horses? I did not know that."

"Of course, they do. I doubt that most people understand that horses can hear everything, and they like to tell me things because I am interested. Horses only have each other to speak with, so it is like having an extra horse to talk to when I am there."

Mayrin hugged him. "You are the most unusual male I have ever met. I am so glad we are bonded."

"And I am so blessed to have met you."

"When you leave to meet with Praetor Makinti on the morrow, take the biggest one to ride. Even being on a horse will mean he is more likely to take you seriously."

"I will, despite the fact I prefer to ride the other. The

larger mare speaks all the time and never keeps quiet. She is quite boring for a horse."

They retired for the night, each thinking about how they might achieve their greatest desires.

***

When he reached Eeglos, Haydar asked for Praetor Makinti and was directed to where he was enjoying his morning meal.

Haydar approached the Praetor's table dragging his feet. "Please forgive me for being so presumptuous, Praetor Makinti. I need to ask you a most important question."

Makinti glanced up, his eyes wide in surprise. "And who are you?"

"My name is Haydar."

"What is this presumptuous question you have for me?"

"I would like for you to see me speak with your horse."

"What?"

"I would like to speak to your horse."

"Speak to my horse? Are you joking? Plus, he is huge, and you are quite little compared to him. I am concerned you may be injured."

"I promise you I will not get injured. I am always comfortable with horses."

Makinti seemed intrigued. "Why do you want me to see this?"

"Sire, I wish to become a horse trainer, and I know I

can be successful at it. I have a way with horses, and no matter their size, they will never hurt me. I am aware you are a friend of Praetor Bardu. I am hoping you will mention me to him to request that Lord Eduardo nominate me to become his Horse Master."

Makinti leaned back in his chair. "Whew. You have epic dreams, young Haydar. Particularly for such a little person."

"Please let me show you what I can do. It will not take much of your time, and my very life depends on it."

The Praetor scratched his head, and knitted his brows together. "You are an exceedingly bold young male to request such a thing." He rubbed his jaw. "If you guarantee it will not take much time, I find myself oddly curious to see what you can do." He stood. "I will give you my time, but you better not waste it, Haydar. Follow me."

Makinti left the hall, followed by Haydar, and headed to the stables.

When they reached the stable building, Makinti spotted a mare tied to a post. "Is that yours?"

Haydar nodded.

The Praetor asked the stable hand to fetch his horse, and when it was outside, minus its saddle and bridle, he turned to Haydar. "So, impress me with your abilities."

Haydar grabbed a mounting stool and brought it beside Makinti's mount. He climbed up so he could reach the horse's head.

Makinti stiffened, but the horse lowered its head toward Haydar, who began whispering to it. The horse nickered and breathed in Haydar's face and then rubbed its nose on his cheek.

Haydar's mare whinnied. He turned at once and pointed a finger at her. "Be quiet. You talk far too much. I am speaking to someone else now. You will have to wait."

The mare dropped her head and pawed at the ground.

Haydar went back to speaking with Makinti's horse, who kept nodding and nickered often. At last, Haydar turned to Makinti. "He told me his name is Prince, and he says I should ask you if you will allow me to sit on his back."

By this time, Makinti was staring at the two of them, his mouth open, and his eyebrows raised. "Er … are you sure?"

Haydar beamed and nodded. "I am very sure."

"Then mount."

"I agree that I am short Praetor Makinti. Could you help me get onto Prince, please."

Makinti laced his fingers together and Haydar set his boot in place. When Makinti lifted him, Haydar achieved his dream. He was sitting on a massive horse's back.

He laughed and laughed and tears ran down his face.

The horse nodded up and down, whinnied and snorted, and lifted his front feet slightly off the ground, forcing Haydar to clutch at the mane.

Haydar reached down and patted Prince on his neck and thanked him, tears still streaming from his eyes. He slid his other leg over the neck, and holding onto the mane slid down to the ground.

Makinti kept shaking his head. "I would not have believed this if I had not seen it myself."

Haydar looked up at him. "Will you now agree to speak with Praetor Bardu?"

Makinti shook Haydar's hand. "In a turn or to, I will be visiting Kaylin on behalf of Thane Cathked. Both Bardu and I will speak to Lord Eduardo on your behalf."

Haydar smiled. He felt such a joy in his heart that when he approached his mare, he threw his arms about her neck and kissed her on her nose. She rubbed her face on his forehead and blew hay-scented air on his face.

He turned back to the Praetor. "You have my deepest thanks, Praetor Makinti. May all your journeys be joyful and safe."

"Farewell Haydar. We have been well met."

Haydar pulled himself up onto his mare's saddle and set off for his home.

**

His ride back to Mayrin and the farm was slower and he took the time to gaze around at the beauty he saw in his land. *I hope I will find Kaylin as beautiful, and I hope Mayrin will like it too.*

When he arrived at their small house, Mayrin ran out to meet him. "What happened? Tell me everything."

He slid off the mare and rushed over to Mayrin and

held her close. "I believe I was successful. I am so glad you persuaded me to take the action I needed."

After grooming his mare and giving her extra oats, he headed in for his own evening meal.

That eve, after their meals were done, he and Mayrin enjoyed each other without worrying about creating offspring.

***

Within fourteen turns, Makinti rode up to the farm where Haydar and Mayrin lived.

Haydar noticed Makinti's face was solemn. *Oh no. He was not successful. I will not be Horse Master of Kaylin.*

Makinti swung down from Prince and sauntered over to Haydar and Mayrin. "You have a fine house here. It is small, but you must be most comfortable."

Haydar waited.

Makinti laughed and clapped Haydar on the back. "But you need to pack up everything and leave it. Kaylin waits for you." He beamed. "Horse Master."

THE BUSTA

Enemy of the Crosa

When Azidon and his daughters were helping the humans of Pridden in the earliest beginnings of the world, they almost always found there were already other groups of creatures that aided the humans in adjusting to the conditions of living in the lands. On rare occasions, Azidon and his offspring brought forth other creatures that helped in certain areas.

Azidon laughed when Ssayleese showed him a Ponti for the first time. "It resembles a young one's picture of a horse. You are making a joke, are you not, Ssayleese?"

"No, this is not a horse. It is a Ponti, and I made it like that deliberately. It does appear to be a little ugly, but it is most practical for some of the lands in Pridden. Horses are beautiful but delicate creatures in many ways. They cannot walk with ease in mountainous areas. Pontis are the most sure-footed creatures and can handle rocky and unsteady areas with ease. They are slower than horses, but they are also much stronger, can carry much larger loads, and can travel much further before they need water and sustenance."

"I see your point, but what have you come up with to handle these nasty creatures the humans refer to as Crosa?"

147

Ssayleese shuddered. "These Crosa are horrible. They are so grossly fat and they resemble long tubes of blubber with horrific heads. They have rows of poisonous teeth lining their jaws, which are difficult to avoid. Despite the fact that they are so fat, they move with amazing speed."

Azidon screwed his face up in disgust. "They sound quite repulsive."

"They are," She shivered, remembering. "They make ingenious traps to capture prey. The Crosa reside in a scorching hot, arid area called the Hellesmouth Desert. They prepare the sand so that it swirls, and the prey get caught in a whirlpool of sand, from which they cannot escape. Trapped in the whirling grit, their prey fall through the sand to the Crosa homes below the Hellesmouth."

"I would suggest this is one hunter we need to help the humans defeat."

Ssayleese grinned, showing teeth. "They already have help. Quite by accident, I have discovered a natural enemy, and they are sentient creatures called busta."

"Busta? I have never even heard of such an animal."

"They are not animals. As I said, they are sentient, and are quite unique. When they stand on their rear legs, they are almost as tall as Rifellans. They can walk on all fours with equal comfort. They have incredible strength, and fine white hair covers their entire bodies. It appears to others as if they are wearing fur coats. They have no need to wear clothing, as we do, because where they live is hot. Sometimes they make use of loin cloths. I am not sure why. Their faces resemble those of humans, except for their teeth. They have massive fangs that almost appear too huge for their mouths. The fangs are so sharp, one would not be remiss in thinking they had filed them to the points of needles."

"How do they help the humans?"

"The best way would be for you to observe what happens when humans and busta work together. You would enjoy seeing this."

"I would like to observe it."

"I regret there are no groups who are crossing the Hellesmouth at this moment, so you will have to be satisfied with my descriptions. First, I shall describe how the busta handle themselves without humans. If a busta is caught in a Crosa trap and falls below the sands, it can kill the Crosa with ease by mounting the disgusting creature and delivering a fatal bite to the rear of the neck. The busta enjoy the Crosa eggs and find them an exceptional delicacy."

Azidon raised his brows. "You did not create these busta?"

"No. They are intelligent enough to survive most challenges. Busta never seek Crosa nests by themselves. They travel in pairs, and on the odd occasion, in threes or fours. When a busta falls into a Crosa trap, they kill the Crosa and collect the eggs. Once they have completed gathering the eggs, they hoot to indicate they have killed their enemy. The busta on the surface carries a line woven from vines found in the forest in which they live. When they hear the hoot, the surface busta throws the line into the trap and the busta below ground grabs it and is hauled to the surface by the other."

"That does indicate intelligence."

Ssayleese shrugged her shoulders. "However, the challenge is that sometimes the surface busta may not be strong enough to free their companion from the sands. The busta in the Crosa trap has plenty of eggs below ground to survive for a length of time, but if they are not rescued before the supply is all eaten, they could starve and die."

"How do these busta help the humans?"

"The desert is huge, and if humans need to travel further south in their land, it is far quicker for them to cross the Hellesmouth. In order to do so in safety, they form an alliance with the busta. They always travel in groups of three or four. If the human falls into a Crosa trap, the busta will jump in to rescue him or her. The busta kills the Crosa and then collects the Crosa eggs before doing anything else. They consider it their payment for guiding humans to safety across the Hellesmouth. Once the busta has collected the eggs, they hoot to indicate they are ready to climb out. Another human or busta on the surface will tie a line to a horse's saddle horn, and throw it down the trap. The horse will stand firm while those below climb to freedom."

Azidon nodded and smiled. "It sounds like the busta and the humans have solved their mutual problem without your intervention."

Ssayleese laughed. "They have indeed. But they have shown me how species can work together. I remember this when I find humans in other areas that require help. I may not have created the busta, and I do not know who did, but I could create something with similar intentions should it be needed."

Azidon frowned, his face apparently buried in thought. "You do not have any idea who created the busta?"

Ssayleese shook her head.

"Could your sibling have been responsible?"

Ssayleese laughed aloud. "I doubt that. If Caleesh created a hunter for the Crosa, it would have been much more attractive to look at and, I suspect, would have had fewer teeth."

Azidon squinted. "Interesting. Busta are unique creatures. It would have taken someone or something equally unique to have created it."

"It matters not." Ssayleese shrugged. "They exist."

THE SHA-HEE

The Androgynous Shape Shifters

When Pridden was first formed and populated by humans, the seeds for another race were planted as well. North of the land of Glowen in the interior of Pinacle Rock, the shifters first appeared. Yet they were not many, but one.

The intelligent being experienced awareness. *I am Sha-hee. I am one with many parts. I can create myself as many.*

The Sha-hee realized that the caverns in Pinacle Rock were almost endless so it began to allow "the many that made up the one" to fill the chambers of the rock with its beings. Over time, tall beings, clad with long robes and dark hoods, filled the rooms in the system of caverns. To any viewer, they appeared as pale, hairless, sexless creatures with eyes that contained no irises. To a human they looked like paintings of blind people, with blank opaque eyes.

The Sha-hee arrived as multiples of itself. Sha-hee was pleased with the results of the creation of its many parts. It searched the area near it and found the ocean and the land, and experienced sky and earth. It divested another part of itself as a huge creature that moved sinuously in the cool freedom of water. It experienced a delight when other parts became many flying creatures. But like Sha-hee itself, the flying ones kept themselves isolated in caverns on the land.

Sha-hee understood its primary role was helping the many humans who populated most of the world in which it found itself living.

The first requirement, Sha-hee understood, was that it needed to remain a secret from the humans who roamed the world of Pridden. Its main instinct called for self-protection, so the secret of its existence needed to be kept, but should a major challenge threaten these humans, they would require knowledge of Sha-hee. So, the shifter planted a code in the minds of the leader and later the multiple leaders, that would be triggered if such a need ever arose.

Sha-hee experienced completeness when it understood what its primary function was. As the awareness of the challenges of Pridden expanded within Sha-hee, a new function became necessary. The island that Pinacle Rock was a part of contained a limited number of growing things. Sha-hee examined the way the humans reproduced and understood that unchecked reproduction might be the cause of challenges to supplies of food and other sustainable items in the future for this beautiful island.

There was no question, that human reproduction on the island needed to be limited.

Sha-hee contemplated the complex problem for many turns and found a simple solution. Humans had a clear vision in their minds of who they wanted for a mate. A part of Sha-hee would shift into the visioned being and remain in that shift as long as Sha-hee remained close to the human. Sha-hee was curious as to how humans accomplished this. Did Sha-hee have no control over this ability?

Sha-hee spent time in contemplation of this new experience. The great benefit was that as humans and Sha-hee were biologically different, no offspring could result from their union. Sufficient humans mated with each other on Glowen so they would continue to be birthed on the island. Thus, the island's population would always be static, and the food supply would always be sufficient for the humans who inhabited it.

Again, the Sha-hee was satisfied. Sha-hee would limit the visions it accepted from humans, thus keeping the growth among humans on the island in a state of homeostasis.

The shifter continued to keep the knowledge of its existence secret from the human population of Pridden. It did the same with its extensions in the water and air over the land of Glowen. If humans wandered too close to the aboveground exit from Pinacle Rock near Krugg Menyd, the flying parts would attack. They would not kill the trespasser, because their reason for being was to supply protection for all humans.

If the potential invasion came from the ocean near Pinacle Rock, the huge creature would swim close to the invader and appear dangerous in the extreme.

The Sha-hee could read the minds of all of the sentient creatures in Pridden dealt with challenges almost before they occurred. The greatest benefit Sha-hee possessed was that it could insert thoughts into those minds.

***

For hundreds and hundreds of passes, the Sha-hee had protected Pridden, without triggering the knowledge of them in the minds of the humans. While the world was not always peaceful, because sentient beings are imperfect and tend to find faults where none exist, they thrived, because the lands contained a huge expanse of arable earth.

As the humans moved to cover the entire area of Pridden, they divided it into six different lands, each inhabited by humans of different appearances. Each land developed leaders who helped set up laws and methods of governance. Even though all lands had people of different shapes, colors, and sizes, they accepted each other most of the time. There were, of course, times when one land would bear a grudge with another, and fighting did occur. Fortunately, the fights never threatened the entire population of Pridden. Humans soon realized that war was an expensive proposition. The Sha-hee scrutinized these conflicts with deep concentration, but rarely needed to interfere.

Much of the time, the people of Pridden tolerated each other, and peace always brought prosperous times.

***

However, a time arrived when the balance in Pridden shifted. In the most southern of the lands, Morden, a man rose to power, who was the antithesis of a good leader. He ordered the killing of the land's current leader and became responsible for fear and resentment among the inhabitants. The leaders of the other lands looked away, asserting that the situation was no business of theirs. Such a challenge must be left to the residents of that land to solve. However, the people of Morden were fearful and inexperienced in such battles. Sha-hee became concerned and after examining the situation, considered that it might have to intervene. This caused Sha-hee's first experience with bouts of pain and confusion. The shifter might have to separate a part to deal with this complex and dangerous situation, and this might cause unknown repercussions for Sha-hee. It was a not a being which had been created to handle violent challenges with ease. Its primary function had always been peace.

***

A being such as Sha-hee, never acted in haste. Many turns passed as it prepared to separate a part to deal with the precarious situation in Morden.

Before it created a separate entity, something quite unexpected occurred. An unknown woman appeared in Pridden. Where ever she travelled. she challenged the status quo. She upset established customs, annoyed a number of humans, and possessed a mind the Sha-hee could not penetrate. Despite how often she caused problems, she was also appreciated by several. No one like her had ever existed on Pridden before

Consumed by curiosity it had never experienced before, Sha-hee arranged for her to appear before it, deep in the caverns beneath the Pinacle Rock. It requested the enormous water portion to bring her to the caverns from the passage at the base of the Rock. When she confronted the shifter as a tall robed figure, she complained that it had drowned her in the water. It seemed that she meant she had perished. Sha-hee was unable to understand why she appeared so annoyed because it was obvious that she was alive. At the beginning of her visit, Sha-hee found it difficult to communicate with her mind because it switched rapidly from a vision of one person to another. Sha-hee could control what most of the humans did but was challenged by how quickly and unexpectedly this woman's mind switched back and forth. It requested she keep her physical distance from it so that it could maintain but one vision.

The visit with this woman was extraordinary. The Sha-hee did not penetrate her thoughts at any time.

She asked about this. "Why can I close my mind, yet you tell me others on Pridden cannot?"

The shifter shook its shoulders because it experienced humor. "I am unaware of why this is. You are unique to this world." It appeared as the strongest vision of someone she knew. Presenting someone she was familiar with would make her more comfortable. What Sha-hee found odd was this woman did not appear concerned about the alien experience. Sha-hee concluded she was accustomed to unusual experiences.

To attempt to explain its existence to this woman, Sha-hee introduced her to the many parts which resided in the chambers of the cave beneath Pinacle Rock. It also taught her a way to strengthen the ability to conceal her thoughts from any other being in Pridden.

She asked, "You tell me parts of you are bonded with Glowens, yet you, as their mates, are never seen with them in public. Why do they not reveal your presence?"

"I removed the memory of how they met me. The part of Sha-hee they bond with always remains in the familial homes with the bonded Glowens."

"Do you always wish to remain undiscovered?"

"I do. It is vital to my survival. As far as we are aware, you are the only person who is aware of our existence."

"Why the secrecy?"

"I cannot exist if many are aware of me. I would burn out from the stresses and cease to be."

"Do you know where or when you came from?"

"That is something I never question. I am Sha-hee. I exist to aid the people of Pridden. That is a sufficient reason for me." Sha-hee shook its shoulders again. "I find our conversation amusing. I am Sha-hee. I exist, therefore I am."

She blinked rapidly. "I am not sure I understand you completely. I will use what you have taught me about closing my mind to protect the secret of your existence. I promise you."

"I thank you. On the morrow I will have five of my parts

escort you to the land so you can continue your journey. I have foreseen that you have a most important service to perform for Pridden."

Sha-hee left the room, recalling his conversation with the unusual woman. *She may be the one.*

***

The shifter spent many more turns observing Pridden and its challenges. It also followed the woman as she continued her journey. Sha-hee experienced humor at how she caused enormous challenges for herself with the Glowens. They were unable to understand why she would consistently turn down their advances. She had broken some rules implying she was available for mating. Her guide appeared to have reached his limit of patience with her, but the Leader of Glowen found her amusing and appreciated her presence.

She did, as promised, keep the secret of Sha-hee, and she daily practiced strengthening the veil on her mind.

The shifter felt a deep concern when she traveled to the land of Baklai. There, the rules she broke were punishable by death. Sha-hee prepared to intervene if necessary. Sha-hee suspected she would solve the challenge in Morden. Convinced of this, the shifter waited. However, somehow, she persuaded another, this time the leader of Baklai, to spare her life.

When she moved on to Morden, Sha-hee marveled that the woman secured the protection of the sentient snakes, who referred to themselves as the Kokas. Sha-hee and the Kokas had enjoyed many lengthy conversations, as they both wished the best for the humans of Pridden.

The final act of the drama in Morden showed Sha-hee how the woman cared for the lives of others. When Sha-hee saw how deadly the current leader of Morden had become, it was astonished that one person could contain such evil.

Sha-hee then perceived how many of the people of Pridden banded together to benefit each other. They fought the evil leader and ended the potential war. They clearly demonstrated the need for ensuring that all humans treat each other with respect and kindness.

Sha-hee sat in its favorite seat and contemplated the world it inhabited. The woman had asked many questions, which had in turn, answered many for Sha-hee.

Pridden is a fine world. It is one filled with respect, love, and peace.

LIANDOCK

The Metal Master

A small whirlwind whipped past Liandock, making him spin in its wake. He coughed, spat sand from his mouth, and counted slowly to ten. "I'm going to have to kill my sister."

He brushed sand from his hair and growled at her, "Irina, you have to stop running around like an anxious Wullawerth. You have sand flying everywhere. You're living on borrowed time, young woman."

"And you, Liandock, are grumpy and boring. You have lived only four more passes than me, but you act old." She raised her arms and turned in circles. "I need to practice running, because I'm going to be the head of guards at the Keep when Murwenna takes over as Lord of Rifella. I will have to be fast to be a worthy warrior."

"Murwenna will not come into her birthright for at least another ten passes. You have time. But you need to slow down. I had my eye on a beautiful gemstone, and the sand buried it."

Irina stopped and stared up at him. "Are you sure you do not want to be a warrior too?"

Liandock gazed down at her. He smiled at the little snub nose, sprinkled with freckles. He could not help himself. *She looks so innocent when she tilts her head like that. Perhaps I will not kill her just yet.* He sighed. "No, I have no wish to be a fighter. I love the beauty of stones and the way they nestle into the metal designs I create. I intend to be the most famous Metal Master on all Pridden."

Irina raised a blond eyebrow. "That does not sound exciting. I will wager our parents will not view it as an acceptable calling."

He smiled at her. "You are wrong. Our parents are aware of my wishes, and their only desire is for me to be happy in my choices. You are right about one thing, though. The joy I find in using stones and gems and metals is a calling. They speak to me and tell me secrets."

Her bright blue eyes widened. "How can stones have secrets?

He ruffled her hair. "You doubt me? I do not understand how the language of gems and stones operate. Perhaps I can show you. We are not far from the Crystal Dunes. Let us go and find a crystal for you, and it will tell me secrets about you."

Irina grinned and jumped up and down. "Yes, we must do this. I will get canteens and you must saddle a horse for us." Without waiting for a reply, she ran back into their home.

Liandock's heart warmed as he watched her run. He adored her, even though she often annoyed him. *She understands me almost as well as I do myself.*

He turned and ran to the stable. By the time Irina arrived, flushed and grinning, he had saddled and bridled his horse. She held up two canteens.

He mounted and reached down to grab her arm and lift her into the saddle in front of him, and they set off for the Crystal Dunes. The Dunes, Rifella's extraordinary cache of glorious gemstones lay close, but the day was hot, and horseback shortened the distance from their home.

Liandock took his time.

Irina chatted nonstop, asking question after question. "What makes you think stones have secrets?"

"You remember Mannin? I was quite taken with her, and I believe our parents thought she might one day become my mate. While we were on our way to that camping trip in the Torrenton Forest, she picked up a small crystal. I asked her if I could examine it. As I held it, I knew that Mannin and I would never bond and that she would, in her future, mate with a warrior from Pakanna and would live there with him."

"She did do that. What words do the stones use to talk to you?" She frowned. "I think our parents were sad she did not stay to be with you." Irina sniffed. "I always thought she was a bit stupid."

"Irina, that is not kind of you."

"Well, she was."

He stopped the horse. "We cannot take this animal further into the Dunes. I forgot to bring padding for its hooves. We cannot afford to injure them on the sharp crystals."

He lowered his sister to the ground, and slid from the

saddle.

Irina headed straight for the Dunes but recoiled from the blinding sun bouncing off the crystals.

"Wait. Do not forget your mask." Liandock reached into his saddle bag and withdrew two masks fashioned from dark wood. Each sported slits for their eyes.

Irina returned to his side and grabbed a mask from him. "Thank you. I was so excited to see how you read the gems. I must have forgotten about protecting my eyes."

He pursed his lips. "Fine warriors are always concerned with protecting themselves from potential dangers. You cannot help another unless you help yourself first. Pay more attention, Irina."

She hung her head. "I am sorry. I know you are correct. I promise I will be more aware of what I am doing."

He put his arm around her shoulders and hugged her to him. "Not just because you wish to be a warrior. You are important to me."

She snuggled into the hug, and smiled up at him.

His heart skipped a beat. *My little sister can be so captivating when she smiles.* "We will not go too far into the Dunes. It is part of the Hellesmouth Desert, and we only have a limited amount of water. There is a flat rock to your left. We will sit and search the area around it and are bound to find some beautiful crystals."

Irina nodded, and they walked over to the rock and sat. She leaned over and began searching through the gems, as if hoping to find something that appealed to her.

He gazed at Irina again. *She is still young, but when she reaches her mating age in five more, four-season passes, she will be a stunning young woman. There will be many young warriors at her door.*

He searched the area in front of him. As he reached down, a frisson of a strange vibration attracted him. He picked up a magnificent green stone, gazed at it for a moment, felt the calling of it, and pocketed it.

"I love this one, Liandock." Irina held out an oblong crystal in a glorious red. "It reminds me of the colors in the sky when our star is sliding below the horizon. What does it tell you?"

"Do not rush this, Irina. Hold it, and I will wait until it speaks to me. Stones are never impatient."

They sat together in silence, and Liandock closed his eyes, waiting for a message from the red stone. "Oh, Irina. This is indeed a fine stone. It tells me you will be a wonderful warrior and will serve at a Keep. But you will not serve Murwenna."

"But --"

He held up his hand to silence her. "You will meet a fine warrior, and the two of you will bond."

Irina scowled. "I do not need to bond with anyone to be a warrior on my own. Males are silly, and they are annoying."

Liandock laughed. "You will discover, Irina, that not all

167

males are silly. This one will be invited by a Lord to hold the title of Praetor at his Keep. The two of you will travel to the Lord's land, and you will serve together."

Her eyes were bright with keen expectancy as she looked up at his face. "Which Lord will we serve? What is the name of my supposed future mate? Are you sure he will not be stupid or annoying?"

He laughed. "The stones do not tell me everything, my impatient sibling. I can give you no more information."

Her shoulders slumped. "Crosa curses. I wish they told you more."

Liandock shook his head. "Irina, that is not an appropriate expression for a young woman of breeding to use."

She pursed her lips at him. "You use it."

"I am older than you."

She sighed. "Did you find any stones you liked and needed for your adornments?"

"I found a most important one." He brought the green stone from his pocket and held it up to the light.

"Oh, that's beautiful. Who is it for?"

"An exceptional woman. A stranger I have yet to meet. She will need this for her protection."

Irina's face crinkled up in puzzlement. "You have no idea who?"

He shook his head. "Not yet."

***

Pridden had circuited its star five more times when Liandock looked up from his work. He was hammering silver metal into a series of bends and twists, when Irina appeared at his doorway. He smiled at her. "What is it? You are blushing. Unlike your normal self, you seem to be unsure."

She moved without her usual grace. "I need your advice."

Oh dear, what has she done now?. "You need my advice? You have never needed it before. Why now?"

Irina shifted about, and avoided his eyes. "Um. Bardu has asked me to be his bond mate. Is he the one you foresaw in the stones?"

His heart lifted. *Bardu? He is the perfect mate for my sister.* "Oh, Irina. Do you love him?"

She nodded.

"Then he is the one. Accept him. Do not wait. He is perfect for you. I believe he is to be Praetor for Lord Eduardo of Kaylin."

"The only thing that is not perfect is that you and I will be separated. I will live in Kaylin, and you will be here in Rifella."

She seemed so sad and forlorn that Liandock laughed aloud. "We will not be separated, sister-mine. Lord Eduardo has requested I come to Kaylin to take up residence as their Metal Master."

Irina's face filled with joy. She threw herself at Liandock and hugged him. "Caleesh has bestowed us with good fortune."

"You are squeezing the breath from my body. Bardu is most fortunate. You will be a mate worthy of a Praetor."

Irina peered up at him. "It is most unusual for Lord Eduardo to request you to serve in the capacity of Metal Master. I wonder why he asked this of you."

He frowned at her. "I do have a reputation of being at one with the stones and crystals of Pridden. Plus, I believe he is anxious to have Bardu as his Praetor. I suspect he made sure to cement that relationship by having us in the same land. Eduardo is a brilliant man. He knows you would chafe if separated from me."

"Are you at peace being away from our home land?"

He laughed at her and tousled her hair. "I am at peace, and I know full well who I am." His breath filled and warmed him inside. "Irina, I was never meant to be a warrior. If I had remained in Rifella, that pressure would always be there. I am well satisfied with my lot."

She sighed. "If only you would also find a bond mate, Liandock, my world would be perfect. There are so many females who would mate with you in an instant, yet you turn them all down."

"None of them are the right one."

"Yet you bed so many. Why are none of them the right female for you?"

He shook his head at her, feeling the strange emptiness in his heart. "Although I am not a warrior, I am still a male.

I do have needs." He sighed. "Do not trouble yourself about me. Now go and begin the preparations for the mating ceremony. In a few turns, we will all depart for Kaylin."

***

Irina entered the sitting room of the house she and Bardu now occupied. "Where are you, bond mate? Lord Eduardo will be wondering why we are so slow."

"He never thinks of us as slow. You are always impatient when we leave for our annual tour of Kaylin."

Irina pretended to scowl at him, but could not hold her expression and finally burst out laughing. "You know perfectly well, mate of mine, I have not met with my brother in more than three seasons, despite the fact he lives but two turns from us. I need to make sure he is well, and is happy."

"With a sibling like you to take care of him, I guarantee he is happy." Bardu pulled her into a hug and kissed her.

She snuggled into him, reveling in the warmth and comfort of him. "I only wish he could find a bond mate who is as fine for him, as we are for each other."

"Irina, he is a grown man. Allow him the freedom to find his own mate."

"I just want him to have as wonderful a life as we do." She pulled back, and her face lit up. "I will take Glo to show to him. I was so surprised when Lord Eduardo gifted me with a pyrock. He told me he has always thought it necessary for his Praetor to possess a pyrock, so that when they tour Kaylin, they are able to contact him without delay. He also said males are less nurturing of pyrocks than females. So, I was given Glo instead."

Bardu tapped her on the nose. "So, worry about the well-being of Glo, and allow your brother to worry about himself."

***

Liandock appeared at the gates of his small village, arms outstretched to welcome Irina and her mate. "Welcome to Lanfair." He walked over to Irina, his kilt swaying like that of a warrior in ceremonial uniform, helped her down from her horse, and drew her into a tight hug. "I have missed you, Irina. It has been many seasons since you visited me."

She just grinned and clung to him.

Holding onto Irina, Liandock strolled over to Bardu and held out his hand, and they performed the complicated Rifellan greeting between men. Liandock bowed his head to Bardu. "Praetor, have you yet managed to bring my sibling under control?"

Bardu's eyes widened, and he stared at Liandock in mock horror. "Control her? Are you mad? If I attempted to control her, she would force me to sleep in the stables."

Irina hmphed, and glared at them both.

Liandock gazed at Bardu, his face set in a serious expression of curiosity. "In the stables, Bardu. Would she truly do that?"

"Liandock, I have no idea why you never warned me what a vicious mate she would make. I am forced to believe that if she had her way, she would geld me."

Unable to contain themselves any longer, the two men burst into laughter.

Irina stood still, hands on her hips. Eyeing the two of them, she gave a long audible sigh. "Are you both quite finished?"

They smiled at her, and with one on either side of her, they headed into Liandock's section of his house. Just before they entered, Liandock tilted his head at the stable master, who nodded and took control of their horses.

Irina called out, "Stop." She rushed over to her horse and took a small cage from the pommel before running back to the two men. "I must show you my gift from Lord Eduardo."

Liandock guided them toward the dining lounge. "It is time for a noon-turn meal, so we can sit, and you can show me the gift."

They sat at a table in the dining hall, and a serving person brought them food and drink.

Irina placed the small cage on the table in front of her. She beamed up at Liandock. "Meet Glo." She reached into the cage and withdrew the warm furry pyrock. With a proud smile, she presented the small creature to her brother. "Is she not adorable?"

Once Glo had been shown to them all and had passed

admiring examination, they settled down to eat and enjoy a lively conversation.

Liandock gazed at his sister and her mate. *They love each other so much. I am so glad Irina found a mate worthy of her.*

After the meal, Irina asked to visit his workshop again. "I love seeing all the new stones you have found, and all your new metal creations."

Liandock turned to Bardu. "Do you also wish to visit my workshop?"

"No, I have seen your workshop before. However, since I am aware you have made changes to the buildings of the village, I will examine what you have done. Some of these changes, might be worth recommending to other villages in our land."

They left the hall, and Irina and Liandock headed for his workrooms.

Irina gazed around Liandock's workspace and exclaimed in delight. "Amazing. You have expanded the length of your workshop. And you have put all the display cases in the cool side of the room. I approve."

"I have not made you any metal adornment in many seasons. I will do so now." He removed his shirt and, bare-chested, approached the kiln and opened the door. He donned massive protective gloves, picked up a stone clamp to remove a small pot of melted silver, which he poured onto a slab with thin lines carved into it. Once done, he placed the rest of the melted silver back in the kiln and closed the door.

He carried the slab to a section of stone, which was set near a doorway, through which a pleasant breeze blew. He removed the gloves and set them aside.

"While the silver hardens, let us sit over here." He led them to seats in the cooler end of the room. In front of them were trays of cut crystals and smoothly polished rocks of all colors and sizes. "You may choose a stone or a crystal."

"Before I do that, I want to ask about your attire. I have always wondered about the long leather boots you wear, done up with laces that reach up above your knees. Why so high?"

"When the metal comes from the kiln, it is molten and could cause great pain if it landed on my skin. It tends to splash on the floor, so my legs are most in danger. The boots protect me."

"You are always bare-chested when you work, so I know you do not need protection for your upper body."

"I only use small pots of molten metal, and pour it downwards so there is no possibility of any landing on my upper body. As you can tell, the heat is intense in the workshop, and this keeps me cooler."

"And the kilt?"

"Ah." He grinned. "You are now no blushing untried female. You are a mated woman and no doubt understand males more than you did as a child. A kilt allows air the ability to flow around my male parts. It is much cooler, and..." He grinned again. "I have a tremendous sense of freedom."

Irina blushed a pale pink. "Oh."

She eyed him. "I have realized something, brother. You are a most handsome male, and if any woman walks into this workshop and catches you in this state, Rifellan pheromones or not, she will be most taken with you." She shook her head at him. "You could have any woman you want. Why have you not had them?

He stared down at her. "Who says I have not?"

Irina turned red this time. "Oh Liandock, really."

"I told you before, Irina. While not a warrior, I am a male with strong needs. I would be a fool not to enjoy what is available."

Irina swallowed.

Liandock placed a tray of crystals in front of her. "Enough about me. You may choose a crystal."

She put out her hand to hover over a dark blue stone with a circle in the middle of it, but Liandock grabbed her hand. "No. Not that one. It is not for you."

Startled, she withdrew her hand and reached instead for a pale pink stone, shot with streaks of silver.

Liandock smiled. "This is indeed for you, but not just yet. I will place it in a silver cage and hang it from a chain in this corner. It will wait for you, and when you retrieve it, it will give you immense joy."

Irina shook her head and stared at him, a puzzled expression on her face. "I will wait for it. But do not make me wait too long." She gazed around the familiar lines of his workshop. "Liandock, I see that you still possess the glorious deep green stone that you found at the Crystal Dunes, before we left for Kaylin." She cleared her throat. "You said it was for someone who would need the protection it would give. You have kept it for so many passes. Have you still not met the woman you say it is destined for?"

"I have not. I keep the stone because it is for someone who is exceptional. She will need much protection."

"So, who is it?"

"I do not know, my dear one. But I will when I see her."

***

For the next seven passes, Irina continued to visit Lanfair once every fourth season to sit in peace and comfort in Liandock's old workshop. Peace had come to Kaylin, and although Liandock no longer lived there, his memory lingered on throughout Pridden. The village of Lanfair was maintained as a remembrance of a fine Metal Master. Pridden became an example of a world of peace and prosperity, due in part to the care of Lord Eduardo and his sibling, Lord Markallo.

Irina entered the workshop and found a chair. While seated, she heard Liandock's voice as if he sat beside her. *It is time for you to accept your crystal.* She rose and walked over to the corner where the necklace rested. She lifted it and placed it over her head and experienced a warm glow within her heart.

Liandock's voice spoke again. *My dear sister, Irina. The joy this crystal represents is for you and Bardu. The progeny you bear within you will bring you both much pride and happiness. Your daughter will become a warrior of note, and your son, will use this workshop to become an even greater Metal Master than I.*

You will bring new life and love to the world of Pridden.

GODRITH

The Tapestry Master

Godrith, sat on his parent, Elgranith's bed, receiving information and orders from him. While Godrith's hair had begun turning gray at more than fifty passes, Elgranith's hair at ninety passes was pure white and thinning.

Elgranith patted his progeny on the arm. "I am so sorry I waited for so many passes to mate again so you could be birthed. I missed my first mate so much I was overcome with grief for many passes. But your female parent was such a wonderful female, I only wish I had met her sooner." He sighed and had a coughing fit.

"Elgranith, should I fetch the Healer?"

"No, it is not necessary. Simply get me some water. The Healer cannot fix what I suffer from. It is, regrettably, the effects of age. It is why I am sorry I did not give you life earlier. If I had, I could have decided to retire and turn over the Mastership of our Tapestry Hall to you much sooner. I also regret your female parent contracted Red Rash and never told anyone she had the disease. I had at least hoped she would be available for you after I joined Caleesh."

"She was a stubborn woman. What is done is done, Elgranith. You cannot change the past."

"I am well aware of that. I fear I cannot last more than a season. And when I leave this land, you will become the twenty-third Tapestry Master in Shendea."

Godrith shook his head slowly. "Are you sure I am ready to be called a Master?"

"You are. You have been trained by the best Master, Shendea has ever experienced. Also, your gray hair assures me you have been studying for more than sufficient passes."

Godrith laughed. "Best Master of Shendea? In that, Sire, you are correct I have heard from so many Shendeans how extraordinary you are as their Tapestry Master. I hope when you do join Caleesh you will look down on us and be proud of me."

The old man coughed again. "Godrith, the Tapestries you have worked on are brilliant in both their color and design. I am positive you will surpass me before you reach sixty passes."

Godrith felt his eyes water. To avoid being seen to cry, he put his arms around his parent and hugged him.

Elgranith patted Godrith on his back and returned the hug. "Please do not be sad for me. I have lived with the joy of creating Tapestries my entire life. I helped complete two that my parent's parent began as a young apprentice. You will complete at least two others he also began later in his life. I hope you will complete the glorious one I designed for Lord Murwenna's parent when I was first appointed Tapestry Master."

"I do anticipate those completions with pleasure. There are so many of yours that I suspect I will not survive to view completed." He frowned and tilted his head. "I must ask you something, Elgranith. I have often toured the back caverns of the Tapestry rooms, and have found some strange tapestries. All the tapestries are complete, but are unclaimed. There are some I find dark and almost frightening. Why are they there?"

"They are, as you said, unclaimed. You may take some time to check the records to find out which families ordered them, and advise them they can claim them." Elgranith shrugged. "Tapestries are so costly I am always surprised to find any are unclaimed. But. of course, the majority of families who order them are either royalty, or those close to royal lines."

"What about the fearful somber ones? Should I also find the families for them?"

"It is our duty to return all Tapestries to the families they were ordered for. If no descendants of the family exist, you may offer them to anyone in Pridden who desires them."

"What about the horrible ones? If they have no families waiting for them, can I destroy them instead?"

"You can, but you must not destroy them within the Keep. The energies released by them would suffocate those in our Keep. You will remove them to a place that is not well populated. I suggest somewhere close to the Burning Rock Mountain, where I hope the energies will be dissolved by the fires of that Mountain. But I urge you to never, ever destroy any Tapestry within the Keep."

"I will not. I will always take anything which needs to be destroyed to Burning Rock.

When Elgranith coughed some more, Godrith handed him water again.

Elgranith held his hand to his chest, and breathed. "Thank you, that helped."

Godrith returned the glass to the bedside table. "I need to speak with you and get some of your ideas for two of the tapestries we are working on. Plus, I just located a dye that will give the threads a most unusual color. It is a cross between blue and deep purple. It also has a type of shimmer to it, not gold or silver, just a shimmer."

"It sounds magnificent. Can you bring me an example of the thread?"

"Of course. I want you to see it. I will also bring the design for the Tapestry Lord Rhognor has requested. He wishes to honor Halfin, who joined Caleesh a brief time ago. He wishes a small Tapestry so it can be completed within ten passes, and then he can display it on the wall of his office."

"Have you estimated how small the Tapestry would need to be for it to be completed in less than ten passes?"

"I have done that, and perhaps when I meet with you on the morrow, you will approve my calculations."

The old man yawned. "Godrith, I look forward to your visit on the morrow, but I am tired now and need to sleep.

Make sure you do not just work all the time. Be aware of any female for a possible mate. You have gone too long without one. Make sure that when your time comes to join Caleesh, you have a talented heir to pass on the mantle of Tapestry Master."

"You know it is not easy to find a mate within the caverns of this Hold, but I do look. I will not let you or Shendea down." He laughed and held Elgranith's hand. "Sleep now."

Godrith left the room and headed for the Tapestry area. He paused at the entranceway, closed his eyes, and breathed in the scent of freshly cut brynosh, and the fragrance of the flower dyes that imparted such glorious colors to the threads. He opened his eyes and the flood of glorious hues assaulted his vision.

A woman he had never seen before ran up to him, holding a spool of thread in the new purple/blue color, wrapped in a clear cover. The light from the thread shimmered back and forth, and sent shafts of color on the walls. "Sire Godrith, is this the color you wished to use on the new tapestry? Your assistant requested I bring it to you."

He took the spool from her. "It is magnificent. Notice how it reflects on the walls. I am convinced Lord Rhognor will agree that this represents the Lady Halfin at her most beautiful." He looked down at the woman. "What is your name? I do not think we have met before."

She smiled up at him. "I am Marrisa, and my parents were growers of brynosh. However, my sibling and his family are now in charge of the farm, and I am no longer needed there. I have always been fascinated by the tapestries, so I have come here to learn. I arrived here about twelve turns ago and have been serving as a runner. When I first heard that brynosh became the thread of Tapestries, I had to learn more about them." She peeked in the weaving room, her face filled with delight. "I did not imagine they could be so beautiful."

"What position do you wish to occupy, Marrisa?"

"I think I would like to create colors of threads that are so unique they make the tapestries more beautiful than ever. I would also love to do some of the weaving." She laughed. "I want to do everything."

He grinned at her. "If you wish to learn everything about creating tapestries, I am sure we can give you the opportunity to work in each area. The thing you need to experience first are the completed Tapestries in the storage area. I am not due to bring my design to Lord Rhognor until the morrow, so if you come with me, I will introduce you to our completed works."

"Oh, I would love to, Sire. I have never seen a completed Tapestry before. My parents were simple farmers, so we were not on invitation lists for royalty."

"Follow me."

They traveled through the rooms of the Tapestry workshop finally entering an enormous room filled with hanging works of art. Godrith clapped his hands, and all the glows in the room burst into light.

184

Huge frames divided the room into many sections, and against one wall stood a number of glass cases containing darker Tapestries.

He turned to Marrisa. "This is where the finished Tapestries are stored until the families who ordered them can arrange for their removal. What you might not understand, most likely because you have never viewed a completed Tapestry before, is the unusual qualities they possess."

Marrisa appeared puzzled. "Unusual qualities?"

"Yes. Come." He took her over to a huge tapestry hung from a frame. It was filled with beautiful flowers of all colors; a shoreline with swimmers jumping; vineyards with plump grapes filling the vines; tiny villages; and in the center, an enormous, well laid-out Keep. The colors and design were stunning.

He took her hand and, holding it back from the tapestry, nodded at her. "This one was ordered by the Thane of Glowen who was the parent to Brennan's parent. It took over seventy passes to complete. The current Thane, Brennan, will be visiting in five turns to claim it for his Keep." He waited. "Touch it, and it will tell you why these Tapestries take so long to complete."

He released her hand, and Marrisa touched the silky furry threads of the picture. She gasped. "I am there. I can see the flowers and feel the grasses around me and I can touch the horses' noses. I can also smell the rich scent of earth. How can this be?"

185

He pulled her hand away. "Do not keep contact with it for too long. The experience can become addicting. As to the how, it is something we have never understood. How can a simple plant fiber, whose natural color is beige, convey such vivid emotions and such extraordinary visions?"

He gazed down at her and was struck by the glow of joy that transfixed her. She was beautiful. He had not noticed this before.

He removed the roll of the blue purple thread from her hand and them unwrapped it from the clear covering. "I want you to touch this, and tell me how you what emotions it evokes."

She touched the bare thread. "Oh, how marvelous. I am experiencing intense love for this thread. I am warm and cosseted and safe."

"Perfect." He covered the thread again. "This is for Lord Rhognor's small tapestry, so he can recall his Lady Halfin. It will allow him to remember her always."

He clapped his hands, which turned off the glows on the walls. "Come again on the morrow, after the noon-turn meal, and I will find you a position in the Tapestry Hall."

She followed him out.

His thoughts roiled inside his head. *She can discern emotions from this thread so clearly. She's an unusual woman. I wonder what other talents she has.*

***

On the morrow, Godrith set out for Rhognor's rooms and travelled the halls immediately after the morning meal to keep his meeting with the Lord. After being admitted to the Lord's presence, Rhognor ordered tea for them both.

They waited in silence for the attendant to return.

Once they were seated with their tea in front of them, Godrith cleared his throat. "Lord Rhognor, may I go over the design I have created to honor your Lady Halfin?"

Rhognor moved his cup so the handle stood at ninety degrees to him. He nodded, both to Godrith and in satisfaction of the positioning of his cup.

"You told me many things that made her significant to you. You mentioned her unconditional love for you, her beauty, her love of animals and the plants of Shendea. However, I also took the opportunity to speak to many of the people of Shendea, including the Healers. They all gave me additional facets of her personality."

Rhognor smiled at him. "I never considered that. An excellent idea. I am glad you thought of it."

Godrith clasped his hands in front of him, as if in prayer. "They spoke of her incredible kindness, her love of the offspring of people and of animals and many birds. They also mentioned she could communicate with all living creatures. The boradai permitted me to speak with them about Lady Halfin, and they insisted I should also include her deep spirituality. She was the last of the Enchanters, and the boradai suggested to me that this was also the opportunity to acknowledge the benefits the Enchanters gave our land."

By the time Godrith finished his speech, Rhognor's eyes glistened, and he swallowed. "I had no idea my people loved her so much."

"They did, my Lord, and they still do. However, as I viewed all these wonderful attributes of the Lady Halfin, I realized that if I put everything into the Tapestry, it would be huge, and I know you would like a memory for you within a ten-pass span. Thus, I have created two designs." Godrith placed them on the table. He pointed at the smallest one. "The first will be the memory Tapestry for you, and will contain the most cherished memories of yours. It will be completed before the ten passes have concluded." He pulled the large one forward. "This second one will be the Tapestry that includes everything about her and is a celebration of her life and of all Enchanters. The second one, neither you or I, will ever see completed. But it will be one all Pridden will be able to view. This Tapestry will be the finest that Pridden has ever possessed."

By this time, tears ran freely down Rhognor's cheeks. He wiped his eyes on the sleeve of his robe, and cleared his throat. "You have done me and my Lady the greatest honor ever. Your Master Elgranith will be bestowing upon you the designation of Tapestry Master soon, but I acknowledge you as Tapestry Master for Shendea this day."

"You honor me, my Lord, and it is your right to do so. I gratefully accept, but please do not mention this to anyone else. I do not wish Master Elgranith to ever consider we are concerned about his pending trip with Caleesh. I wish him to enjoy what life he has left for as long as possible."

"Godrith, I will grant you, my silence."

Godrith left the Lord's rooms with his designs.

*****

He had been working at his desk when Marrisa entered the room.

"Sire Godrith, have you decided where I can best serve?"

He turned around. "Before I decide, since you have been here twelve turns, you must have worked on some areas already. I would like to try an experiment." He rubbed his forehead. "I know it is a little soon, but you do understand some of the emotions of the colored threads, I think we might discover how you enjoy weaving. I can seat you with Paraneen, who is working on one which Lord Lanerch of Kaylin ordered some time ago. The Lord wanted a tapestry that would show the beauty of his land. I am not sure whether Master Elgranith or his parent designed this. Would you be amenable to this, although you have no experience in that department?"

"It sounds wonderful, and I promise I will work extremely hard to prove I am capable with weaving."

"Fine. Come with me, and we will get you started. If you need to know who designed any specific Tapestry, you can always consult the records."

He led her to the first weaving room and they waited while the woman at the loom finished tamping down the row she had just completed. "Paraneen, this is Marrisa, who has joined our Tapestry group today. I would appreciate it if you would train her how to weave." He turned to Marissa. "Paraneen is our most skilled weaver." He left the weaving area.

Paraneen glanced up at Marissa. "I would be honored to help you understand the art of weaving. Please sit here beside me."

Sitting at the back of the tapestry, Paraneen demonstrated how she wove her bobbin, filled with brilliant blue thread, over and under the alternate warp lines. After about six sets through the warp, she used the sharpest point of the bobbin to tamp down the thread to form a complete band of color. "It is most important to tamp the thread down so that it is tight. If you do not, the threads may separate once the tapestry is moved."

Marrisa gazed with curiosity at the back of the Tapestry before her and saw bobbins filled with many colors of thread hanging, waiting to be used again. "Paraneen, how do you know what the front is like?"

"Look through the warp lines." She pointed at the wall in front of the Tapestry. "See the huge mirror? That is what the front's appearance is, and off to the side is the original design. I can always view what I have accomplished."

"I am so impressed with your skill. How many passes have you been doing this work?"

Paraneen smiled. "Since I became twelve passes in age. When you are young, you learn fastest and retain your skills best. So, these were my initial training passes. When I reached fourteen passes, I was not allowed back into the tapestry room until I gained eighteen passes. Then I was allowed to work at this full time. I adore what I do." She patted Marrisa. "It is time for the noon-turn meal, so we will eat in the Keep's dining hall, and when we have finished our meal, I will demonstrate again, and then, perhaps I may give you an opportunity to weave a few lines."

"Really? Oh, Thank you."

***

Marissa did not get the opportunity to begin weaving, because just before they left the dining lounge, an apprentice rushed in looking for Godrith. He was so distracted everyone began to worry about what was happening.

Marissa stepped up to him. "You said you are looking for Godrith?"

The man nodded.

"Have you checked his design office?"

"I am new to the Keep, and I do not know where that is."

"Come, I will take you." Marissa led the young man to Godrith's office.

He rushed in without knocking. "Sire Godrith, you must come with me at once. Master Elgranith is calling for you."

Godrith, without asking about the problem, rushed after

the man and Marissa, curious, followed.

At the doorway to Elgranith's room, Godrith ran to his bedside, but the young apprentice waited outside the door.

Elgranith was coughing violently and could not get his breath.

Godrith yelled to the apprentice. "Get a Healer. Now!" He lifted a glass of clear liquid from the table beside the bed, held Elgranith up from his pillow and brought the glass to his lips.

The old man managed a sip, but although the coughs eased a little, they did not stop.

Godrith massaged Elgranith's back, and it appeared to be slowing the coughing a bit more.

"Can I be of help?" Marissa asked.

Godrith startled, appeared to see her for the first time. "Bring more water."

She ran into the small kitchen attached to the bedroom, located a glass, and filled it with water from a huge jug sitting on the counter.

She held it out to Godrith, but he shook his head. "Put it on the table." He turned and scanned the room, frustrated. "Where is the Healer?"

At that moment, Deleth appeared and shooed Marissa from the room. In mere minutes, Lord Rhognor also entered the room, accompanied by one of his councilors.

Marissa found herself shunted aside, so she returned to the Tapestry room.

The room was filled with people all chattering to each other, faces screwed up, and brows creased in fear and doubt. No one worked on tapestries or any tapestry preparation.

Then the chattering ceased, and all was silent. No one moved or spoke. They waited.

It was approaching the time for an evening meal when Godrith appeared, his eyes red, with Lord Rhognor and his latest councilor.

Rhognor spoke first. "I am here to tell all of you that Tapestry Master Elgranith has left us to join with Caleesh. We will be holding the pyre for him in two turns near the Crimson Cauldron. and you are all given leave to attend should you wish to."

He put his hand on Godrith's shoulder and pulled him forward.

"Because of Master Elgranith's departure from our presence, I wish to announce the news that Godrith, Elgranith's heir, has attained the title of Tapestry Master of Shendea. In four turns, we will celebrate his achievement. There will be no more work today in Shendea, and we will all have the time to decide how we wish to mark two such momentous events."

***

When he first received his new position, Godrith found the workers in the Tapestry rooms were overly formal with. It took only a few turns before they accepted his word that he was still the same male, and his name was still Godrith.

Marissa went back to learning how to weave from Paraneen, who continued to demonstrate before allowing Marissa the opportunity to try on her own.

Marissa was itching to attempt weaving. "Paraneen, I believe I do understand how weaving is done. Am I ready yet to weave lines on my own?"

"I think you may be able now, but one last time, I would like to test you on the pressure you need to place on the bobbin, and I also want to watch how you handle the rolls of thread. Once I am happy you are comfortable with that, we can allow you to try on your own."

When Paraneen felt Marissa was ready, she set her to work on a small Tapestry for a family in Kaylin. Marissa had worked on this for about five turns, when one morning, she began to smile. Such a good mood spread throughout her body, that she burst into song.

Paraneen stared at her, so Marissa laughed. "I am just enjoying myself. The weather is fine, and I am happy."

Paraneen stopped her own work and came over to where Marissa sat. "Put the bobbin down."

Marissa looked up at her and laughed. "Why? I am doing a wonderful job."

Paraneen repeated her order. "Marissa, put the bobbin down. Now."

Marissa put it on the bench beside her. Her good mood evaporated, and she frowned at Paraneen. "You do not have to be so grumpy with me."

"I am not grumpy with you. Come with me. It is important."

Marissa stood and followed Paraneen from the room, still frowning. They walked through the corridors of the hall and entered Godrith's designing room.

He looked up from his desk. "What is it?"

Paraneen pointed at a chair and said to Marissa, "Sit."

Godrith nodded at his best weaver. "Ah. She is a super sensitive."

"I am afraid she is. I am so sorry Sire."

Marissa glowered at the two of them. "What are you two talking about?"

Godrith smiled at her. "I will tell you in a moment." He turned to Paraneen. "I can handle this. You may go back to your weaving if you wish."

"Thank you, I do. I was just about to change a thread for the next section." She left the room.

Godrith shook his head. "I am so sorry, Marissa, but we cannot have you weave. You are known as a super sensitive. You may have brushed a thread on your bobbin or on a thread roll by accident. You might have touched the tapestry. You are so sensitive to the moods set up by the colored threads that you began to exhibit their emotions. If you allow these emotions to go unchecked, you could end up losing your mind. I know we could put gloves on you, but the tapestry would suffer."

195

Marissa lowered her head. "Oh no. Does this mean I cannot work in the Tapestry rooms?"

"Relax. It does not mean that in the least. You could spin the brynosh into threads, you could create new colors, and you could dye the brynosh threads. There are also many other things you can do, provided you wear gloves. The only thing you would not be able to undertake is the weaving."

"So, I will not have to leave, Master Weaver?"

He smiled. "No, you can remain here, unless you keep calling me Master Weaver. Remember? My name is Godrith."

She blushed. "My apologies, Godrith. I forgot."

"I cannot spend the time with you at this moment. Come back to this room after the noon-turn meal. I will discuss with you the other opportunities in the Tapestry Hall." *She is a beautiful woman when she blushes like that.*

She beamed. "Thank you." She left his office.

***

Marissa did return after the noon-turn, and Godrith showed her all the possible jobs she might wish to perform. Over the next full season, Marissa worked at a variety of positions, but ended up assisting Godrith with many of his needs as Master Weaver. They met each morrow and discussed the potential challenges of the day, working on solutions that might be needed. Over time, they became a team of their own. Marissa could always guess what Godrith might need even before he knew it. He was delighted and admitted to himself that Marissa was one of the brightest people in the Tapestry Hall.

After working together for more than two passes, they were studying a new design in his office late one turn, and she leaned over him, pointing at a specific color on the parchment. She turned her head and stared at him and, without warning, bent her head and kissed him.

Godrith, enjoying the warmth of her lips, closed his eyes and leaned closer to her. *What am I doing?* He opened his eyes and drew back from her. "Marissa! No! We cannot."

"Why not?"

He stammered. "We are colleagues. And I am old enough to be your father." *She is so close, and her breath smells like roses.*

She moved closer to him again. "You are wrong. I am only thirteen passes younger than you."

"That cannot be. My hair is gray. Yours is a beautiful brown." *It is like silk against my face.*

"My family have always appeared to be much younger than our passes. The difference between us is of no matter. I love you, and I want you."

Godrith stared up at her, open mouthed. *She has bewitched me. I cannot resist her.* He did not pull back from her next kiss. He groaned as his body ached for her.

He broke the kiss, pushed back his chair, stood, and wrapped his arms around her. "You are so beautiful. I have always been taken with you. But--"

"No buts Godrith. I have always wanted you, and I am tired of waiting for you to touch me as a female. I love you, my foolish male. Kiss me."

With an order like that, how could he refuse? His body responded instantly. He wanted her. No other, just her.

She breathed roses at him and pressed her body into his. "Godrith, please love me."

That day marked the first one of the rest of their lives as bond mates.

BRENNAN

Thane of Glowen

Farraden Pen Taddyn sat in his private quarters engaged in a thoughtful conversation with his mate, Terenease. "I am aging, my dear. I regret we have not been blessed with off-spring of our own. I must make a decision as to who will rule our land when I join with Caleesh."

"You worry about this far too soon, Farraden. You are still a young and vigorous man. You are many passes from leaving the Thaneship to another."

He laughed and put his arm around her shoulder. "I do not plan on joining with Caleesh yet. But whoever takes over my role needs must have the necessary training. The truth is, my love, someone should already be in training, because the role is a heavy one, and requires much preparation."

Terenease snuggled up to him. "You worry too much about being a Thane. I see lines forming on your brow. You are far too young for such worries." She reached her hands beneath his robes and began to rouse him.

Farraden was helpless to her ministrations, and responded without hesitation. He slipped her garments from her body and spread kisses over her skin, and within minutes, she moaned in delight. All else forgotten, he swept her up in his arms carried her to their bedroom, and deposited her on their bed. Shedding the rest of his garments, he spread himself over her and, with his body, gave and received mutual pleasure. With a roar like a lion, he reached his apex, and they fell apart, each gulping air — sated with blissful release.

Gazing over at his mate, Farraden laughed aloud. "You are a wicked female. You distracted me from an important discussion. I can rarely resist your charms. But now you must pay for your sass. Get dressed, bring some Orenberry wine, plus bread and cheese to my office, and we will complete the discussion of my potential replacement."

***

After eating and drinking, but only one glass of Orenberry wine, Farraden shook his head at the list of four names. "I believe I should start with the list of traits a Thane should possess. That way, we can find someone who meets those qualities instead of attempting to choose someone whom we think might be appropriate for the job."

Terenease frowned at him. "I suggested that in the first place."

He sighed. "You were right." He turned the parchment over and began a new list. "A Thane must love his people, and needs to have an enormous amount of patience."

"Farraden, a Thane's primary responsibility I believe is to rule a land where the people can live their lives in freedom, have fair trade with other lands, and also possess the respect of the rest of the people in Pridden." She frowned. "The latter is the one thing I perceive where we should make improvements. We both know that while our Orenberry wine is always in demand, we sell little to Kaylin. They think of us as people of loose morals, and are convinced our attitudes toward the thrills and delights of life are profoundly wrong, since we appear to have the desire to experiment with many others."

He frowned at her. "Well, their minds are profoundly closed to our ways of living. I believe we should consider requesting that our people be far gentler when dealing with those from other lands and refrain from acting in too liberal a manner in their company."

"I think you should meet with Lord Lanerch and attempt to find out if he will persuade the Kaylinese to reconsider their attitudes toward our people." Terenease held out her hands. "You could mention that we will request our citizens be more circumspect when they are among folks from Kaylin."

Farraden stroked his jaw. "Interesting."

Terenease raised a finger and grinned at him. "I hear he has chosen a new heir, young Eduardo. Perhaps you could point out it would help if he can instill the new ideas within Kaylin when Eduardo takes over the Lordship."

"My love, you are the wisest of females. And you have just indicated a Thane should also be a powerful diplomat."

"I believe we can re-examine the list of potential candidates now that you have a list of valuable traits for a Thane."

He smiled. "I will begin a new list, placing the four names I have considered along the top, and beneficial characteristics down the side. I think it will show me who the best potential heirs might be."

They began the new list. It was unfortunate that the males and females he had considered did not show many of the ideal temperaments. He realized he had overestimated them.

Farraden sighed. "We need more names. Let us spend the next few turns having meals in the Keep's communal dining lounge, and visiting as many young males and females and their families as possible."

"Would you consider an heir from another land?"

"No, we must find an heir within Glowen. It is important our future Thane understands our land and its people, from his or her birth. I caught your nod, and I am happy you agree. We will begin our search on the morrow, starting with our morning meal in the Keep dining hall."

***

They had retired with a new sense of purpose to find a suitable heir. The bed so comfortable and both their minds exhausted from all the planning, they fell asleep without any delay.

Farraden grunted when an elbow thumped him in the ribs.

"You wanted to dine in the Keep Hall for our morning

meal. If you do not leave your bed this moment, we will be too late to meet new potentials to be your heir."

He groaned as he lifted himself off the bed. "Terenease, this time it was your fault. I was ready for sleep, and you tempted me again. You are not the best mate for a Thane who has so many challenges to consider for his people. You offer too many temptations for me to stay focused."

"Such nonsense. You have a superlative warrior as your Praetor, an excellent Horse Master, a perfect councilor, and four other talented advisors on your council. And you are only forty-eight passes in age, yet you complain about a lack of stamina. If you are not careful, I will have to seek another, stronger male to share my bed."

Farraden sat up abruptly. "What? You would consider an additional mate?"

She sniffed at him. "If you do not stop complaining, I might."

He laughed aloud and drew her toward him. "You are a most wicked, wicked female." He stood, lifted her over his shoulder, and headed for the personal. "I shall wash you of all your sins, and all I demand is that you scrub my back."

Once in the shower, they washed each other, but Terenease smacked him when his hands began to rove over more intimate parts of her body. "No, there is not time for fun. We must find an heir for you."

He shrugged and they, dressed and headed for the Keep dining hall.

Terenease scanned the room from the door of the hall. "Find a table for at least eight people. We will want others to join us."

"I do not envisage a problem there. All the citizens of Glowen want to sit at a meal with their Thane."

Terenease shot him a glance and snorted.

"What was that for?"

She rolled her eyes. "No one likes an arrogant Thane."

He glared at her. "I am not arrogant."

She patted him on the arm. "True. You are not." She smiled up at him. "And, the people do appreciate you. They know they are fortunate you guide them and our land so well."

He put his arm around her waist and led her toward a large vacant table. Many followed their progress with smiles.

As they sat, a couple with three young offspring walked over. The male bent his head and asked if he and his family might join them for the meal.

"Of course, Please sit. What are you named?"

The family seated themselves and the parent answered. "I am Draskin, and this is my mate, Gennin. I wish to ask for your help, my Thane."

"I will be willing to help any way that I am able. What is your need?"

"As you can see, I have three offspring. Both of my female progeny are delighted by the growing and preparing of wines, and since I manage a small vineyard, I have been able to find them positions to help them with their futures. My male progeny, however, has no interest in wines, neither in the growing of the grapes nor in the preparation or the fermenting of them to produce wine. Is there any possibility you could suggest what position he might seek at your Keep, my Thane?"

Farraden eyed the young male. "So, you are not attracted to wine production. What does attract you?"

"I would like best to do many things. To perform only one function seems a waste of talent that might be put to many uses. I enjoy keeping track of how things are made and how they are sold. I would like to prove that many of the items we prepare could be presented in a way that they become well known in other lands." He blushed and bobbed his head. "Glowen has many beautiful things that I am sure no other lands are aware of."

Farraden stroked his jaw. "Interesting. What is your name?"

"I am called Brennan, my Thane."

Farraden spoke to Brennan's parents. "I believe we might have a potential position for him. Have him come to my office within the Keep on the morrow after morning meal, and I will talk with him to determine how his capabilities might best serve Pridden."

Draskin thanked the Thane profusely, and he and his family rose from the table and left the hall.

***

Terenease laid out the dishes for the evening meal, which the kitchens had just delivered. "So, my love, are we going to eat our morning meal in the dining hall again on the morrow?"

"No. I am meeting with young Brennan on the morrow, and I want to find out more about him. Something about the young man appeals to me. I think he is very bright and I also believe there is an excellent sense of humor behind that solemn demeanor."

She cocked her head. "He reminds me of you at his age. He has a similar build, and his eyes have a considerable deal of mischief in them. He may end up being a handful."

"I do not think so. I discern in him a strong sense of purpose and an ambition to achieve much in his life. I suspect he may be the one we are seeking."

"We have only met one possibility. Do you not think we should speak to more young males? We could also interview women."

"I am just as surprised as you that I may have found someone without much delay," He stroked his chin. "I think Brennan may be the perfect young man whom I would wish for as my heir."

***

Farraden was pleased that Brennan appeared at his office door as soon as he had completed his morning meal. "Good morrow Brennan. When we first met you mentioned you are interested in many things. I will give you the opportunity to help out in a number of jobs within Glowen to discover which position you are most qualified for, and which you enjoy the most." He passed a note to the young man. "Here is a list of positions, and I have advised those who are in charge that you will be joining them to help with their areas of skill."

Brennan grinned. "These appear very exciting."

"You may find them so. I will first have you reporting to our head of kitchen, and then to my Keep manager. You will work with them each for seven turns. After that, I will send you to the vineyards, the flower gardens and, of course, to the Stinger Keeper."

Young Brennan's eyes shone with excitement. "I get to do all these things?"

"Yes, and after each seven-turn session, we will meet and discuss how you coped, and I hope also answer any questions you may have. I will, of course, speak with the heads of each of these departments, to get their assessments of you."

"Thank you so much, my Thane. This is a dream come true."

"You may have to purchase certain items for each of your trials, and I have advised all of the department heads that I will cover any of the costs. Now report to Grethin at the Keep kitchen, and she will assign you a room, and prepare you for work."

After Brennan left, Terenease strolled into her mate's office. "You did set him a huge number of tasks. Are you not overwhelming him with work?"

"I do not believe so. He is enthusiastic, has a desperate desire to work, and is not afraid of being required to learn new things. I am sure he will do well, and could be an excellent Thane if he passes my challenges."

***

At the beginning of the next season, Terenease strolled into Farraden's office. "How is young Brennen working out?"

He looked up from the parchment he was reading. "I am amazed by how much we agree on many aspects of our land. He has come back from each assignment with excellent evaluations, and often with suggestions for changes that I will make in the near future."

"It appears your fine thoughts about him proved correct."

"I believe so. On the morrow, when he reports for his next assignment, I plan to send him with our sales team to create sales of our wine in the rest of Pridden." He frowned. "But I am not sure about sending him to Morden. Rumors are circulating about potential threats to Lord Taliaferro and his family. I think we will wait until we are aware of what happens there."

"What are you hoping he will achieve?"

"If he handles himself well, I will request his parents foster him to us. He is after all, only sixteen passes. If they agree, I will begin to train him in the duties and obligations of a fine Thane needs to succeed."

"I am glad you find him a superb candidate as your heir. I like Brennan. He is kind, thoughtful, and possesses a wonderful sense of humor." She walked over to Farraden and kissed him on the cheek. "I must admit, I am jealous of him. Since you are paying so much attention to his training, I have been seriously neglected. I may be forced to find a second mate."

Farraden roared with laughter. "I have told you before that you are a wicked woman. I stand on my assessment of you. Even suggesting such a thing, I am sure, would be considered treasonous in any other land."

He stood and gathered her against him.

Terenease knew he was well ready to enjoy time with her. "My memory must be failing. I can barely remember the last time you performed your duty to me as your mate. Since when have you ceased doing your duty daily?"

Farraden attempted to frown, but could not maintain it and chuckled. "I performed my duty, and quite admirably, I must admit, the morn of the previous turn." He kissed her, swept her up in his arms, and headed for the bedroom. "It is obvious you need retraining in the memory of love." He laughed again.

She erupted in giggles, which soon changed to groans of pleasure.

***

When Brennan returned from his lengthy sales trip, he knocked on Farraden's door, and heard, "Come." He opened the door and entered.

Farraden, reading a parchment, stopped striding across the floor, and smiled at Brennan. "Welcome. I am pleased you are back from your trip. What have you learned during your travels in Pridden?"

"I believe I have discovered a way to create increased wine sales with the rest of Pridden." He shifted his feet and gazed at the floor. "I'm sorry, because I cannot speak for Morden as I did avoid entering that land. The rumors that Gritch is seeking to take over as Thane are true. In brief, I learned that he has killed Lord Taliafarro's entire family."

"What? He has killed a Lord? That news has not reached Glowen. Is there any news about how the other Lords will handle this repulsive action by Gritch?"

"I am not aware of anything further as yet."

Farraden shook his head. "Gritch's actions are unforgivable. The rest of Pridden's leaders will need to take action at some point." He walked over to the tassel in the corner, then waved at a chair. "Sit and we will discuss your conclusions."

A knock at the door, indicated Farraden's assistant guard, and the Thane called out, "Come", and ordered drinks for them when the young male entered.

Farraden sat across the table from Brennan. "So, tell me what happened in the other lands."

"I must admit I was not aware of how different from the

rest of Pridden we Glowens view the pleasures of life. The people in other lands do also enjoy pleasure in arts, in nature, and in wine and food. I found out, however, what they do not relate to are the ways in which we view mating."

"Oh?"

"Our people experiment on a regular basis with relationships because they only mate for physical pleasure. I learned that when I reached thirteen passes, and my parents explained most of it to me. It appears that people in the other lands, while they do also mate for physical pleasure, actually form lengthy relationships from emotional ties. They speak a great deal about love, which I suspect means more to them than the act of mating."

"That does appear to be very different from our land."

Brennan cleared his throat. "This should not seem so odd to you, my Thane. Neither I nor any other on Glowen have seen you or my Lady Terenease mate with any other. You both appear to be completely satisfied with your relationship. I perceive much fondness between the two of you. Is it possible that Glowens also appreciate love?"

"I believe many Glowens do, if as you say, you have noticed fondness between my mate and me."

"Yes, I have seen love between you and Lady Terenease. Most Glowens, since everything they do is for pleasure only, experiment often with relationships. The constant change within their connections creates turmoil for the rest of Pridden. A male you met before who was mated with a female

211

may now be with a male, or both a male and a female. I wonder if when a relationship becomes confusing for a Glowen, they decide to switch to a different one. I have many friends who change their mates on a regular basis."

Farraden laughed. "I have never considered my mating with Terenease in that light. You may be correct, Brennan."

A knock at Farraden's door indicated the arrival of their tea. The assistant entered, placed the tray of tea on the table and left.

As Farraden poured the tea, he asked. "Having determined these major differences in our people from the rest of Priddenese, what is your suggestion?"

"I would like to create a training program for our salespeople so that they can promote our products without tramping upon other's views. They would be trained to deal with professionalism with other lands, and to refrain from expressing their physical desire with anyone other than their own people, and then only behind closed doors."

"Excellent. You have my permission to begin the planning of this training now." Farraden patted Brennan on the back. "I also have something else to put to you." He rose from the table and paced around the room. "I would like to approach your birth parents to request they allow you to be fostered to me and Terenease. Would you be willing?"

Brennan jumped up from his seat, and his eyes glistened with excitement. "I would be more than willing Sire. I would be so honored to be your foster progeny."

"I am pleased. And Terenease is very fond of you, so she will be pleased too. Once your parents have approved, I will begin training you in the duties you will require in the future. After a time when you are confident in the role as my foster, I will name you as my heir to the people of Glowen."

Brennan's mouth gaped open and he sank back in his seat. "Oh, my Thane, Caleesh has blessed me beyond my expectations."

Farraden crossed over to Brennan and held out his hand. "Welcome to my family, Brennan, future Thane of Glowen."

***

The passes grew in number. Brennan's training for the salespeople of Glowen proved successful, and Glowen prospered, adding Stinger products to the sale of wines. The Glowen sales teams returned home and spoke about their meetings with the other lands and recounted how they now viewed the rest of Pridden with new vision. Other Glowens learned the same skills and chose to visit Rifella and Shendea and see the wonders that their lands offered. Kaylin still remained too formal to attract many Glowens, and Morden was still too dangerous.

Brennan had not yet found his own mate, but traveling beyond the borders of Glowen afforded him the opportunity to meet many possible young females.

However, when traveling through Glowen to meet with Nisbod pen Iselon, something unexpected happened. Nisbod, who headed the Pod responsible for relationships with the other lands, invited Brennan to dine with him and his family. When Brennan entered Nisbod's dining hall, he was stunned by the sight of a beautiful young female. Her hair fell around her shoulders, a deep and shiny ebony veil. Her wolf eyes sparkled and her mouth formed a perfect cupid's bow. Nisbod introduced her as Lilliwon.

Brennan was immediately smitten.

By the time he had concluded his meeting with Nisbod, Lilliwon had admitted her intense attraction to Brennan. Nisbod appeared thrilled and went out of his way to be as courteous as possible to Brennan. Brennan suspected that Nisbod was more excited that his Lilliwon could mate with a future Thane, rather than find a non-royal young male.

Within four turns, Brennan and Lilliwon mated and declared they were bonded for life.

***

Several passes later, Farraden called Brennan to his office.

Brennan who travelled and worked so hard that he had not seen his foster parent in almost three passes, was astonished at how he had aged.

"I can read it on your face, Brennan, that you think I look old." Farraden sighed. "Our family have never been long-lived, and I'm afraid I will be surrendering to Caleesh quite soon. In two turns, I will announce that my health is forcing me to resign, and will name you as the new Thane of Glowen. I know you will be excellent for our people, and continue to help them through valuable changes. I ask only one thing from you."

"Anything, my Thane. Anything."

"Please watch over and protect Terenease when I am gone. She is also your foster parent, and she is as fond of you as if you were her birthed progeny. Promise me you will see to her happiness as much as is possible. Encourage her to mate again, if possible. She is rather stubborn."

"Please Farraden, do not leave too soon." Brennan swallowed. "And I do promise."

***

In less than one pass, Farraden joined with Caleesh, and Brennan was acknowledged as Thane of Glowen. He and Lilliwon moved to the Thane's Keep, where they did their best to take care of Terenease. However, she refused to mate with any other male. She did, however agree to live in a set of rooms within the Keep.

"My son." She had adopted many Rifellan words, "I loved your foster parent so much. I can never forget him, and thus cannot bond again with any other."

"I will never forget him either, my Lady."

***

Terenease joined Caleesh much sooner than expected. Brennan suspected she missed Farraden too much to remain on Glowen any longer.

Soon after her exit from this life, Brennan met with an odd woman from a land other than Pridden.

He sat in his office, discussing her with Lilliwon over a morning meal. "This woman, Kat, is the making of unpleasant dreams. She has caused nothing but trouble since she landed on our island. She swam naked in Lake Yuffern, and then took offense when approached as a mate by one of the men from the area. She insulted a male and female who are artists and sent a complaint to me that she was being stalked by both men and women in our land." He sighed. "She also ate raw orenberries, and then became dangerous when they attempted to use the pollinators on her to withdraw the poison from her body. In the end, they had to sedate her. The woman has been an enormous amount of trouble."

"You poor thing. A Thane's work is never completed." Lilliwon wrinkled her forehead. "She was one of the first visitors from outside Glowen, was she not?"

"Yes, why?"

"When you trained our sales people to deal with those outside Glowen in a different way, that solved many of the problems the rest of Pridden had with Glowen. Correct?"

"Yes."

"So why not issue a parchment to advise our people how to act with visitors from elsewhere? Advise them that they can be natural and normal around their own kind, but need to act with restraint with others from outside Glowen. In addition, suggest to the leaders of other lands that they advise their citizens to wear labels to indicate the lands they come from when visiting us." She frowned. "Although they should realize that no other lands have the color of our eyes."

Brennan gave her a huge grin. "You, my loved one, are brilliant. I shall begin working on the wording, and hope you will help me prepare a final copy."

"Of course, I will. I am after all, the best mate you could have chosen, and who else could be of assistance to you?"

"True. You are the best mate for me. I wish Farraden were still here so I could tell him of your brilliant idea."

Lilliwon patted his cheek. "I suspect that Caleesh gives him leave to view all of the good that is happening for Glowen."

Brennan smiled at the thought. *I know now how Farraden and Terenease felt about each other. I love Lilliwon in the same way.*

The People of Pridden

DERWYNN

Head of the Thieves Guild

Derwynn, a talented emotional therapist for people who were riddled with guilt through some unfortunate incident, was head of a Guild referred to as the Guild of Removal of Guilt, Fears, and Broken Dreams. He was never sure whether the number of people seeking help from this Guild was limited because of the difficulty of the title or another peculiar situation. He often expressed surprise that so few sought their help and did his best to persuade some of his people to investigate why this was so.

Young himself, Derwynn had never felt overcome by anything negative. He lived a life of plenty, as his parents were of more than adequate wealth and were respected by the people in Shendea.

In order to learn more about people and their challenges in life, he dedicated one full pass to travel through all of the lands of Pridden. It was a pass filled with adventure, as the people of each land experienced vastly different situations.

He was fortunate when on his journey through Rifella, the first land he chose on his voyage, he met a young Morden named Mouse, who fascinated him. He looked exactly like his name, a small man who always covered himself up in gray robes. Mouse kept a very discreet profile and avoided being noticed. However, Derwynn, as an astute therapist, was plagued with an immense amount of curiosity about him. Mouse projected a small, anxious person, who never wished to be the center of attention, and hid in corners. But Mouse was an enigma. Derwynn sensed that behind the small persona hid a being of strength of purpose. He also thought that the real Mouse was, in truth, much physically stronger than the male he presented.

"You appear to be a very timid person, but I do not believe that about you," Derwynn told him.

Mouse's mouth dropped open as if surprised. "What do you mean?"

Derwynn grabbed his upper arm. "This is not the arm of a cowardly and weak little male. It is the arm of a warrior."

Mouse pulled away. "You are wrong in your assessment."

Derwynn smiled. "No, I am not. I have studied people for many passes and am an expert in discovering the emotional and physical elements of a people's personalities. I know who and what you are. I also understand that you wish to keep your true self concealed. You may relax I have no desire to put you in possible danger by revealing who you are."

Mouse relaxed. "I am astounded. I will acknowledge you are the only one who has guessed this about me. You are correct. I do need to keep my true self concealed, and I appreciate you will continue to keep my secret. When the time comes that I am able to reveal what my real identity is, I will advise you of it."

"In the meantime, as my friend, will you agree to be part of our Guild?"

"I will. I believe, however, that you have misnamed your Guild."

"I have been considering this same question for some time. What do you think our name should be?"

"You may think I am being foolish. But the people you help, I believe, do not understand all the words. I suspect their thoughts are far simpler than what you believe. They assume that what you do is take away their disruptive old selves and replace them with bright new shiny selves. If there were not already a Magicians Guild, I would suggest you use that name. I think you would do well to call yourselves the Thieves Guild instead.

"Why Thieves Guild?"

"Think about this. On Pridden we think of a thief as one who removes unwanted things and replaces them with wanted ones. Thus, if you also create a complicated ceremony around the personality change, people will believe you removed what never served them, and have returned to them what they now need."

"Mouse, this is brilliant. You are using words to clarify something I might never be able to explain. So, from here on, we will be referred to as the Thieves Guild, and you are a major part of it."

"Excellent, Derwynn. You might also approach the Healers and request from them certain potions which will appear to create a passage of time, and which the candidates will not remember receiving."

"Mouse, you have helped create a valuable resource for many who do not realize they are sabotaging themselves. I can handle the mental challenges of the candidates and you will handle the practical designs and processes of our Guild."

"We are in agreement, and, once again I ask of you to keep silent about any abilities you may discover about me."

"I will. In two turns we will perform the thieves' ritual for a candidate who I believe will be perfect to our way of performing the ceremony you have suggested. I would prefer it if you would attend."

***

On the designated day, Mouse appeared, wearing a pale gray robe and a long white scarf draped about his neck. The members of the Guild were clad in white robes and all were seated on cushions arranged around a central fire pit. The logs crackled and spat as they burned. A stone path, strewn with white flower petals, led from a black-velvet-draped doorway. Beside the fire rested a white pallet, decorated with yellow flowers with black centers.

The assistants extinguished every second globe in the room and the chamber dimmed. Through the black-draped doorway, Derwynn appeared in a robe of emerald green.

An assistant robed in pale yellow marched two steps behind him. Both men wore white scarves, and a band of yellow on their heads.

A gong sounded somewhere, and through the drapes walked a tall bald man, clad only in a loincloth and covered in scented oil, which Mouse could detect from a fair distance. Two men walked beside him. The three headed toward Derwynn, and stopped beside the pallet, faced Derwynn, and bowed. One of the assistants stepped forward and handed the Guild Master a generous cup of steaming liquid.

Derwynn raised the cup up toward the ceiling of the room. "Today we grant this male's desire." He turned to the applicant. "Do you agree to our help?"

The man bowed again. "I do."

Derwynn handed him the cup, and the applicant downed the liquid. The two assistants eased him onto the pallet, and he sank into a stupor.

Additional assistants entered, bearing more cups of foaming liquid which they handed to the members of the Guild. The hall filled with fog, created by the fire from the central pit and the foam from the liquid. The members passed the cups around after each took two sips. Mouse gazed at Derwynn and shook his head slightly, and Derwynn nodded at him.

Mouse's neighbor tilted his head and regarded him with curiosity. "You do not drink. Why?"

"I am on special assignment and am an observer only."

"I see."

Mouse held his hand to his lips, as Derwynn raised his hand and began to chant a deep melodic sound. The entire hall joined in, and the members swayed to the rhythm of the music.

Derwynn raised his voice again and commanded the unconscious man.

"Your error was a minor one, and the female you chose did not meet the needs you required. You will find what you desire over this night of star set."

The chanting from the audience slowed and then stopped. The fog began to dissipate, and the silence stretched.

A further gong vibrated in the hall, and two helpers entered and carried the pallet from the hall.

The members rose and stretched and slowly headed toward the exit talking quietly among themselves.

Mouse approached Derwynn. "I did not drink of the cup, but I did feel affected by the fog. The ceremony seemed brief to me? But I overheard, that others thought it lasted almost an entire turn?"

"It did. Will you join me for a light evening meal?"

Mouse frowned. "Odd, but I feel no hunger."

Derwynn smiled. "That is quite normal for this ceremony. Although you did not drink from the cup, you sat in stillness for a considerable length of time. However, you will sleep better after consuming a light meal. Join me."

"I will. I assume we will view the result of this procedure on the morrow."

"We will meet again after the morning meal and will see what has occurred to the candidate when he returns to the hall."

***

Derwynn met with Mouse for the morning meal. "Are you more refreshed this morrow?"

"I am, and I have a question for you. What occurred for the candidate during the darkness?"

"This is probably the most important part of the ceremony. Using words, potions, and suggestions, four of my most learned Guild members helped him clear his life of all memories starting from just before he met the woman he wishes to forget. They spoke with him most of the night until they believed his mind had been cleared of those memories. At dawn, they gave him a potion to bring him back to full consciousness. They then bathed, clothed, and fed him."

Mouse nodded. "It makes sense. I must ask, do any of the applicants return and ask for a second ceremony?"

"Only rarely, but we never agree to a second ritual."

They completed their meals and headed back to the ritual hall.

Once again, it was filled with male Guild members, joined now by six females. Chanting began, and the people swayed. Mouse found himself adrift in meditation.

A gong sounded, and the chanting ceased. Derwynn

stepped to the center once more, and two assistants entered the room, escorting the applicant, now dressed in a long white robe. One assistant handed a fizzing cup to Derwynn, who faced the candidate. "Are you ready to rejoin your life?"

The applicant bowed his head. "I am, Master Derwynn."

The Guild Master handed him the cup. "Drink."

The male drained the cup.

Two more assistants entered, each guiding a female, whom they escorted to a position across the hall from the male.

Derwynn retrieved the now empty cup from the applicant. "Choose your life."

The male contemplated the females. He began to move toward the female on the left, but stopped, a puzzled frown on his face. He turned to the female on the right and his face lit up with a smile of joy. He ran toward her, and they embraced, her face wet with tears.

The people in the hall were silent as the assistants escorted the couple from the hall. The remaining female left by a side entrance without attracting attention.

The Guild members rose and exited the hall, chatting with each other.

Derwynn approached Mouse. "Will you join me in my offices, and I will order tea."

Mouse agreed and they set off for Derwynn's rooms.

In his office, Derwynn indicated that Mouse should

seat himself, and he arranged for an assistant to fetch tea for them. "This is the first time you have observed this ceremony, is it not?"

"It is, and I am impressed at how well you helped the male."

"I thank you for your astute observation. It is not something we do often, because in most cases, people should consider their choices before they decide to embark on a specific action. In this case, the male had been pushed by his parents to make an advantageous bonding, but he never loved his partner."

"So, the parents were responsible for the error in judgement."

Derwynn sighed and spread his hands in sympathy for the male. "His life was comfortable with plenty of material things in it, but there was little satisfying emotion. He then met the second female and became aware of the extraordinary joy of mutual love. He did not hate his original mate, but could not forget the passes they had spent together, so he was in constant conflict between his guilt over his duty to her and his emotions for the new female."

"Could you not persuade him to understand that his parents, not he, wanted the bonding and therefore it was their guilt, not his?"

"I attempted all the regular ways of consoling him, but he was too consumed by the guilt to release it. I was convinced the only hope for him would be the ceremony." Derwynn smiled in satisfaction. "I thank Caleesh I was correct in my thinking."

Mouse shook Derwynn's hand. "My thanks, Master Derwynn, for the privilege of seeing the ceremony this turn. I am pleased to be a member of the Thieves Guild. I must leave Shendea and return to Morden, but I hope to be attending other ceremonies in the coming passes."

Derwynn clapped. Mouse on the shoulder. "You know you are always welcome. Go in safety with Caleesh, my friend."

***

After another pass, Derwynn received a moth from his friend, asking permission to bring someone else to a ceremony. Without even asking who he wished to bring, Derwynn assured him, by return moth, that he would be most welcome. He advised him when the next ceremony would begin.

Mouse appeared with an odd female, and explained that she was from another world, and that Lord Eduardo had requested that he act as her guide through Pridden.

Under normal circumstances, Derwynn was adept at understanding people, but he could not read anything from Mouse's visitor. Her mind was barred to him. He hid his surprise.

Mouse and the woman attended the ceremony and Derwynn knew that Mouse spent much time explaining the process to the female.

Once the Guild had completed the ceremony, and later, Derwynn met them for a meal.

The discussion about the candidate and what happened to him continued. The female, whose name Derwynn learned was Kat, insisted that the name of Thieves Guild was incorrect.

Mouse frowned. "Incorrect in what way?"

"You didn't really steal his former life from him. You just made him forget it. And you use potions and tricks to implant new memories in his head."

Derwynn winced at the word *steal.* "Correct. A thief is someone who exchanges an unwanted thing for something better."

She snorted. "No, a thief is a criminal, and he steals for his own benefit."

Derwynn gasped in horror. "We do not steal. We are an honorable Guild."

Mouse appeared equally horrified, his eyes widened, and his lips thinned. "I believe I possess an idea of how you view our name. In Pridden, a man who actually steals is referred to as a brigand. Please do not use the word 'steal' when referring to us. It is a foul insult." He shook his head. "Derwynn's word were clear. He told you a thief is one who exchanges the unwanted for the wanted."

The female opened her eyes as if seeing something new. "Oh, my apologies. I understand why you were upset when I accused your Guild of stealing. I will never again associate that word with you and your members."

Derwynn sighed in relief. "Thank you. We appreciate your understanding."

Kat stood. "Mouse advised me that we leave for the next part of our trip early on the morrow. I am weary and must bid you farewell, as I need be fresh for the journey. My thanks for allowing us to be your guests."

Both men stood as she walked from the dining hall toward her room.

Derwynn looked at Mouse. "A small glass of Orenberry?"

Mouse nodded. "Yes, a much-needed glass."

Derwynn signaled to a kitchen assistant, and they sat at the table again when she brought them wine. "Mouse, how long have you been this female's guide?"

Mouse sighed. "Far too long, and we still have the rest of the lands to visit. She is demanding and wishes to control everything around her. And, she is completely ignorant about our customs and social mores." He drank from the glass. "In one way, I must sympathize with her. She is in a strange new world and appears to miss her home, to which she longs to return."

Derwynn held his glass up to Mouse. "I wish you safety and ease in your journey."

"Thank you, my friend. I am sure it will be a most interesting trip. I shall meet you again when I have concluded my assignment and had success with it."

Derwynn drank. *Mouse is destined for something quite extraordinary. I wonder what?*

The People of Pridden

SSARFF

The Assassins Guild Master

Scaatchi sat stroking his syeth. He touched its nose by accident, and it hissed and bit him. He gazed at it, shaking his head. "Why do you still insist on biting me? You should know by now I am immune to your poison."

Scaatchi, as one of the males who belonged to the group called the syeth trainers, discovered he quite liked snakes. He joined as a young man, apprenticed to the group to learn all he could about syeths, the smallest and most poisonous snakes in Morden. When he first joined, the Master trainers fed him limited doses of syeth poison until he could withstand his first bites from the creatures. He then endured regular bites until he formed a complete immunity to their venom.

Under this constant training, Scaatchi became so adept that they requested he become the head of his group. Rather than train new apprentices, he handed the responsibility to another and spent his time trying to discover a financial use of the talents of the males under his tutelage.

Upon examining some of the others who were fascinated by snakes he discovered that some enjoyed the huge constrictors and used them for comfort. He was intrigued that many Mordens were attracted to serpents but, of course, they did not was to be bitten or squished, and enjoyed discussing them with others. He began to liaise with many of them and, as their numbers grew, persuaded them to join his Serpent Guild.

The membership continued to grow until Scaatchi decided they needed somewhere to meet. He also wished for sufficient room so many of the members could also live there. To achieve that, they would need funds.

The group Scaatchi built up was so new, that he often needed to spend many turns solving new challenges. He made a point of visiting the Magicians Guild, and the Thieves Guild. Both organizations used names that did not, in truth, reflect their purpose. But their guilds solved problems for people, and they chose monikers that described the actual situations they dealt with as closely as possible.

As the passes came and went, Scaatchi aged and became frustrated because he did not settle the Serpent Guild in a comfortable niche. It was regrettable that he joined with Caleesh before establishing a strong effective Guild.

After his offspring inherited his position in the Serpent Guild, something extraordinary happened during the seven-year pass of the outbreak of Red Rash, which terrified all the inhabitants of Pridden. The organization of Healers grew as they helped females with birthing and others to mend broken bones and settle their ailments. One of the most accomplished Healers, Gritha, assigned to the current Lord of Morden discovered something quite exceptional. She found that the Serpent Guild members who were immune to the poison of syeths never contracted Red Rash. She requested some vials of syeth poison from the current leader, and began to experiment. She worked through the entire Red Rash season and was convinced that she had created a potion to protect people from the deadly disease. A better discovery was once that they received the potion, it gave them immunity for life. She was ecstatic, but had to wait another seven passes to verify her findings. However, she did advise all the other Healers of her discovery. Because of the potion, Healers gained popularity in all the lands. But in Morden their popularity was even greater, because Gritha found them a product that helped them to create more funds.

***

The Serpent Guild was delighted and now possessed enough income to begin construction of their permanent Guild. They hired a builder to design a type of Keep and arranged for stone to be delivered from Mont Zumbis, and wood from the Serfa Forest. The construction would take some time to complete because the Healers only purchased the syeth venom about every seven passes.

Once the Red Rash challenge had been dealt with, the latest Lord of Morden, Torrenton, called the current leader of the Serpent Guild, Mindibba, to attend a meeting with him. The Lord indicated it might well be to the Serpent Guild's financial advantage. Mindibba did not hesitate.

He hurried to the Lord's Keep on the northern section of Morden, and met with Torrenton. The Lord invited him to a dinner, and the evening passed most pleasantly.

While they sat drinking wine, Mindibba sensed the Lord seemed reluctant to ask for something he wanted.

Mindibba took a long drink from his glass. "Lord Torrenton, I suspect you asked me here to request something. What can I help you with?"

"I do, indeed, want something from you that I find very difficult to request. You may not know this, Mindibba, but running a land can be more and more demanding with every pass. My people are, for the most part, fine citizens, and they work hard and are helpful to each other. Every now and then, however, there is one who lacks the spirit of cooperation, and cannot be trusted whatsoever. Some also hurt others physically, and sometimes even commit murder to achieve their own ends."

"I had no idea running a land would be so challenging, my Lord. I must admit our Guild members are so devoted that no such thing would ever occur."

"This is why, Mindibba, I wish to request you set a syeth on a person I shall name so that he can no longer be a threat to the citizens of Morden. We will pay a fee for you to eliminate this person."

Mindibba opened his eyes wide. "What?" He was shocked.

"I know, Mindibba I am asking you to kill someone. This is something I have never done before, and it is a vile thing that I am requesting."

"I trust you, my Lord, and am sure you feel your request is just. But it is an extraordinarily demanding thing you ask of the Serpent Guild."

"I know this. However, although I know some in Morden who would perform this task, I do not wish one of my own citizens to bear the guilt. I ask you because you have never lived with this male."

They sat for a while and discussed the full reason why Torrenton required Mindibba to handle the challenge. The Lord expanded on the crimes committed. When he mentioned how the criminal had tortured and killed a young child, Mindibba made up his mind. *He did the unspeakable to that child. Although I dislike thinking it, I have to admit, he needs to be removed from this society.* Mindibba obtained the name of the man and where to locate him. Mindibba spent two sleepless turns making his decision to aid Lord Torrenton.

Upon completing his assignment, Lord Torrenton paid Mindibba a generous fee.

***

At first, Mindibba did not wish to accept a fee, even though he had performed the service, but after much consideration, he decided his Guild needed the funds. In addition, he was convinced the male in question would never repent his vile and murderous actions. He had given the assignment to one of his best syeth males, and once the contract was complete, the Serpent Guild received its payment, which allowed them to continue the construction of their Keep, and Mindibba put some aside to help all the young offspring in Morden.

Over the next fifteen passes, Mindibba received additional requests for similar help from other Lords and Thanes. Mindibba insisted upon absolute proof that the people to be eliminated deserved their fate. While the leaders believed these situations should be dealt with by residents of their lands, they, like Torrenton, had no desire to place such a burden on their own citizens. Mindibba did, indeed, eliminate some of these criminals, but preferred, if possible, to banish them to the area called Air Wyth, where survival appeared unlikely. The people Mindibba dumped there were not left with any tools, horses, water, or food. Mindibba comforted himself by deciding that if any of these foul males survived, it would be Ssayleese who would make the decision.

The fact that the Serpent Guild solved these problems for other lands became general knowledge among the criminals who felt they had the right to rob or murder others. These foul males began to refer to the Guild as Assassins. Mindibba hearing this, was horrified at first. But he realized if he adopted the name, it would become a deterrent to people against performing something lawless. Plus, in his mind, the word assassins meant they were assassinating crime. Despite his fears, most of the people of Pridden acknowledged that the service the Guild provided was much needed. They also knew that non-criminals had nothing to fear from them. Mindibba did not allow his members to threaten any other citizens.

Mindibba continued to flourish as leader of the Guild and expressed pride when the assignments led to the completion of the Guild's Keep. His joy increased when to his delight he met a mate of his liking and they produced a male offspring by the name of Saraf. The youngster began his initial steps to becoming a syeth trainer, but he discovered he received more satisfaction in dealing with the running of the Keep and the Guild itself. He enrolled in all the training needed to become a warrior and understood that becoming a leader of people required a variety of skills. When he graduated as a suitable heir for Mindibba, his name was changed to Ssarff to indicate his new status.

***

During the ensuing five passes great changes occurred in Morden and the rest of Pridden. Most of the lands gained new Lords as the heirs inherited the positions, but the bloodlines for Wielders weakened, and the lands expanded the leaderships to include Thanes. Morden was hit by more change than most. Gritch, the epitome of an evil male, assassinated Lord Taliaferro and his family. For some reason, none of the other leaders hired the Assassins Guild to deal with him. If the leaders in the rest of Pridden were questioned, they looked away and said they would not interfere, a resident of Morden would have to ask for that type of help.

Gritch in order to protect himself, made sure his personal guards frightened the citizens by claiming the Assassins were free to eliminate anyone in Morden at their own pleasure. These lies worked so well that the people had no idea who to fear most — the Assassins or Gritch himself.

When Gritch died, many suspected his progeny, Galdin, had killed him. The heir was satisfied to allow the fear of the Assassins to continue. It served his desire to keep his people living in a state of constant terror.

***

Once again, change caused a further ripple of fear to course through the Mordens. Galdin sent a message to Ssarff to attend him. The Assassin was reluctant, and his second-in-command, Ssestin expressed his fear to him. "You know he cannot be trusted."

"I am aware of this, and I plan to use what little power I possess to present myself as a formidable foe."

Ssestin stared at the Guild Master and shook his head. "Master, you are not formidable in any way." Ssestin understood that most people at the Guild saw a stunningly handsome male. His skin was a light bronze, like those of southern Morden, and his dark black hair stubbornly refused to remain straight. True, his ochre eyes sported a gold vertical slit, but the majority of females at the Keep found him that much more attractive.

"Not as I appear at this moment. But by the time I arrive at The Thane's Keep, I promise I will be most formidable."

He left his quarters for the stable, where a young male supplied him with a magnificent animal.

After leaving the Keep, Ssarff rode through forests, avoiding exposure in the fields and grasslands on his way to the Thane's Keep. During his ride, he called on the trickle of Wielder powers he had inherited from his parent, and slowly adjusted his appearance. When he arrived at the gates, he presented a changed man.

The guards showed him to Galdin's door, and he slipped into the room.

***

Galdin watched the tall thin man appear at the edge of the door and appeared to slither into his hall. The hood of the man's long black robe, thrown back, revealed a bizarrely smooth pate, and Ssarff's face, so pale in color as to be almost white, displayed not a single visible hair. Bereft of eyebrows or lashes, his skin, free of any blemish, stretched taut over his jawline. His eyes sank deep in their sockets, and his expressionless face hinted of danger and hidden evil.

He strode toward the throne and inclined his head in the short bow of equals. "Sire, you asked for me?"

Galdin stepped down and the two men clasped arms.

"Ssarff, I require your expertise."

Ssarff, his face stripped of all emotion, gazed at Galdin from dark ochre eyes, with that terrifying vertical slit of gold. An ancient memory of serpents reminded all who viewed him as one who trafficked with the slithering and dangerous creatures of Morden. The personae he displayed terrified the Keep guards even more than Galdin did. "The Assassin's Guild are always more than willing to aid the Thane of Morden."

Galdin nodded, revealing no emotion by making sure his own face remained concealed in the shadow of his hood. *This man is dangerous and formidable but, if well managed, will make a fine ally. I only wish I could read his thoughts, but his mind is one of the few closed to me.*

***

Ssarff stared at the Thane. "What is it you wish me to do, Galdin?" *I know how much he hates it when I do not use his title. His fear of me and his inability to read my thoughts, however, keep him in his place.*

"In recent times, a woman has appeared who is said to have come here from another world. She has plans to take over Pridden with abilities of which we cannot even guess. Eduardo's own councilor, who is a citizen of Morden, has informed me of her evil plans. We cannot afford to let her wander through Pridden unchecked. I do not wish you to use a syeth on her as yet. I want her brought to me so I can uncover her plans for our world."

Interesting that he does not want her eliminated but only captured. "It sounds like an odd request We are not usually involved in kidnapping. Why do you want us to capture her rather than eliminate her? Before I make a decision, I would need to have more information about this woman and the situation she is creating."

"Of course. Please sit, Guild Master Ssarff, and I will have my guard bring us Orenberry wine."

"I would prefer some of your magnificent Canobwint tea so I can focus clearly upon what you need."

"That does make sense, Guild Master." He called out to the guard, who ran into the room. Galdin gave him a hasty order, and the guard disappeared.

"Galdin, do you have a fee in mind for this job?"

"I do indeed." Galdin pulled a piece of parchment from inside his robe, unfolded it and handed it to Ssarff.

Ssarff read it and nodded. "The fee is reasonable, providing there are no unseen challenges. However, I need to understand why you wish this woman captured."

At that moment a knock sounded on the door. When Galdin called out, "Enter", a kitchen helper entered with a tray of tea, mugs and some small edible biscuits.

The helper placed a mug of wine in front of Galdin and tea in front of Ssarff.

Ssarff startled by the dark red dried-blood color of the wine, kept his face impassive. *He is drinking Blud wine, not*

Orenberry. How did he persuade a wine merchant in Glowen to supply him with this? He sipped at his tea, checking for any unwelcome additions. "I would appreciate obtaining as much information as possible about this woman. I gather she is currently in Kaylin?"

"Yes, but I believe she will do her best to head for other lands, so it would be easier if we stop her now."

"We Assassins cannot enter Kaylin with ease. Lord Eduardo would certainly do anything to rebuff us. Do you have any males in Kaylin who will be willing to aid us?"

Galdin nodded. "I do. His name is Drainin, and he is Lord Eduardo's primary councilor. He has spent time examining the strange woman's motives and is much alarmed by her plans for Pridden. I will make arrangements for him to be at a certain place to meet up with you and any men you may take with you."

Ssarff raised his eyebrows. *Does he really think I'm fool enough to do as he expects?* "No Galdin. I will not go to Kaylin. If only my foot soldiers are in Kaylin, it will allow me to claim ignorance of their mission if they are caught by Eduardo."

Galdin blinked rapidly. Ssarff had no idea if it meant he saw the wisdom in Ssarff's words, or became astounded that Ssarff refused him.

As they talked further, Ssarff became far more curious about Galdin's motives. He made a decision on the spot to agree to the contract. *I will send Ssarassin. He looks almost exactly like my current disguise. Should I also tell Eduardo what Galdin plans?* Ssarff decided he would delay delivering the woman to Galdin until the Assassins met her and evaluated the situation.

***

The raid in Kaylin proved disastrous. Of the five Assassins Ssarff sent to bring back the woman, only two returned unscathed one of which was Ssarassin. At least Galdin had paid half the fee for the contract, but withheld the balance because they did not capture the woman, nor did they bring her his Keep. Ssarff used the initial half to help the families of the three dead Assassins.

However, Ssarff appeared twice more at Galdin's Keep as his hairless, tall, pale persona with the sunken ochre eyes. He knew this view of himself made Galdin more than uncomfortable. Galdin presented a contract to capture the woman, and after he increased the fee more than three-fold, Ssarff reluctantly agreed. The contract for the raid in Shendea was made with the assurance that the Assassins would receive help from Hesginn, the Gray Magician and head of the Magicians Guild. This time, Ssarff, convinced that Galdin withheld much needed information, sent only four Assassins. The group was led by a novice syeth guard, who was not bright or devious, but always followed orders. When the guard was told to report to Hesginn, he assumed it was for his final orders.

The Shendean incursion ended worse than that in Kaylin. Ssarff suspected Galdin was unaware of Hesginn's perfidy. Hesginn told the syeth leader that Rhognor was in league with the strange woman and ordered him to launch a syeth at Rhognor. The stupid young male believed him obeyed. The tragedy was that Lady Halfin threw herself in front of her mate, and the syeth bit her instead. She perished from the poison.

The small band of Assassins captured the woman, and fled for the tunnel linking Shendea to Morden.

Lord Rhognor, by now apoplectic from the loss of his mate, swore vengeance and raced with his guards to kill Hesginn and rescue the woman from another world. In the melee, only one Assassin escaped and sought refuge at the Guild's Keep.

By now, Ssarff became convinced that Galdin had an intense and hidden agenda and that perhaps she was not a problem, but a means to some other end. When Galdin proposed that Ssarff enter Rifella to capture her, Ssarff agreed for a considerably higher fee, all of which had to be paid up front. *Galdin craves to have this woman in his hands with such desperation that she must be able to give him something he wants or needs. But what might it possibly be?*

After returning from Galdin's Keep, Ssarff met with his second-in-command, Ssestin, to discuss the new contract.

Ssestin expressed alarm. "Master, you cannot trust the Thane. It appears his desire to capture this woman is madness and is without reason."

"It confuses me why he would want her. From the little I have learned she causes challenges wherever she travels. I heard a rumor that Eduardo has persuaded her to complete a task for him. How he plans to repay her appears unknown." Ssarff narrowed his eyes. "Perhaps it would be to our advantage to capture this woman but keep her for ourselves. If we retained control of her, would this give us an advantage in our own dealings with Galdin?"

"Master Ssarff, I suspect that might prove dangerous for the Guild. He is becoming more erratic in his dealings with the Morden people. He increases his personal guard by capturing young Morden males and forcing them to serve with his guards. The numbers are becoming so overwhelming that they are feared by most Mordens. At some point, I suspect they will rebel."

"A rebellion would benefit all of Morden. I would be much happier with a Thane who appreciates his people, rather than deals with them with increasing violence." The faint smile on Ssarff's face hinted of danger and retribution. "I will send a small number of Assassins to Rifella, and we will capture the woman, but we will bring her back to our Keep. According to Galdin, Melindar, Murwenna's sibling will be our contact in Rifella. She and Tiwellan, who is one of Murwenna's councilors, are afraid of the dangers posed by the woman we are to capture. The Thane claims both of them worry that Murwenna does not sense the potential hazard and is putting Rifella in danger. I am considering sending a small group of the Syeth Guard Unit to deal with the woman."

***

Once again, primarily due to Galdin's lack of understanding of people he thought would aid him, the Rifellan attempt was an unmitigated failure. Ssarff lost four of his best Syeth Guards, and once again, used the fee to help their families, rather than refilling the coffers of the Guild.

When Galdin called Ssarff to meet with him again, he had a different query. Ssarff agreed to a colossal fee for the Assassins Guild to unmask an apparent secret held by the Glowens. Galdin was convinced the secret would enable him to more than double the powers he already amassed by stealing them from others — those he eliminated from Morden. He indicated that Ssarff would be helped by a male who handled the sale of Blud wine from Glowen, Emrys pen Godron. This male, it appeared, was just as curious as Galdin to learn the secret of Glowen.

When he returned to the Guild, Ssarff sent for Ssestin. "Galdin wants my help again, but I am so reluctant to do anything for him. I am convinced we need a new Thane. Morden requires a Thane who is gentle with his people and is not possessed by the need to bolster his own importance." He strode over to the tassel and pulled it. "I had been considering sending a group of fourteen to deal with the Glowens, but I have changed my mind."

248

At that moment, a knock at his door caught his attention. "Come," and a young guard entered.

Ssarff ordered tea and food for him and Ssestin.

Ssestin closed the door behind the young guard when he left to fill the order. "You said you have changed your mind, Master. What is your plan now?"

"I am going to send just you, Ssestin. You are my most trusted councilor, and you are more mentally adept at understanding challenges than most of my guards. If anyone can discover the secret in Glowen, it will be you. When you meet with this Emrys, do not let him know you are the only one from our Guild. Let him believe the others are hidden and will remain so until we find out more about the secret."

"I will."

The young guard returned with Ssarff's order, and placed it on the table.

After he left, Ssarff sat with Ssestin, his second-in-command, planning how best for him to enter Glowen, and how he might remain unseen during his time in that land.

***

After almost seven turns, Ssestin returned from his visit to Glowen, and rode up to the Keep. He left his horse at the stable, but gave orders to feed and groom the animal. He went to his own quarters to shower the travel dust from his body, and then headed for Ssarff's office.

The Guild Master greeted Ssestin with a clap on the

shoulder and suggested he sit while they enjoyed a noon-turn meal together. "I am most anxious to hear what you discovered in Glowen."

Ssestin appeared discouraged and shook his head. "The only secret I discovered was that Emrys illegally supplies Galdin with Blud wine. But --" he brightened, "I met the woman and I do not believe she is a danger to anyone. I traveled on the same boat as she did to Baklai. The odd thing was someone killed her horse on board the boat, and Thane Cathked is most unhappy with her. Her name by the way, is Kat, and I like her."

"So why do you think Galdin is after her.?"

Ssestin shook his head. "I do not know and cannot guess why he wishes her at his Keep."

"I have been ruminating about this. Consider this. She is under Eduardo's protection, and we both know Galdin has aways envied Eduardo for his Wielder abilities. We have both heard many times that if Galdin meets someone who has a power he covets, he kills them and absorbs their power." Ssarff frowned and shook his head. "I am not quite sure what sort of magic he possesses which allows him to do this, but his power does seem to be increasing."

"Sire, how would that bring him more power?"

Ssarff leaned back in his chair. "What if Galdin believes Kat has a close enough relationship with Eduardo, that he would go to Galdin's Keep to rescue her if she were kidnapped?"

250

Ssestin's mouth dropped open. "So, he would be able to kill Eduardo? That is so peculiar, it just might be true."

At that moment a moth flew in through Ssarff's window. He grabbed it and listened. "Galdin again. He wants me to meet with him," He sighed. "Again."

"Master, please. Do not go. You cannot trust Galdin in any way."

"I will go once more because I need to discover what his agenda is. However, will you have two of our best Assassins accompany me, unseen, and ensure I get there and back alive?"

Ssestin agreed and arranged for two guards to accompany Ssarff and remain invisible. They were never to lose sight of him.

***

Ssarff returned to the Assassins' Keep and called for Ssestin to meet with him. "It is late Councilor, and I need my bed. However, I also require food. Join me and I will advise you of my meeting with the Thane."

They sat at the table in Ssarff's quarters and ate.

"What happened, Master?"

"I am almost convinced Galdin is not of sound mind. We are supposed to attend Baklai to capture this Kat and bring her to his Keep. Believe me, I have no intention of that happening. I wish you to head to Baklai and help protect this female, because Galdin told me his ally in Baklai is Kerdinon, Cathked's mate. When Cathked discovers this, I shudder to think of how he will react. He is not acknowledged to be a forgiving male."

Eager to help Kat, Ssestin headed for Baklai the following morn, and arrived in the land to discover she was accused of treason because she viewed a Mating of Horses -- something, that, in Baklai, was illegal for women to do. She had been placed under arrest to be escorted by a guard out of Baklai. Ssestin followed at a safe distance to allow him to keep watch over her. However, later that night, the Border Hut at which she stayed fell under attack by Kerdinon and her personal group of guards. Ssestin remained out of sight from Kerdinon's guards and quietly entered the hut later. He made his way to Kat's room, cut her bonds, and left her a knife. Before he left her, he told her she would be welcomed by the Assassins Guild in Morden should she decide to visit their land.

Just as Ssestin was preparing to depart, Cathked arrived at the Border Keep and caught Kerdinon in the midst attack. Despite the fact that he once loved her, he arranged for her death.

Ssestin fled Baklai and reported this information to Ssarff, who complimented him on his swift thinking.

***

When he learned that Kat was headed toward the Guild, Ssarff prepared to meet with her. He found her attractive, but she was also demanding and constantly engaged in power struggles with him. However, he also recognized the guide who accompanied her through Pridden was Mouse, who was often referred to as Galdin's man. Ssarff sensed an unmistakable power emanating from the small gray male, and became convinced that Mouse definitely was not Galdin's man.

Challenges increased. Ssarff and his second-in-command, Ssestin, were soon forced into war by Kat, his own people, and by Galdin's cruelty to the people of Morden. The ensuing battle with the vicious Thane resulted in an excessive amount of bloodshed, particularly since it took place in the terrifying Kennes Swamp, home to masses of dangerous creatures.

Ssarff's guards, together with groups of people from all over Morden and legions of Rifellans, finally achieved victory over Galdin and his reduced guard unit.

With the ousting of the Thane by Mouse and the combined forces in Morden, the Thaneship was available, and many of the people gathered near the Thane's now vacant Keep begged Ssarff to take over. Even Ssestin expected Ssarff to accept but he refused.

He had much more to do in repairing his Guild's reputation within Morden.

However, he was more than satisfied and at peace with simply being the Guild Master of the Assassins.

BALLINOR

Praetor for Lord Rhognor

Ballinor closed his eyes in frustration, and tried to block out his mother's strident voice and his father's growls. He was being attacked from both sides.

"Ballinor, it is time for you to decide what you plan on doing with your life." Apella, his mother, chided him.

His father, Havelock, chimed in. "You could easily obtain a premier position in Murwenna's personal guard unit."

Ballinor frowned at them both. "I am a warrior, and it is all I have ever wanted to be."

Apella waved her hands in the air. "Ridiculous. You have the talent and a family with enough connections to be more than only a warrior. You should seek the advice of Praetor Arrogol. I am positive he can suggest an advantageous posting that will still allow you to be a warrior, and place you in an important position."

Ballinor frowned at them both. "You do not understand. I do not wish to remain in Rifella. I long to see other lands, but still be a working warrior."

His mother tutted at him. "Then speak to Arrogol. He understands where warriors are needed."

"I have only met him once. Why would he help me?"

Havelock rolled his eyes. "Are you being deliberately obtuse? Your mother's words are true. Arrogol is familiar with our family and is quite aware of the influence we hold in Rifella. He will agree to see you."

Ballinor held up his hands as if in surrender. "Fine, I will arrange to see Arrogol on the morrow. I hope both of you are correct in your knowledge of him."

***

Ballinor received a reply that the Lord Murwenna's Praetor, would welcome a visit, and inviting him to join him for a noon-turn meal at his home just inside the gates of the Lord's Keep.

When Ballinor arrived, Arrogol invited him in to his small dining area and urged him to sit at the table. Arrogol joined him while one of the Keep's kitchen assistants brought their meal, accompanied by mugs of Orenberry wine.

Arrogol held up his mug. "Enjoy." He drank. "It is fortunate you wished to meet with me, Ballinor, because I also desire to speak with you. So, tell me what you wanted from me."

"I have spent most of my life training to be the best warrior I can. I now understand it is time for me to put that training to use. But I would appreciate being posted somewhere other than Rifella. I love my home, but I want to visit other lands and meet other people. Would it be possible for you to help me obtain a post other than in Rifella?"

Arrogol grinned. "Your visit, Ballinor, is timed to perfection. I have received a request from Lord Rhognor's councilor, Hesginn, to supply the Lord with a Praetor. I believe you would be perfect for the role, as I have watched your progress and seen your dedication as a Rifellan guard."

"You are considering me as Praetor to Lord Rhognor?"

Arrogol beamed and nodded. "Yes. Can you think of any reason why you could not fill that position?"

Ballinor grinned, stretching his mouth. "I cannot think of anything I would like more. I met Lord Rhognor many turns ago, and I admire and respect him. I believe I would be an excellent Praetor for him."

Arrogol leaned over and clapped Ballinor on the shoulder. "Then drink up. We have solved both our challenges." He took a sizable gulp from his own mug. "It would suit all of us if you could leave for Shendea within the next four turns. Can you be ready by then?"

"I can indeed."

"If you enter Shendea via the Carrog Pandy Bridge, I would suggest it will take you about four turns to reach Lord Rhognor's Stronghold. That should be sufficient time to travel with your own horse and any other items you will need. Remember, the winter seasons are fierce in the northern part of Shendea. Contact Healer Fenneth, as she will be able to advise you about needed clothing. If you require additional armor, contact Merrindock at Pakanna by moth, and you can take a short detour and pick it up it when you leave

257

for Shendea."

"My thanks for the information. I will contact my mother, and she can move mountains. I will be prepared."
They both rose, and Ballinor headed back to Restin, but first sent a moth to his parent to request her help.

***

Ballinor's parents purchased a home for him in Roothnal, the location of the primary guard unit for Shendea, and he travelled there to furnish it and store the supplies he brought with him. When he arrived in Roothnal, he took a turn to meet with the bulk of the males in the guard unit, and they also warned him he should take his warmest clothes with him. One of them cautioned, "This season, the area near the Lord's Keep will be buried in snow and ice, and the traveling will be challenging in the extreme."

He brought three horses with him to Shendea. When he travelled there, he had planned to leave one in the stable attached to his house in Roothnal. For the trip to the Stronghold, he would use the second horse for his luggage, bulky because of the extra clothing he needed for warmth during the trip. The third, he would ride.

Ballinor spent the first night in Roothnal, but early on the morrow, he sent a moth to Hesginn to advise him that he would arrive at the Stronghold in three turns. He set out immediately, aware he would not reach the first inn until the star set for the night.

He stayed at the well-used Vendi's Inn and, early the following morrow headed for the Ponti Inn where he would exchange his horse for a Ponti. His baggage would not weigh as much because he would don extra clothing and the heavier coat lined in warm fur.

By the time he reached Ponti's Inn, a few flakes of snow were already falling.

A stable hand waited for him, and led Ballinor's horse and baggage animal into a warm stall. "Praetor Ballinor, I will feed and water your horses. When you have completed your noon-turn meal, return here and I will have a Ponti for you to ride. Your baggage is now light enough so it can be secured to the back of your saddle." He sighed. "It will be challenge enough for you to carry it yourself to the Stronghold."

Ballinor walked to the massive door of the inn, and grabbing the iron handle, pulled it aside and entered.

A blast of toasty warm air enveloped him and the din of conversation and laugher greeted his ears. The innkeeper waved him over to a table and deposited a mug of heated mulled wine. The Praetor sat down and drank the heated drink with appreciation, enjoying the passage of the wine as it slid down his throat.

He gazed around the room and spotted a table of small Baklai males, sitting close to the fire roaring in the grate. Near them, red-faced, fleshy Glowens laughed and mocked each other. Beside their table, a spacious one occupied by Rifellan warriors, clad in leather armor and fur held the center of everyone's attention. Well away from the Rifellans, a pair of dark-haired, pale-faced Mordens sat wrapped in black robes and sullen silence.

A well-endowed female placed a plate of stew in front of him, and Ballinor dug in with relish. The ride from Vendi's Inn, while short, had stimulated his appetite.

He finished his meal but drank only half the wine. He did not wish to fall off his Ponti because of two much alcohol. He exited the inn and discovered snow had increased and already lay in swirling patches on the ground. He stepped back inside to add a warm shirt over his other clothing, and then donned the heavy furred coat. He wrapped an additional scarf around his head and neck and walked to the stable carrying his much lighter bag.

The young stable hand led him to his Ponti and tied his baggage tied on the rear of the saddle.

Ballinor heaved himself onto the Ponti's back. *I can feel the animal's bones. Not a comfortable perch.* He gripped the reins and set off, following the guide supplied by the inn.

The innkeeper at the Ponti Inn had advised him, that he should reach Half-way Haven before the star settled below the horizon.

The snow increased and some flakes turned to ice pellets which stung his face. *This is going to be a nasty ride.* The wind rose, sending dead leaves skittering across the hardened ground. He drew the scarf tighter around his face, blinking as the flakes turned to ice as they covered his eyelashes, reducing his visibility. *I hope I do not have to visit Lord Rhognor often in this season.*

Ballinor would have been prepared to swear the ride to Half-way Haven took an entire pass, but he and his guide did arrive before the star disappeared below the horizon.

With gratitude, he handed his Ponti to the waiting stable hand and pushed his way through the iron barrier of an attractive building. Inside, he headed for a table, shedding his coat and scarf, and hung them on a series of hooks just inside the door.

He sat at a table beside a sputtering fire in the grate. A massive pot, suspended from the middle of the arched oven, bubbled with something that emitted the delicious odors of roasted, spiced meats and vegetables. The meal, probably wullawerth, teased his nostrils, and he enjoyed every mouthful. However, he needed to stand every few moments, to ease the ache of Ponti travel.

***

Before he fell into his bed, he spent time soaking in the huge tub to ensure a deep night's sleep. The bath contained steaming heated water laced with herbs to relax muscles.

He woke the following morrow, his body free of aches and pains. He felt remarkably well and ready to attack the mountain.

After a hearty meal of klim mixed with nuts and fruit, Ballinor met with his guide.

"I am sorry Sire but we must now climb the right crag of the clogs, known as Bar Braich. This is where Lord Rhognor's Stronghold is located. It will be challenging. The rains that tend to fall, during this season often become solid ice, and it is far too cold for most Shendeans to leave the Stronghold. During this season we usually rest indoors."

"Why are you guiding me there now?"

"We are, at times, required to bring someone to the Stronghold, so on those occasions, we climb."

Ballinor put on his coat and wrapped his scarf around his head so that only his eyes were exposed, and he slid his arms through the straps on his baggage so it fit snugly across his back. This meant he did not have to carry it as he followed the guide.

They began the climb and even though he was a seasoned and strong warrior, Ballinor's progress soon slowed. Each foot seemed encased in stone, which he dragged along the solid path. His breath became labored despite how fit he normally was. *I shall have to train to handle this mountain with greater ease.* His guide did not have as much difficulty.

As they climbed, he marveled at the sharp stone ridges thrusting up to the sky like knives. The landscape, so desolate and lonely, caused him to shiver, not with cold but with a sense of apprehension.

Rhognor's Stronghold loomed ahead, an enormous opening in the mountain, with two massive ironbound doors flanking the entrance. Both creaked as wheels and gears groaned to open them wide enough to allow Ballinor and his guide access to the front hall. As they entered a massive room with arched ceilings and stone carved walls a marvelous blanket of heat enveloped him, and Ballinor sighed with pleasure

Along one wall, rows of hooks, attached to the walls, bore many cloaks, shawls, and hats. A lower shelf supported piles of hand coverings of thick wooly material.

"Praetor Ballinor?"

He turned and stood face to face with a female in a blue robe. "You must be Healer Deleth."

She smiled. "I am. Councilor Hesginn intended to meet you here, but Lord Rhognor needed him. The councilor apologizes and asked if I would agree to meet you. If you will follow me, I will take you to the rooms that have been designated for you whenever you are in the Keep."

He followed her through halls and past grottos and rooms off the many passages. "My thanks. I did not my armor or other spare clothing with me because of the season's inclement conditions, I needed space for my warmest clothing."

"I believe your permanent station is Roothlan. I suspect you will begin to discover what things you will need to have doubles of. There is a great deal of distance between Roothlan and Lord Rhognor's Keep, too much distance to require you to be constantly traveling to fetch some item you have forgotten at either place. This is not how Praetors live in the other lands. Shendea is a far more challenging land to reside in. The Lord is well situated here. He is protected not only by the rocks of Bar Braich but also the weather extremes, and the fact that this is the only entrance to his Keep aids his protection as well."

Ballinor smiled at her. "Indeed, and I, as his Praetor must live where I can leave quickly to defend the border or accompany the Lord on one of his inspections of his land."

Deleth grinned. "You understand us already, Praetor."

She reached an ornate door carved with symbols from Rifella. "These are your rooms, Praetor. Lord Rhognor is a little further down the passage, and his door has leaves, vines, and flowers on it. Lady Halfin, his mate, loves nature, and so everything Lord Rhognor does for her is a celebration of the outdoors and forests from which she came."

Deleth handed him the key for his rooms.

"My thanks. When does the Lord wish to meet with me?"

"He has invited you to join him for your morning meal. He will send an assistant to bring you to him. Make sure you sleep well this night. A first meeting with Rhognor can be interesting. He is knowledgeable and possesses a mind that is extraordinarily quick."

Ballinor thanked her again, and as she walked down the passageway, he inserted the key in the lock and entered his rooms.

He gazed around his quarters, well furnished with all

the necessities, and distributed the few items he brought with him. His stomach informed him it was time for a meal. After his trek to Bar Braich, he did not wish to wander the passageways searching for the dining hall, so instead, he walked over to the tassel and tugged it twice.

A knock came at the door and the kitchen apprentice appeared with a fragrant stew and a mug of mulled wine. "Praetor, I do not know your preferences as yet, but our head of kitchen suggested this would be appropriate for a Rifellan guard. My name is Crestain."

"Thank you. This is perfect for now. Is the dining hall far from my quarters?"

"Not at all. When you leave your rooms, turn left, proceed down the passageway and turn left again at the fifth entrance."

"Thank you. You do not need to pick up my tray until the morrow. I need to sleep."

The apprentice nodded and left.

***

Ballinor woke to the sounds of birds singing and sat up abruptly. *Birds? I am in the Stronghold. It is carved from a mountain. How can there be birds?* He bounded from his bed, showered, and dressed to meet with Rhognor for the morning meal. Ready to leave his quarters, he opened the door at a knock.

A young female in a blue robe stood waiting. "Praetor

265

Ballinor. Lord Rhognor is ready for you. Please follow me."

He found her attractive. "I assume you are a Healer. What is your name?" He followed down the passageway.

She smiled. "I am Grenneth, Healer Deleth's assistant. She could not meet with you this morrow because she is attending a birthing."

"I understand. Can you answer a question for me Grenneth?"

"What is the question?"

"I am sure we are in the Stronghold, but I hear birds."

She smiled. "Lord Rhognor created a forest for Lady Halfin in one of the halls and placed birds, animals, and many growing things in there."

They arrived at a door carved with the greenery of nature.

She knocked at the door, and from inside came "Come."

She looked up at him. "Please enter, Praetor."

"You are not invited?"

She shook her head, turned, and walked away.

Ballinor opened the door, and bowed his head. "Lord Rhognor, I am your new Praetor, Ballinor."

Rhognor rose and motioned to a beautiful carved wooden table, set with sparkling crystal glasses, shining silverware, and crips white linens. "Ballinor, in private, we do not stand on ceremony. Call me Rhognor when we are alone." He pointed to a delicate ethereal female already seated at the table. "Please meet my mate, Enchantress Halfin."

Ballinor bowed lower this time. "My Lady."

She laughed a delicate tinkling laugh. "Rhognor and I are of the same mind, Ballinor. Please, in private refer to me as Halfin. Too much formality can become tiresome."

Rhognor clapped him on the shoulder and guided him to the table. "Sit. Our meal will arrive soon, and I am hungry."

As Ballinor sat, Rhognor joined him.

At that moment, someone knocked, and the door opened for two kitchen apprentices, laden with trays bearing a variety of dishes, an enormous teapot and three delicate mugs. They deposited the dishes and mugs on the table. "Would you wish us to serve, my Lord?"

He smiled at both the females. "It is not necessary for this meal. We are enjoying a casual morning meal. You may clear the dishes just before the noon-turn."

They both bobbed their heads and left the room.

Rhognor straightened the serving spoons so they lined up with the dishes. "Please do serve yourself, Ballinor." He grinned at his mate. "If you do not, Halfin will consume everything. She owns a prodigious appetite."

Halfin giggled. "He is joking, Praetor. He always insists I eat more."

They passed the dishes around, serving themselves, and then dug into the meal.

As he ate, Rhognor asked about Ballinor's background, his parents, and about his training as a warrior. He constantly fiddled with his cutlery and glasses, moving things in alignment with each other.

In the beginning, Ballinor was distracted, but he soon understood that this constant movement was Rhognor's idiosyncrasy, and he quickly got so used to it, he no longer noticed the constant movements.

By the time they were drinking tea, Ballinor realized that Rhognor had learned everything about him, but he had learned little about the Lord.

Rhognor stood suddenly and reached for the hand of his mate. "Halfin, we need to attend the noon-turn with my councilor Hesginn and our Horse Master. Please forgive us, Praetor, but we have much to do this day."

Ballinor jumped to his fee. "Of course, Rhognor. Shendea has such a fine reputation, I am sure there is much for you to do."

Rhognor nodded at him. "I would suggest you spend the next few turns becoming familiar with the Stronghold. Learn where everything is located, and meet with Hesginn and my other advisors. Three turns from now, you and I will meet with all my advisors, and then you should return to Roothlan. Under normal circumstances, you will spend most of your time there." He laughed. "You cannot be an effective Praetor if you are locked up in my Keep for too long. As my Praetor, I am sure you are aware of your two specific duties. First, you are the primary line of security for Shendea. The second duty is that you will accompany me and Halfin when we tour our land each season."

Ballinor nodded. "Excellent, Sire. I look forward to our meeting and will make note of any other duties you may require from time to time."

They left Rhognor's quarters and Ballinor returned to his rooms.

***

Ballinor wandered the caverns, grottos and passageways of the Stronghold for two turns. He made notes on where everything and everyone was located, and soon he was able to wander around without getting lost. He also studied the maps of Shendea, all the entrances to the land, to be prepared to discuss all the requirements of security for both Shendea and the Lord.

After the morning meal of the third turn he made his way to Rhognor's quarters to meet with the Lord and his various councilors.

Rhognor invited him to sit on his left, and the Thaumaturge Hesginn sat on his right. The Horse Master, who also resided in Roothlan, Healer Deleth, and two additional councilors were at the table.

Rhognor ran an excellent meeting. He kept the attendees focused and steered them back on topic if they brought up unnecessary items.

These meeting with all his advisors occurred once each season. However, Rhognor had access to Hesginn, Deleth, and the other two councilors at any time he needed. Ballinor soon understood that Rhognor was a fine leader. His mind was sharp and he did not delay decisions.

After the full council meeting, when the others departed, Rhognor invited Ballinor to stay for a further meeting, this time with Halfin. Ballinor was impressed when Rhognor briefly summarized what the group discussed, and asked for Halfin's feedback.

Over time, the pair captured Ballinor's heart. Both could easily view the cause of problems, and they made decisions that were brief, quick, and always in the best interest of Shendea. Ballinor covered up Rhognor's fussiness whenever possible. Halfin, he adored.

Ballinor and the Horse Master became friends, partly because they both resided in Roothlan. When he discovered that Deleth possessed extraordinary prophecy abilities, he asked for her help in his love matters. Hesginn was the only one of Rhognor's councilors who disturbed him. While he appeared capable, there was always an underlying oddity about him. If Ballinor remained truthful with himself, he disliked Hesginn.

Ballinor loved his posting, and although he wanted a mate of his own, his life was happy for the most part, and he was content.

Once each season he visited his parents in Rifella, almost always for three turns. They caught up on their achievements, laughed, ate and drank, and enjoyed their reunions.

***

The female from the other world, Kat, who visited, guided by Mouse, whom Ballinor respected, turned much of his world upside down. The woman was ignorant of many of their customs, and had a tendency to control everything around her, and proved to be annoying. When she was attacked by a foolish male, she rendered him incapable of escape by using a form of defense she had learned on her world. Kat, demonstrated the defensive move to his guard unit, and while Ballinor accepted her help, he later told his unit not to use it. In his opinion, the technique lacked flow and demonstrated too much violence.

He invited Kat to his home for a meal because he found her attractive. But his attempt at seduction failed. He realized that some other male held importance in her life

He did not regret seeing her leave. His love life had other needs.

***

Rhognor sent for him, as it was the time for the Lord and Halfin's regular time for their trip around Shendea. Surprised to realize that the female, Kat, traveled with them, he found it a difficult trip. Once again, Kat caused challenges. Lady Halfin needed to threaten her when she attempted to remove a boradai from Shendea. But everything erupted when they reached Blain. Some Morden Assassins entered Shendea via a tunnel through Clog Arth, intent on capturing

Kat. In the ensuing battle, an Assassin aimed a syeth at Lord Rhognor, but Lady Halfin threw herself in front of him. The syeth bit Lady Halfin, and the poison acted too fast for anyone to save her.

Ballinor realized that Hesginn was responsible for the assassination attempt on the Lord. As members of Hesginn's gray magicians fled into the tunnel with their captive Kat, Lord Rhognor, enraged by the death of his mate followed with Ballinor and his guards fighting for their lives. Rhognor yelled in triumph as he ran his sword through Hesginn, killing him instantly.

Ballinor fought to keep the gray magician traitors away from the Lord and was stabbed a number of times and ended up crushed among the fighting men. He lay exhausted and bleeding profusely in the tunnel until the victorious guards found him and carried him back into Shendea.

Rhognor commanded the guards to take him to the Stronghold to Healer Deleth. They created a pallet, covered in soft padding, and moved as fast as they could. It was fortunate it was the growing season in Shendea and bearers moved him up Bar Braich to the safety of the Keep without contending with atrocious weather.

Deleth moved him to the infirmary and gave him a number of shots of sedatives to allow healing to occur. From time to time, Ballinor achieved a near conscious state and heard worried voices, but he soon faded again. Delete and her assistant Healers worked with little rest to heal his broken body. Rhognor often stayed at his side.

After about ten turns, Ballinor returned to consciousness. The worried faces of Deleth and Rhognor hovered over him. When he tried to talk, all he could manage was a feeble croak.

"What happened?"

It took time for him to be able to move, sit up, and eventually walk a bit. Daily, Rhognor came and assured him that his job as Praetor would be held for him and that his second-in-command was performing any needed tasks. Ballinor's parents visited him, but they were both aging and the trip was too difficult for them to come often.

Ballinor felt heartsick that he had not been able to attend Lady Halfin's pyre when she joined Caleesh. He spent almost as much time reassuring Rhognor about Lady Halfin as the Lord did assuring him about the job of Praetor.

Almost an entire season passed before Ballinor could resume his duties as Praetor. But much had changed. He missed Lady Halfin so much. He was convinced he had failed her by not protecting her, as his job demanded. He sought council from Deleth who turned him over to Anwen, one of her assistants.

Rhognor, when he learned of Ballinor's guilt over Lady Halfin, called him to meet with him. "Ballinor, you did not fail my Lady Halfin. She threw herself in front of me to save my life. She chose what she did. I know how you acted and how fast you were when you went after the traitors. I want to assure you, that the position as my Praetor is yours for life. I cannot think of a better male for the job than you."

Ballinor's guilt eased somewhat, he returned to Roothlan, and asked Anwen to visit with him whenever she could. They grew closer, and he realized she was the woman he had searched for all his life.

He asked her to be his bond mate, and when she said yes, both of them had tears in their eyes.

Anwen resigned as Deleth's assistant but continued to practice her healing techniques.

The season and passes came and went, and one morning Ballinor woke and found himself aching from the damage his body had suffered so many passes ago. He was aging, and understood he would not be able to be as effective as a Praetor any more.

He and Anwen visited Lord Rhognor and advised him that Ballinor needed to resign as Praetor.

Rhognor regarded them both. "I found gray in my own hair this morrow. You may resign. I doubt it will be long before I retire and hand the Lordship to another. I thank you for all your years of service."

As they left to return to Roothlan, Rhognor considered his final wish for them. *I hope the people realize they had the best Praetor in Shendea in the person of Ballinor.*

MURWENNA

Lord of Rifella

Lord Texstra, Lord of Rifella, thought his head might actually explode. He had, on the previous turn, experienced the first twinges of aches in his bones. Now he was faced with what seemed to be an unsolvable problem. *Am I becoming old and infirm?* He headed for the dining lounge in the Keep to consult with his mate. "Annaleena," he called as he saw her at a table for six. "I need your council." He joined her at the table. "Are our sons and daughters joining us for this meal?"

"They do not often join us. Why do you ask?"

"I need to talk to you about them, and I think it best if we were alone for this discussion."

"What have they done now?"

"It is more about what is happening to me." He reached out and took both her hands in his. "The fact is, I am beginning to ache when I do too many physical things. My body does not recover the way it used to and I am positive I found a gray hair three turns ago." He groaned. "I am aging, and I need to be considering who will be my heir for the Lordship of Rifella. I must make that decision soon."

"Why now?"

"If I leave to join Caleesh without making a choice, these progeny of ours will battle for the Lordship. And even worse, I need to begin the training for whichever one I choose so that they have the skills they will need to lead our people."

She nodded. "You make sense. But, my beloved mate, you are not becoming an old man just yet. I am two passes older than you, and I am not aching."

"You do not have the cares of leading people like these Rifellans. I am so burdened with being a Lord."

Annaleena sniffed. "Burdens? Cares? How do you think I cope with a mate who demands as much as you do? Plus, I survived being the one responsible for raising four offspring. When you complained about them, who do you think persuaded them to finally train to become warriors?" She sniffed again. "Burdens indeed."

He grinned. "I am just complaining. You did a fine job of raising them. I would normally consider calling one of my sons an heir, but none of them appear to have an interest in being Lord of Rifella."

"Have you asked them for their thoughts on becoming the Lord?"

"I have. What an eye-opening experience. I met with our eldest, Mendehar two turns ago in my office. I thought he would be pleased to think I considered him as my heir."

Texstra thought back to the day Mendehar strode into his office and sat next to him in a leather chair. "What do you wish to discuss, Sire?"

"You are my eldest son, and as is the tradition, I would tend to pick you as the heir to the Lordship of Rifella. I wish you to advise me what you think of this situation."

"I do not want to disappoint you, but it is the last thing I would wish to be. I have been traveling through Rifella for the pass that has just ended, and have spoken to people all over our land. I have also considered all types of things I might turn my hand to. I spent the best time of my life in Orkanna, and have discovered I adore the sea."

Texstra frowned. "What would you do on the sea?"

"Sail, Father. Sail. I have worked on a ship which plies the waters from Orkanna up to the Mora Waters, delivering goods between Rifella and Shendea. We deliver Rifellan produce to Shendea and we bring back Red Rash potion and swimmers caught and dried by Shendeans for Rifellans to use as foodstuffs. I have been offered the role of first mate on this vessel. I intended to ask for your blessing in accepting the position."

Texstra leaned back in his chair. "What you have told me is a surprise, but I would never deny you something you enjoy doing so much. Answer me one last question. Do you prefer to become a first mate on a ship, over ruling Rifella as a Lord?"

"I prefer to sail, Father."

"If that is the case, Mendehar, I give you my blessing to do what you most desire."

"Thank you. I suppose you would like me to tell this to my mother."

"I would indeed."

The memory faded and Texstra found himself sitting with Annaleena.

He grinned at her. "Mendehar did come and tell you his plans, did he not?"

She nodded.

"So, you know full well he will not be a candidate for an heir to the Lordship."

"I do, but I never was told why Marlberg had not accepted the position."

"I sent for him to discuss the possibility, and he replied with a moth."

Annaleena's mouth dropped open. "A moth? To a Lord's request?"

"Yes. He has decided he prefers the self-indulgent lifestyle of the Glowens. He began spending more and more time on Glowen and has now retired to Kammerdow. He often spends time at Lake Yuffern, and has no wish to return to Rifella. He enjoys mating with many males and females in Glowen. Their predilection of mating with whomever they wish appears to appeal to his desires. I am most disappointed, as I thought we had shown him a lifestyle appropriate for a Rifellan warrior."

Annaleena rose from her chair went over to Texstra and hugged him. "My poor mate, I am sad that Marlberg has proved to be such a challenging son. However, it is clear you now have only two choices."

"I believe Murwenna is the perfect choice. She loves the people of Rifella, is thoughtful, and will rule our land well. She has a sense of strength that surpasses that of her siblings. She will make an excellent ruler, and unlike her siblings, she is the only one to display Wielder abilities. And Melindar, without Wielder abilities, could only be a Thane"

"You do realize that Murwenna has chosen a female as her mate. The only reason it matters, is because our line as Lords of Rifella may end with her."

He shrugged. "We shall see. I will arrange to meet with her on the morrow and establish what her desires are."

***

On the morrow after the morning meal, Texstra arranged to meet with both Murwenna and her bonded mate, Janella.

When a knock sounded at his door, he rose and admitted the two of them. "Come, sit at the table. Tea is already served."

Murwenna hugged her father before she sat. "You seem very solemn. What is the problem, and how can we help?"

"I have a most important question to ask you. I am not as young as I once was, and aging is beginning to take its toll."

Murwenna chuckled. "You believe it is time to choose

your heir, and you want to ask me to fill the role." She laughed aloud at his frown. "I am well aware, of my siblings' views on the matter. Mendehar wishes to be a sailor. Marlberg is not suited to be a Lord of Rifella. He appears to have not only embraced Glowen traits but has also almost become one. And, Melindar has no magical abilities."

"Murwenna." He raised his brows. "Have you been listening to the conversations between Annaleena and me?"

"I would never do such a thing. I am merely observant."

He sighed. "I have always known this about you. This is one of the major reasons you are qualified to assume the role of Lord of Rifella when I leave this world. It is also important for you, Janella, to agree to this. You are bonded to each other, and Lord or not, Murwenna, one should always be in sync with one's mate. Are you both in agreement?"

Janella smiled. "Of course, we are, Lord Texstra. We discussed this some time ago, knowing full well the day would come when decisions needed to be made."

"There is one other challenge for you both. Heirs."

Murwenna laughed this time. "We have discussed this as well. We are considering making an arrangement with a trusted male to provide what is needed. I promise you, before I join Caleesh, Rifella will have a suitable heir."

Texstra relaxed his shoulders. "You two make me so proud." They all stood and he gathered them both in a hug. "Janella, you are also like family to me. I wish both of you the best life possible. You will make a fine ruling family for

Rifella."

***

Within the next four passes, Annaleena discovered the life of a mate to a Lord became more onerous as she needed to be part of a ruling family. At one morning meal, she broached a discussion with her mate. "Texstra I am beginning to feel my age, and I am weary of the requirements of being the Lady of Rifella. Our offspring are not our responsibility any more, and all of them except Murwenna, have moved away from our home. Do you not think it may be time for us to retire?"

"You are thinking much like myself. My hair is now gray, and I observe a few strands of the same color among your beautiful locks. I will put pen to parchment and prepare the speech for my people within the next five turns. We must first advise Murwenna. She is ready to assume the mantle of Lord. I am astounded at how well she has learned to be a fine ruler. I must admit, she has even taught me a few embellishments I had not considered. Rifella is safe in her hands, and her mate Janella is without a doubt, a supportive partner."

"The ceremony to celebrate Murwenna becoming the Lord will take place five turns after your retirement announcement. Are there any robes or specific clothing required for either you or Murwenna?"

He looked at her with a blank expression. "I have no idea. I suspect you should ask our Taylor, Wealin."

"Of course. I will contact her and will arrange for whatever is required for either of you."

***

On the turn following the celebration of Murwenna's investiture as Lord of Rifella, Janella, yawning, joined her for the morning meal. "I am surprised how many of our people came to help you embrace the role of Lord. There were far more than expected. Your mother advised me this was because the people of Rifella love and respect you."

"Annaleena has always been right before, so I hope she is also correct this time."

"I am sure she is." Janella paused and regarded Murwenna with a serious expression. "You have just reached your thirtieth pass. It is time for us to decide how we will have offspring."

"I have already given this some thought. We cannot decide with any carelessness upon the perfect male. He must have family with a history of power. I am, as you are aware, a Wielder, and in order to achieve a Wielder offspring, whichever male we choose must have a Wielder among his ancestors."

"You cannot choose one who is attractive at least?"

"No. It matters not how pleasant he is to view. He could be incredibly ugly but have the needed power in his line."

Janella laughed. "Perhaps that would be a good thing. That way, you would be unlikely to fall in love with him."

Murwenna screwed up her face in disgust. "Oh no, Janella. I will not mate with him. I have been speaking with the Healers, and they will have Healer Wynneth of Kaylin come to Rifella to help with the process."

"Process? What do you mean by process?"

"It is most clinical. The male will deposit his seed in a container, which will be brought to me at once, and Wynneth has a way of depositing it within me that will result in a potential babe."

"It sounds odd, but at least you will not be tossing me aside as your mate."

Murwenna pulled Janella up from the table and kissed her. "Never. You are my loved one."

Janella sighed. "We do not have time for that. You are due to attend a meeting of your councilors."

"I will begin the list, and when I meet with the councilors, I will request their backgrounds. Who knows. The male I seek may well be among them."

***

Janella sat waiting when Murwenna returned to her private rooms. "So, did you find an appropriate male?"

Murwenna threw herself onto the comfortable couch, beside Janella. "I believe so. I think I found two who might be appropriate."

"Do not keep me in suspense, Murwenna. Who are they?"

"One of them is only a weak potential. Grendel is part of my honor guard, and he was in attendance this morrow, so I put my question to him. He has a distant relation who was the third brother of his maternal parent's parent who was believed to have some Wielder abilities. However, he is also getting close to the age of retiring as my guard."

"I suspect the potential Wielder abilities in his line would be weak."

"I would agree."

"So, who is the other?"

"Someone I did not suspect. My Praetor Arrogol."

"He is a fine-looking male. The resultant babe would be sure to be handsome."

"Three parents back, the female had some Wielder abilities, so the line is more direct. Plus, he is a friend, as we attended warrior training together. I can also bribe him, if necessary, because he needs something that only I can give."

Janella laughed. "From what you say, there is no question who would be the ideal male. What does he need?"

Murwenna grinned, smirking at her thought. "He is attracted to Olwyn. But her family wish her to bond with someone closer to royalty. If I endorse the joining of Arrogol and Olwyn, her family will have no choice but to approve."

Janella laughed again. "You resemble a child who has been hiding in the dessert kitchen and has eaten her fill."

"I would like to invite him for an evening meal with the two of us. It is important that he realizes you are in agreement with the arrangement."

"Should we also invite Olwyn?"

"No. She is a woman with strong beliefs, and I suspect she will rule their household when they bond. We must get his agreement, and then it is up to him to persuade Olwyn to consent."

Janella threw her arms around Murwenna. "We will be parents, my love. I am so happy."

Murwenna stood and reached out for Janella. "We will be, and I sense the perfect way to celebrate."

Hand in hand, they headed to the bedroom, shedding clothes as they went.

***

Murwenna and Janella met with Arrogol in their private living room on the following morrow after the noon-turn meal. Both were seated at a table laid for tea.

He strutted into the room in his normal manner.

Murwenna held back a grin. *He does believe he is Caleesh's gift to all females. Why he feels the need to do so when he is aware that Janella and I are bonded is beyond my knowledge.*

He gave a slight bow. "My Lord." He glanced at Janella and bobbed his head. "Lady Janella."

Murwenna gestured at the third chair. "Oh, stop preening, Arrogol. Sit down. We have something to ask you."

He sat, and pursed his lips in obvious annoyance. "You

told me always to be formal if other people were around."

Murwenna rolled her eyes. "You understand very well, Janella is not 'other people.' She is my bond mate. Behave yourself."

"You have never invited me to your private area before. I did not guess what I needed to expect."

"We have been friends for many passes. You know that if I wished to find fault with something I would have you come to the council room."

Arrogol raised one eyebrow. "I did not think of that. So, am I to understand you wish to ask me something more personal?"

"Yes. You must be aware that since I was named Lord of Rifella, I am in an unusual position. Despite my current choice of bond mate, I will be required to eventually have an heir of my own."

He eyed her, raising a querying eyebrow. "So?"

"I would request that you be the male parent of my heir."

Arrogol's eyes grew huge and his mouth dropped open. "Er… er…you want me to…to…"

"Relax, my friend. I do not want you to mate with me. What I wish is for you to supply me with your seed. The Healers will handle everything else."

His brow wrinkled up, almost as if he was in pain. "You want what?"

Murwenna sighed. "Arrogol, this is not difficult to understand. I wish you to donate some of your seed to me."

"But you do not want to mate with me?"

"No, I do not. I am so sorry, but in truth, I am not attracted to you in the least. All I need is your seed."

He hung his head, shaking it slowly from side to side. "This is very odd. I am not sure I like the sound of this."

"I can make your decision beneficial to you."

"How?"

"I notice there is attraction between you and the Lady Olwyn, but her parents do not see you as an appropriate bond mate for her. Does she love you?"

"Yes, and you are correct that her parents feel I am unworthy of her." He growled. "I cannot understand why. I am Praetor for Rifella after all."

Murwenna grinned at him. "They may not think you are worthy of her. However, Arrogol, if I suggested to them that I would approve a bond between the two of you, I will be willing to wager a few chits that you will suddenly become worthy."

His eyes lit up. "You are correct, they would. If I agree to donate my seed to you, you will intervene with Olwyn's parents on my behalf?"

"I give you my word as Lord of Rifella that I will."

He thought a bit.

Janella and Murwenna waited for his reply.

"I will do it." He smiled at them both. "Did you choose to ask me so that you hope your babe will also be a good-looking male?"

Janella said. "That was but a minor part, Arrogol. I did most of the research for Murwenna. Your background, while fine for fathering a potential Lord, did give us one concern. You are healthy, and your ancestors have all been healthy as well. Only your arrogance was a negative, but we decided that Murwenna's ability to be diplomatic would outweigh that challenge."

He looked startled by her words.

Janella rose. "Murwenna and I thank you for your agreement. We will have Healer Wynneth of Kaylin contact you with all the details when she arrives at the Keep."

"Should I tell Olwyn?"

"You should wait until Murwenna has spoken to her parents."

He stood and bowed to both the women and exited the room.

Once the sound of his footsteps had faded, Murwenna turned to Janella with joy. "We have chosen well. Arrogol's seed will be perfect for our heir."

Janella agreed. "The fact that he is a handsome male is a good thing, despite what I said. We do want our son or daughter to be beautiful."

***

As the turns rolled by, Murwenna became pregnant with the help of Arrogol and the Healers. The people of Rifella were all so excited and many older females prepared booties, blankets, and swaddling for the babe.

The Lord's pregnancy proceeded as with most other women. When she gave birth to a son, the entire land celebrated. The people were excited, and they showered Murwenna's babe with gifts.

Arrogol gained in reputation as the male parent of the babe, and he and Olwyn were bonded. Murwenna's prediction proved to be accurate. Olwyn did control both Arrogol and her household.

Texstra was also proved correct. Within a few turns, the people of Rifella considered Murwenna to be one of the finest leaders Rifella had ever been blessed with.

The People of Pridden

290

THONTOOK

The Master Weaver of Kaylin

Everyone in Kaylin thought of Thontook as a grandfather figure. His body was well-padded, his hair liberally streaked with gray, and his eyes always shone with mischief. Like all Kaylins, he was fair-skinned but his eyes were an unusual gray-green in color. It was fortunate that he kept his hair tied at the back of his head, because his beard exploded from his chin and resembled a chaotic bush. Many thought he enjoyed the fact that his hair and beard were such anomalies. His appearance confirmed for them that he was a man who loved life, and avoided being thought of as normal. The people of Kaylin loved and respected him.

Many people dropped by the Weaver Hall to exchange jokes with him because he always had a collection of new amusing anecdotes. Those who worked with him, however, were particularly impressed with his abilities as the Master Weaver.

From his early years, Thontook had wished to do nothing but work with color. As a result, he had created some new and unusual hues. From time to time, he helped the Tapestry Guild create different shades which projected the most interesting emotions. He and Tapestry Master Godrith often

291

met and discussed colors, shades, and hues, and the emotions they generated in people's minds. Kaylins and Shendeans would pass them seated at tables in either land, enjoying a cup of tea, and shake their heads when they overheard their impassioned conversations,

Thontook's latest assistant, Tantinata, had been with him only three passes, but already she adored him. Her own male parent had perished from Red Rash, so the Master Weaver became her substitute male parent.

Tantinata visited her home in Trigoran on a regular basis, and her long-suffering female parent was subject to her entreaties each time. "Really, you should consider meeting Master Thontook. He would be the perfect mate for you, and then I could refer to him as my male parent."

"Will you cease these silly ideas? I have no desire to find another mate. Plus, your Thontook sounds exhausting. I am retired, and I have a perfect circle of friends to enjoy life with. Tantinata, you have also not considered that your Master Thontook may have no desire to replace his deceased mate either."

Tantinata grumbled. "I miss my own parent, but he cannot be here. Master Thontook would be a reasonable substitute. I would like to be his progeny."

Her parent shook her head in frustration. "Well get him to adopt you, you stupid female."

***

Tantinata returned to the Weaver Hall and peaked in Thontook's office. "Master Thontook, may I ask you a question?"

"You may, but why so formal all of a sudden?"

"Well, it's a kind of formal question."

He turned around and raised bushy eyebrows. "A formal question? How odd."

Tantinata scuffed her foot on the floor, and stared at the ground. "Promise you will not be angry?"

He stared at her and scratched his head. "Angry? Me? When have I ever been angry? Come on. What is the question, annoying assistant?" He laughed at his own humor.

"Thontook, do you have any progeny?"

Now he appeared more astonished than ever. His eyebrows had almost merged with his hairline. "Progeny? No. Have you met someone who has claimed I am their parent?"

She shook her head. "No, Sire. But, since you have no progeny, and I have no male parent, I think it would be an excellent idea if you adopted me."

He blinked rapidly, shaking his head as if ridding it of annoying insects. "What did you say?"

She stood in front of him, hands on her hips. "I said, I think you should adopt me."

Thontook leaned back in his chair. He opened his mouth as if to speak, hesitated, and closed it. He opened it again. "Why? What problem would that solve?" He held up a hand. "Wait, before you answer that, bring me some tea and sit."

She stared at him, a frown on her face. "You already have a tea on your desk. But I will sit." She dragged a chair beside him and plonked herself on the seat.

He waited for her to speak, and when she remained silent, he cleared his throat. "So, why?"

"I think you should adopt me because this is the best position I have ever had, and I adore working with you. However, I am aware you have had to fire other assistants in the past. I would not recover if you fired me." She nodded with emphasis. "If we were family, you could never fire me. That way, we would always be together."

Thontook opened his mouth again. "Oh." He stood and began to pace the room. "Tantinata, this is the most flattering thing you are suggesting, but…" He rubbed at his forehead. "You know we live in Kaylin. Maybe other lands consider this normal, but not Kaylin."

She opened her mouth and stared at him. "What? Thontook! Really. I was not suggesting anything in the least improper." She stood and shook her finger at him. "What you are suggesting I meant is outrageous. I am without a male parent, and you have no progeny. I adore you as a parent, and I know you are fond of me. I think we would be excellent as family. A parent and an offspring. Nothing more."

Thontook walked over to the chair and dropped in it. "I need to sit again. I was not suggesting anything more. I do understand you are asking for adoption, but I am sure no young person has ever suggested such a thing before. You took me by surprise. I never considered that I might desire to have progeny. I do not know what to say."

She slowly walked over to the seat beside him, and sat, her lower lip trembling. "You are angry at me, and you think I am foolish for being so bold."

He stared at her face, and began to laugh. "Tantinata, the quivering lip is well done. You have been manipulating me, you wicked female."

"Perhaps, but only a little. I do love working with you more than I can say, and you do often feel like parent to me. I wanted to hear you say you would never fire me." She grinned at him. "I was talking about you to my female parent, and I told her how much I enjoyed my time here. I suggested she should bond with you so you could become my parent too. You would not believe how angry she became, and then," Tantinata giggled, "then she suggested you should adopt me." She laughed and patted Thontook on the hand. "I thought it might be fun to see how you would react."

"You gave me heart palpitations instead."

"You are just grumpy because I came up with a better joke than you." She raised both her hands in the air and pretended to cheer. "All Pridden will declare it to be the best joke ever."

He sniffed. Loudly. "I will admit it was amusing, but not the best one ever. I myself have created better ones before you were even birthed."

"You, Sire, have delusions of adequacy." She stood and

pick up his cup of cold tea. "Sit here and recover, I am going to get us both a fresh cup of tea."

She walked out of his office, humming so that only Thontook could hear her.

So, she believes she creates better jokes than I. We will see.

***

The two continued to work together in perfect harmony over the next two passes, although Thontook had not given up the desire to create a more satisfying joke of his own.

Prior to the annual delivery of brynosh add wullawerth hair, Thontook met a new apprentice healer, Ranneth. Within a season, they bonded, and she produced two female offspring, who he was pleased, inherited her beauty. Thontook forgot about jokes for a while, but wandered around with constant smiles for everyone, the epitome of a proud parent.

Tantinata became an older sibling within the family, despite not having been adopted.

The Master Weaver and his family prospered, and his reputation for cloth of all colors became legendary.

Five passes later, Tantinata burst into his office. "I have created something wonderful. Look." She handed him a roll of thread.

He was standing at his desk, but he peered at it. "Silver thread is not that unusual."

"No. See this." She unrolled some of the thread. As she

moved it through her fingers, it also flashed gold, green, and purple.

"Stop moving it." Thontook picked it up. "What color comes through when it is woven?"

She beamed at him. "I am almost positive that they all will."

"You mean you have not tried that yet?"

"No, I wanted to show it to you first."

"By Caleesh, you are unbelievable. We must find an empty loom. Now."

He searched a couple of chambers and found one in a back room. "Bring the thread here." He set up the warp threads on the loom, grabbed a shuttle and loaded the thread on it. His nimble fingers kept the shuttles swishing between the warp threads, and the heddle bars clacked as he raised and lowered them. The resultant rhythm was mesmerizing, and Tantinata found herself swaying to the sound. Thontook wove a band of the color about the width of a forearm.

He stopped and contemplated the result. "Oh, my." His voice was hushed, almost reverent. "The thread you have created is one that Caleesh herself would bless. As you move the cloth, the colors shift and soar like light does through a crystal. It is the most magnificent thread I have ever witnessed."

Tantinata's eyes misted over, joy pouring from her heart.

He caught her hands. "How did you do this?"

"You made a suggestion to me one day, Master. You said, 'Imagine what might happen if we could create strands so thin that they are almost transparent and use a different color on each. What would it be like when strands of different colors are wound together to create a useful sized thread?'"

"I remember, but I said that about three passes ago."

"I know, but the thought intrigued me so much, I have been working to create that ever since. Today, I succeeded."

He reached out and caught her in a bear-crushing hug. "Tantinata, you are fast becoming a Master on your own."

She coughed. "You are little too strong, Master. My abilities are there because you have trained me so well, and you gave me leave to try new ways of doing things."

"Sorry." He released the hug. "I am so glad for you. I will gently remove the band of cloth I wove, and we will take it home to show to Ranneth. I want her to see what two great minds can create. I will advise her I am naming you as my heir to become the next Master Weaver."

Tantinata gawped at him. "Will she not be upset that you will not be placing the designation on either of your off-spring?"

He shook his head. "No. They are both so young. It would be more than thirty passes before they could gain enough knowledge and enough practice to be able to do what you can already accomplish. And that is assuming they even want to follow me into the making of cloth."

He gazed at Tantinata, smiling. "I am going to give you

your journeyman status on the morrow."

"Master, do you definitely mean all that you have just told me?"

"I do. After the time we have spent together, working with colors and cloth of all designs, even though I never followed up on your joke, you are much like an offspring to me."

Tantinata burst into tears.

Thontook frowned and appeared startled. "Tears, my wonderful assistant. Why tears?"

"No one in my entire life has ever said anything so wonderful to me. I love you, Thontook, almost as if you were my real parent."

She hugged him this time.

Thontook blinked rapidly to hold back his own tears. He sniffed. "Come. We will take this portion of cloth home. Ranneth will be thrilled when she sees it."

***

On the morrow, Thontook called all the workers in the Weaver Hall to a meeting after the morning meal.

When they were assembled, he held up the piece of the new cloth and announced. "We have a new and beautiful thread we can use for particular special types of clothing. I want you to meet the female who designed this." He pulled his assistant forward. "This is Tantinata, and today, she earns her Journeyman Weaver badge. Help me congratulate her."

The entire room burst into applause. They whistled and stomped and cheered. Tantinata could not help herself. Tears streamed down her cheeks.

Thontook beamed at the crowd. "You will have to forgive her. I have no idea how she managed to create such marvelous thread with such leaky eyes."

Laughter enveloped the hall, and the people approached her and congratulated her, some hugging her as well.

Thontook smiled at the throng of people surrounding her. He faded from the scene and returned to his office. Once there, he tugged at the corner tassel. When the young apprentice arrived at his door, he asked for a large pot of tea. "Oh, and before you bring the tea, would you send someone to fetch Seamstress Brith to meet with me here."

The young male, bobbed his head and set off down the hallway.

***

The assistant arrived with tea at the same time as Brith. Thontook directed him to place the tea on a small table in his office and invited Brith to seat herself.

Thontook took his own seat and poured tea for the two of them. "Brith, I have something extraordinary to show you." He picked up the piece of cloth made with the gorgeous new thread. "What do you think about this?"

Brith gasped. "It is the most glorious cloth I have ever seen. How did you create it?"

"It was created by my Journeyman Tantinata. She claims I gave her an idea, and she has spent almost two passes creating it. You are the seamstress. What do you believe is the best use of this cloth?"

"There is only one possible use of a cloth of such magnificence. Royalty. In any ceremony for a Lord or a Thane, they should have robes or gowns made from this fabric. No other should ever wear it."

Thontook clapped her on the shoulder. "I knew you would have the perfect solution. I shall have Tantinata begin creating spools of the thread, and only she will weave the cloth from it. We will weave enough for many passes, and it will be stored safely in one of our back caverns."

"Excellent, Master Thontook."

He grinned slyly at her. "Perhaps this might call for some Orenberry wine, my dear."

Brith grinned. *I would rather have tea, but he needs me to have a drink of wine with him.* "Be sure to water mine, Thontook. I do not have enough body to drink it full strength."

By the time Brith finished her drink with Thontook, she was already feeling the wine, even though he had indeed watered it. She headed back to her rooms in the Keep and, locking the door to her studios, decided to take a much-needed nap. *Oh my. I cannot handle wine, but I also cannot refuse Thontook.*

***

As the seasons passed, the spools of glitter thread, as Tantinata name it, filled a cupboard kept for thread of immense value. She wove the thread into cloth, and before the close of the next four passes, there was sufficient material to create the first garment for a celebration for a new Lord.

By the time the new Lord had ruled for an entire pass, Thontook, bent by age, with his hair grayer than ever, retired from weaving to spend more time with his beloved, Ranneth and their offspring. He shook his head at himself as he remembered the laughter he and Tantinata had shared. *I never did discover a better joke to play on her. But I did not need to.*

Tantinata was named Master Weaver of Kaylin.

PYROCKS AND BORADAI

Pyrocks

No one knew the actual origins of pyrocks. Because they first appeared in Kaylin, many suspected the Wielder Lords were responsible. However, Wielders did not create pyrocks they were merely the ones who discovered them.

Lord Lanerch, when first named the heir to the Lordship of Kaylin, was a young man who existed as a prime example of curiosity. He wished to learn all he could about the land of Kaylin, and often sneaked off to explore the countryside.

He noticed the dark entrances of caves in the Clog Nordad and was eager to discover if anything lived in them. He entered the closest cave and found it cool and sweet smelling. The odor surprised him because, as he walked further in, he encountered what he thought were strange bats. He could not view them close up, as they flew further into the cave as he approached.

As he continued to follow them, he heard a tiny squeak from a side grotto. He found what he thought was an injured small bat. As he extricated it with extreme care, he discovered a creature completely different from anything he had ever seen before.

The gray ball of fur shook itself, stretched its body and extended a pair of leathery wings.

He examined it with care. "You poor little thing. That is what is wrong with you your wing is torn."

It squeaked again, exposing a long pink tongue and two rows of tiny and remarkably sharp white teeth.

Lanerch would not leave the little animal on its own. It would need medical attention. He took off his outer jacket and, with gentle hands, wrapped the furry little animal in the thick fleece to protect it and keep it warm.

By the time he got the creature back to the Keep, it had fallen asleep, curled in a tight little ball. He removed it from the jacket, and called for his assistant to find him a small wooden cage so it would be safe. It had not attempted to leave, so Lanerch relaxed and had his Healer summoned to help him repair the wing. By this time, the small cage had arrived, and Lanerch lined it with a warm fleecy piece of toweling.

When Wynneth, the Healer arrived, he showed her the creature's wing. "Oh, my Lord, you will need to bind up the wing so it can heal on its own." She reached for the creature and it backed away and hissed. "Oh dear. I do not think it wishes me to touch it. I will give you instructions and you will have to be its healer. Spread the wing, gently, because I am sure it hurts. Now, put this unguent on the slice along the wing and with slow movements, place the two pieces together."

As he did so the little animal gave plaintive squeaks and blinked rapidly.

"My Lord, take this piece of linen and lay it across the inured wing and wrap it in place, being most careful not to move the tear apart." She nodded at him when he did so. "Excellent. The last thing is to lift it into the cage without moving the wing to let it heal on its own."

When he did the little creature gave a small trill similar to a purr and curled up on the soft material in the cage, keeping its wing still.

"I also think you should give it food and water."

He stared at Wynneth with furrowed brow. "What do you think it might eat?"

She shrugged. "I am not sure, but I would try klim, if I were you. It is a most nourishing substance which we use for traveling. Try that, and also give it plain water."

"My thanks, Wynneth. I will watch it with focused intent and keep you informed of its progress. I wonder what kind of an animal it is."

"I will contact my sibling in Shendea. The Healers have many old documents with histories of people and of various animals. I will let you know what I find."

When Wynneth left, Lanerch called for his assistant and asked him to bring some klim and a bowl of water.

When the food and water arrived, Lanerch settled himself in a chair, with the cage and the food on the small table in front of him. He opened the cage door, put a small amount of klim on the end of his finger, and held it under the sleeping creature's nose. It woke, blinked, and licked the klim from his finger. He gave it three miniscule amounts on his finger before the creature seemed satisfied. Lanerch then poured a tiny amount of water on a teeny dish and placed in front of his furry friend. It lapped up all the water, emitted the smallest burp, tucked its nose under its front paw, and slept.

Lanerch smiled at the sound of a faint snore. *Somehow, I have a pet. I have no idea what you are, but we appear to be linked somehow. I shall call you Link.*

***

Three turns later, Lanerch responded to a knock on his door. "Come."

Wynneth popped her head into his office. "I have some information for you, my Lord."

"About my little creature?"

She came into the office and sat down without an invitation. She was, after all, one of the most important people at the Keep. She was the Healer. "I have had word from my sibling. She found old records in the Healers' section of Lord Rhognor's Keep. Your creature is called a pyrock, and it is most useful. Pyrocks were used for sending messages, but somehow fell into disuse when moths became more common. You can write out a message, tie it to the leg of the pyrock, and it can instantly deliver the message to your desired destination."

"How does it do that?"

"Nothing in the documents indicated that anyone ever knew the answer to that. From what I have read, they have the ability to project themselves to another location without any delay. And one other major thing. Once you have bonded with a pyrock by touching it, no other can ever bond to it. That most likely indicates why it hissed at me. You are now the only person who can touch this creature. We will need to create a small tube to carry messages that can be attached to a foreleg with ease, but in a way that no other person will need to handle Link."

"Why is it so important not to touch another person's pyrock?"

"They become most confused, and that confusion can often result in their death."

"I shall begin to design a tube as you described."

"Excellent. Deleth sent a messenger with a drawing of what was used in the past."

"What else can you tell me?"

"All pyrocks are female and, every now and then, might produce an egg. If you keep the egg warm for about seven turns, when the egg is hatched, the new pyrock can be bonded to someone else.

Lanerch was delighted to be the only person to have a pyrock, but he often wondered often if Link was lonely. He considered heading back to the cave where he found her but for some reason, was unable to ever locate it again.

He often took Link from her cage to talk to her, enjoying it most when he fed her. "I am so sorry I cannot find your friends." He stroked the little creature until she fell asleep, and he returned her to her cage. He perfected a metal tube that clung to her foreleg, and often send messages to Wynneth and Deleth, because they both understood how to handle pyrocks.

As he aged, Lanerch became concerned about what would happen to Link when he joined Caleesh. The problem was that neither Wynneth nor Deleth knew either.

Wynneth brought Eduardo to Lanerch, to protect him from Morden's cruel Thane, Gritch, and Eduardo became the heir to the Lordship of Kaylin. Not long after Lanerch announced that Eduardo would succeed him, Link laid an egg. Wynneth advised Lanerch that Eduardo should begin touching the egg daily, without handling Link.

Eduardo did so, and when the egg hatched, the new pyrock bonded happily with him, who became equally smitten with the little creature. Eduardo named his Blink, a name with which the pyrock seemed to approve.

After a number of passes, Lanerch expired in his sleep. When Eduardo called on him, he found Link curled on Lanerch's chest. When Eduardo touched Link, although he was reluctant to do so, he discovered the pyrock had left this life as well. Eduardo gazed at the two of them and felt his eyes fill with moisture.

When three turns passed, Lanerch was laid upon his

pyre, and Link was placed on his chest. Both joined with Caleesh. Many viewing the pyre shed tears, moved that their Lord had been joined by his fondest companion, the pyrock called Link.

***

Boradai

When the first Lords of Shendea decided to create a Stronghold from the miles of caverns in the mountain of Bar Braich, they were sure all the caves and grottos were bare of living things. It took much work to create a comfortable, warm, and productive Keep. Many brooms swept the dust accumulated over the ages, and the males transported the heavier furnishings. The females carried linens, cooking utensils, and everything needed for preparing a home for the hundreds of people residing in a wooden structure in Finrase.

As families and various groups of like-minded groups moved in, they created teams of specialized people. The current Lord was assigned a series of rooms in the most secure portion of the caverns, with his councilors in a nearby section. A communal kitchen and dining area found plenty of space, and some of the tallest caves became the perfect domain for the Tapestry makers. Many smaller sections became homes for the Rifellan guards and their weapons, seamstresses, and the Healers, and others for the many items needed on a daily basis. The final benefit became the appearance of a market where the residents of the Stronghold might purchase anything they needed.

During the many passes required to create the final comfortable Keep, several grottoes and passages remained unexplored, waiting to be found to be useful.

During the term of Lord Rhognor, something unusual was discovered. In reality, it was his mate, Lady Halfin, who found the boradai. She returned to her boudoir from the evening meal and, startled, found an odd animal ensconced in the middle of their bed. It reminded her of a tiny cat without discernable ears, brown fur, and shiny black eyes. Its delicate nose shone bright yellow, and stubby legs and short fluffy tail completed the appearance of a rather comical but benign creature. Halfin wanted to cuddle it but hesitated a moment. She reached out a tentative hand out and spoke. "What on this wonderful earth are you?"

As she touched the animal, a glorious voice addressed her. *I am Blaine, and you are receptive. Your touch has bonded us. We will always talk. But please do not speak in the noise. My mind can understand your thoughts and you can be aware of mine.*

"I can listen to you in my mind?"

Blaine winced. *Please do not use your loud speak. It hurts my head, and I cannot understand the loud words. I understand your thought words well.*

I am sorry to have hurt you. I will be careful not to

speak aloud when I am near you. I have never seen anything like you before. What species are you?

I am a boradai.

Why did you suddenly come to this Stronghold?

We did not come. We have been here always. We did not show ourselves to many in this place because most were doing too much loudness. But then you came here, and you are not like the others. We had ascertained your thoughts, and they are of kindness and peace and love for all creatures. The only others who can bond with us in this way are those your kind call the Healers. They too are creatures of quiet contemplation.

Thank you so much, Blaine, for becoming my friend. Lord Rhognor has been so good to me in creating my beautiful garden with many plants and animals. Your presence completes this. I am so happy in my life.

Lady Halfin, I will be with you for along as you need me, you may be assured.

***

Blaine, as a leader among the boradai, had news to impart. *A woman whose brain is quite different from the Healers, has arrived here ins the Stronghold. I sense she will need our help. I wish a volunteer to bond with her.*

Breen stepped forward. *I am willing, it might well be interesting.*

I thank you for volunteering, Breen. I wish you to be

aware that this woman may place you in much danger. I do not know what will occur, but I foresee possible death if you do this and perhaps for other boradai as well. Are you still agreed?

If boradai will learn more and it will be of benefit, no matter what sacrifices are involved, I am still willing.

***

Breen met with the woman Kat, and although her brain did not appear to be as open as that of the Healers, when she and the boradai touched, the woman also listened to the boradai's thoughts. Breen, of course, always understood Kat's thoughts.

What Breen found delightful was that the woman had attracted an enormous black creature, whom she called Shade. He was much like a cathnog, but gentle and filled with a sense of mischief, and he was invisible to all others. Over a number of turns, Shade and Breen indulged in tricks with the woman's guide, a being called Mouse.

Breen discussed the guide with Shade. *I do not know why they call him Mouse, do you? He is an amazing warrior and much larger in stature than how Kat views him. Odd, correct?*

Shade only rumbled in agreement. He did not appear to be worried that he saw things differently than did the woman. Nor did he care that he was invisible to all but the woman and Breen.

The four travelled across Shendea, moving from one minor adventure to another, and Shade kept Breen entertained throughout the journey.

When they encountered the Lady Halfin on the final part of their trip, she knew at once that Breen had been concealed in Kat's bags, and accused the woman of attempting to remove a boradai from Shendea, a crime punishable by death.

Kat defended herself because she was unaware of these penalties but, almost immediately, disaster struck.

Breen send out a cry to all the boradai in the Stronghold. *We are under attack by Lord Rhognor's councilor and others from Morden, and Lady Halfin has been bitten by a syeth and lies dying. Blaine is desperately attempting to help her but I think too much poison entered the lady's veins.*

Blaine's sad cries for Lady Halfin reached the gathering of boradai at the Stronghold, and they all sent vibrations of help.

Breen called out once more. *I am trapped in Kat's bag, and the enemy have captured her. We are about to enter the tunnel to Morden. She has also been bitten, and I must remove the poison from her. I sense she has more to accomplish in Pridden. Sisters send me strength, please.*

Breen, in a desperate attempt to rid herself of the poison once she had removed it from Kat, clamped onto Rhognor's traitorous councilor and began to inject the poison from her body into his.

313

Rhognor, racked with grief, plunged his sword into the traitor, and Breen, unable to send poison to him any longer, began to fail from the poison within her own body. The boradai in the Stronghold overheard her last cry of pain tinged with a sense of failure, and then, nothing.

The fighting over, Blaine spoke to the Healers to tell them that Breen should accompany the Lady Halfin's body to the forest for the pyre to return her to Caleesh.

Lord Rhognor lit the pyre, tears streaming down his face. The fire consumed Lady Halfin, with the tiny body of Breen laid on her heart, and all the people, animals, birds, and boradai alike mourned their passing.

Shade, still with the woman from elsewhere, uttered one last growl and vanished forever.

ABOUT THE AUTHOR

Marilyn, (J. M. Tibbott) is a prize-winning author, a writing instructor, and a substantive editor. She has been writing since grade school, and has continued to study literature and the English Language ever since. She believes there is always something new to learn.

Her works include magazine and newspaper articles, newsletters, online blogs, and story collections. While *The Wielders: Book 7*, is the final book in the Pridden Saga, a myth/fantasy series, book 8, *The People of Pridden*, expands the lives of many of the people who helped Kat during her journeys.

Marilyn. feels strongly that the well-being of any author is maintained by belonging to a number of writer's groups. Since early 2020, some of her groups have morphed into virtual ones.

If you enjoyed this book, please let Marilyn know by writing her at: askme@jmtibbott.com

Marilyn has a monthly newsletter to keep her readers in the know about her progress on her books, and recommendations for other fantasy authors. You can get a copy of this newsletter by requesting a copy at: askme@jmtibbott.com or by clicking on the QR code below

In addition, you can view all her current works by going to Amazon, typing J. M. Tibbott in the search bar at the top of the Amazon page.

A Note from the Author:

I am aware I called this book *The People of Pridden*. As I was writing it I remembered that two small creatures paid a large role in Kat's journey. Blink, her pyrock, and Breen, the boradai in Shendea were very important to her journey. I had to include their stories as well.